THE

HUMANOID

TOUCH

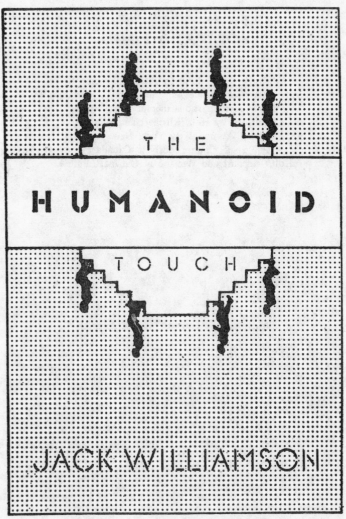

THE
HUMANOID
TOUCH

JACK WILLIAMSON

HOLT, RINEHART AND WINSTON NEW YORK

FOR FRED POHL

Printed in the United States of America

THE

HUMANOID

TOUCH

1

Humanoids Self-directed robots invented to serve and guard mankind.

Keth loved the suntimes. Thirty days of light and freedom, while the kind sun climbed and paused and sank. He loved the clean smell and cool feel of the wind and the sky's blazing wonder. In the first sharp days before the thaw, there was ice for skates and snow for sleds, but he loved the warmer days more. The excitement of green things shooting up, sunbuds exploding into rich-scented bloom, great golden-sweet melons ripe at last. Best of all, he loved the Sunset festival, with the leaves burning red, and gifts and games, and all he wanted to eat.

The moontimes were not so nice, because the ice storms after Sunset drove everybody back underground. Thirty days in the narrow tunnel places, where he was always cold and just a little hungry, with lessons to learn and no fun but the gym. He hated the dark and the cold and the black humanoids.

"Demon machines!"

Nurse Vesh used them to frighten him when he was slow to mind her. She was a tall, skinny woman with a frowny face and cold, bony hands. Her husband was dead on Malili, where Keth was born, and she blamed the humanoids.

"Bright black machines, shaped like men." Her voice was hushed and ugly when she spoke about them. "Sometimes they pretend to be men. They can see in the dark and they never sleep. They're watching and waiting, up there on the moon. They'll get you, Keth, if you dare disobey me."

She made him fear the moontimes, when Malili either stood alone or sometimes hung beside the red-blazing Dragon, never moving in the cold, black sky. He could feel the cruel minds of the humanoids always fixed upon him, even through the rock and snow above the tunnels. Sometimes in bed he woke sweating and sick from a dream in which they had come down to punish him.

Sometimes he lay awake, wishing for a safer place to hide, or even for a way to stop them. Men must have made them, if they were machines, though he couldn't guess why. Perhaps when he was old enough he could build machines strong enough to fight them.

"They'll never get me," he boasted once. "I'll find a way to beat them."

"Shhh!" Her pale eyes mocked him. "Nobody stops the humanoids. Ten trillion machines swarming everywhere but here! They know everything. They can do anything." She chilled him with her bitter, thin-lipped smile. "They'll get you, Keth, if you don't mind me, just like they got your poor, dear mother."

He couldn't remember his mother or Malili or anything before Nurse Vesh had come with his father back from Malili to keep him clean and dole out his quotas and make him mind.

"What did they do—" The look on her face dried up his whisper, and he had to get his breath. "What did they do to my mother?"

"She went looking for a braintree." Nurse Vesh didn't say what a braintree was. "Outside the perimeter. Into jungles full of humanoids and dragon bats and heathen nomads. Never got back. You might ask"—her voice went brittle and high—"ask your father!"

He was afraid to ask his father anything.

"On Malili?" He shook his head, wishing he dared. "Where we came from?"

"And where my Jendre died." Her Jendre had been with his father on Malili. She wore a thin silver bracelet with his name on it. Keth had always wondered how the humanoids killed him, but he couldn't ask her because she cried whenever she remembered him. "Ask your father how." Her voice began to break, and her white face twitched. "Ask where he got that scar!"

He wanted to ask why anybody ever went to Malili. It looked too far and cold for people. He thought it might be better just to let the humanoids keep it, but he didn't say so now because Nurse Vesh had stopped looking at him. She was leaning with her face against the wall, her lean body shaking. He tiptoed away, feeling sorry for her.

His father was Crewman Ryn Kyrone. A tall, brown man who stood very straight in his black uniform and worked in a hidden back room where Keth couldn't go. The steel door stayed shut, with a quick little red-blinking light to remind his father when it wasn't locked.

Sometimes his father slept in the room and brought Nurse Vesh quota points for his breakfast, but he was more often away on Lifecrew business. He never talked about that, or much about anything else.

Not even about the scar, a long pale seam that zigzagged down from his hair and split across his jaw. It changed color when he was angry, and he was often angry. When Keth asked for more than his quota. When Keth couldn't tie his boots correctly. When Keth was afraid to go to bed, because he knew he would have dreadful dreams about the humanoids.

Keth knew his father must have been hurt on Malili, perhaps in a terrible fight with the humanoids. They must be very fierce and cruel if they could hurt a man so strong. Once he asked Nurse Vesh if his father was afraid. Her face grew tight, and her pale eyes squinted blankly past him.

"Brave enough," she muttered. "But he knows the humanoids."

The year he was six, she sent him to the gym every morning. The other kids seemed strange at first, because they laughed and ran and sometimes whispered when the leader wanted quiet. They weren't afraid of anything, and they weren't nice to him.

The leader tried to scold them once, explaining that Keth didn't know the games because he was born on Malili, but that only made things worse. They called him "moonbaby" and mocked the way he talked. One day a larger boy pushed him.

"You'll be sorry!" His voice was shaking, but he didn't cry. "My father—" He thought of something better. "The humanoids will get you!"

"Humanoids, ha!" The boy stuck out his tongue. "A silly old story."

"My nurse says—"

"So baby has a nurse!" The boy came closer, ready to push him again. "My Dad was an engineer in the Zone, and he says there're no humanoids there. He says the rockrust would stop them."

Limping home through the cold tunnels, he wondered if that could be true. What if Nurse Vesh had made up the humanoids, just to frighten him? He found her in her room, reading a queer old printbook.

"You aren't to fight." She frowned at the blood on his cheek. "Or did you win? Your father will be angry if you ran."

"I fell, but it doesn't hurt at all." He watched her carefully. "I was talking to a boy. He says there are no humanoids—"

"He's a fool."

Her lips shut tight, and she opened the book to show him a humanoid. The picture was flat and strange, but the thing in it looked real. More human than machine, it was sleek and black and bare, as graceful as a dancer. He thought its lean face seemed kinder than hers.

"It isn't ugly." He studied it, wishing he knew how to read the golden print on its black chest. "It looks too nice to be bad."

"They pretend to be good." She took the old book from him and slammed it shut, as if the humanoid had been a bug she wanted to smash. The puff of dust made him sneeze. "If you ever fall for any of their tricks, you'll be another fool."

He wondered how a machine could trick anybody, but she didn't say. He wanted to ask about rockrust and how it could stop the humanoids, but she didn't like to talk about Malili. She scrubbed his cheek and gave him his calorie quota, which was never enough, and made him do his lessons before he went to bed.

The next summer he took a recycle route, pulling a little cart to pick up waste metal and fiber. The tunnels were cold, and most of the tokens he earned had to be saved for his winter thermosuit. But one day he found a bright black ball almost the size of his fist, so shiny it made a little image of his face. It rolled out of a trash bin, along with the bits of a broken dish and a worn-out boot.

"A dragon's egg." Nurse Vesh shook her skinny head when he showed it to her. "Bad luck to touch. Better throw it back in the bin."

It looked too wonderful to be thrown away, and he asked his father if it would hatch.

"Not very likely." His father took it, frowning. "Ten million years old. But you've no business with it, Skipper. It must be missing from some museum. I'll see about returning it."

His father carried it back to that always-locked room and never spoke about it again. Wondering, he used to search the moontime sky for the Dragon. It was the sun's sister star, and perhaps the dragons had flown from nests on its queer far planets to leave their eggs here on Kai.

It would have been exciting to watch it hatch. The baby dragon would be too small to hurt anybody. And as lovely as the dark-shining egg, he thought, with glittering diamond wings.

Once he dreamed that it was really hatching while he held and warmed it in his hands. The thing that crawled out of the glassy shell wasn't a dragon; it was a black humanoid.

Another crawled after it, out of the broken shell, and then a hundred more. They crawled all over him, with clinging icy feet, and his terror of them froze him so that he couldn't move or scream. He was stiff and chilled and sweating in his berth when Nurse Vesh woke him.

He always shivered when he remembered that dream, but it had made the egg more strangely splendid than ever. He wondered for a long time if it could still be in his father's room. One day when he came in from his route the place was very still. He peeked behind the curtain and saw the red light winking. He listened and heard no sound. His father and Nurse Vesh were out.

His hand trembling, he touched the door.

2

Cat and Dragon   Twin suns of the binary "runaway star" on whose planets the refugee colonists tried to escape from the humanoid universe.

The apartment was a branching cave, carved deep in solid rock. His father's room was off a long tunnel behind that faded tapestry, far at the back. It was very secret. That was why it was hidden, and why the gray steel door was so thick, and why the light winked to warn his father if it was ever disturbed or left unlocked.

He almost ran when the door swung open, but nothing else happened. He listened again, but all he could hear was his own thudding heart. He tiptoed inside to look for the dragon's egg.

The room seemed very small and bare. A desk with a holophone. A shelf stacked with huge old flatprint books. Blankets neatly folded on the narrow cot where his father slept. A rusty strongbox, with the painted oars of the Lifecrew peeling off the half-open door.

Breathless, he peered inside. Except for a few spilled quota tokens and a tall brown bottle, the strongbox was empty. The dragon's egg must have gone back to that museum. He was turning to slip away, when a picture stopped him.

A strange old flat picture, made with rough daubs of colored paint. The paint had faded, and the silver frame was tarnished black, but the man in the picture looked alive. Looked like his father.

The same black hair and the same straight nose. The same gray eyes, narrowed like his father's when his father was angry. But the man in the picture had a thick black beard, and one hand held a queer old projectile gun.

Nurse Vesh was teaching him to read, and he sounded out the symbols on the darkened silver. Kyrondath Kyrone—

Kyrone! His breath came faster, because that was the name of the great new starship, and his own name too. He stood a long time looking, wishing he knew more about his father and the room and the humanoids.

He jumped when he heard somebody walking, but it was only Nurse Vesh, getting up from her nap. He scrambled out of the room and pulled the steel door carefully shut and went on wondering. Though she and his father never talked about the starship with his name, he heard more about it from the holo news and later from his history tapes.

The *Kyrone* had been in construction out in orbit as long as he could remember. It was to carry people to settle planets of the Dragon, which they hoped would be kinder worlds than Kai and Malili. Later that year, it was ready for the flight. Nobody said that it might meet dragons, but his father tried to stop it.

One day at lunch Nurse Vesh had the holo news on and he heard his father speaking to a meeting. The flight had to be halted, his father said, because the fusion engines would have a rhodomagnetic effect. The humanoids might detect that and find the people who had fled from them to the worlds of the Cat.

Captain Vorn followed his father on the holo, laughing at such fears. The Cat and the Dragon were moving too fast, and the humanoids had been left a thousand years behind. Foolish fears had kept people trapped too long on Kai and Malili. The time had come for another bold escape.

He liked the look of Captain Vorn. A tall, lean man with cool, blue eyes and a quick, brown smile, not afraid of anything. When he spoke next day, his daughter Chelni was with him. She was a sturdy little girl with straight black hair and a stubborn chin. He saw they were fond of each other. He never forgot them.

Or the man with golden hands.

Bosun Brong, his name was. He had come from Malili to be an engineer on the starship. The newsmen said he had been exposed to bloodrot outside the Zone and lost his natural hands. The metal hands were shining golden levers, graceful and powerful. The holo showed them bending steel.

In spite of his father, the building of the ship went on. He used to wish that he had been aboard. Sometimes he dreamed of the happy new worlds the colonists would find. Happy there, they would never be hungry or cold. Far from sinister Malili, they needn't fear the humanoids.

For half a year, the holo carried news of the flight. When Vorn reached the Dragon, he found seven planets. The inner worlds were too hot and dry, and the outer ones were cold gas giants, but one in between looked fit for people.

The first lander went down toward it, and everybody waited to hear what the pioneers reported. They never did report. All signals simply stopped. The newsmen couldn't guess what had happened. One Bridgeman wanted to send a rescue expedition, but the Navarch said it would take too long to build another starship.

Little Chelni Vorn was on the holo again. Her chin was white and shaking. She told the newsmen she had wanted to go with the ship but her mother had kept her on Kai. She blinked at her tears and said she thought the ship was safe, because her father had carried a dragon's egg to make good luck.

"Luck?" Nurse Vesh sniffed. "He's a fool."

That was all anybody knew, till the day Bosun Brong called from the spacedeck. Keth's father was away, but Nurse Vesh let Brong in. A nimble little black-eyed man in a shaggy winter thermosuit, he seemed to know Nurse Vesh, but she backed away from him, looking pale, when he offered his yellow-gloved hand.

"So you're Shipman Keth?" His face looked dead, but his voice was quick and warm. "Crewman Kyrone's son?"

Keth shook his hand. Inside the thick glove, it felt hard and very strong. Nurse Vesh let him sit in the front room and made him a pot of her bitter tisane. Waiting, Brong pulled off the gloves.

"You know about the starship?" Nurse Vesh poured the boiling tisane and stood staring at his golden hands. Her voice was frightened and high. "What happened to Captain Vorn?"

Brong's hands were very deft and clever with the mug. Keth waited, wondering if they had met whatever laid the egg, till Brong set down the cup and told them about the flight to the Dragon, and the new planet they had found.

"Kyronia, we called it." His black eyes looked far off, as if he still saw it. "As wild as old Terra must have been before men evolved there. A fine place, maybe, but it nearly killed us all.

"We had three landers. The first one just disappeared. Went behind the planet on its descent and never came back. The second got down on what looked like a nice safe spot—a wide green plain that looked like grassland but turned out to be a layer of weed that hid a sea of mud. The lander slid down through the weed and never came up.

"We had better luck with the last one. Got down safe on a rocky coast and made three trips back to the starship to ferry our gear and the rest of the crew. Vorn came down on the last flight, with a fusion engine ripped out of the ship to make power for the camp. Then he gathered us together around the landing pad.

"Kyronia, he told us, was our last best chance. With luck and work, we could make it a finer home than Kai. We still had troubles to come, but that was life. Working and risking, making and loving, losing and winning. I liked the way he said it. Standing tall on a granite rock, voice ringing back from the cliffs behind us. We all felt proud—

"Till the humanoids came."

3

Rhodomagnetics   A tachyonic energy spectrum linked to the second triad of the periodic table of the elements: rhodium, ruthenium, and palladium. Analogous to ferromagnetics, which is linked to the first triad: iron, cobalt, and nickel.

Nothing ever changed Brong's dead brown face, but his hands clenched into golden hammers and his voice went sad and slow when he spoke about the humanoids.

"Our lost lander came back that night. We found it on the pad next morning, loaded with humanoids. They had taken the craft without hurting anybody. They always said they could do no harm to any human being. All they wanted was to help us. If we wanted a home on Kyronia, they would build it for us."

He shook his head and made his hands unfold.

"That's what they did, though Vorn tried to stop them. He begged them to let us do it ourselves. To let us build our own houses and open our own roads and clear our own fields. To use our wits and brawn against a wild planet, fighting to tame it. That's what we'd come for."

The gold hands spread and wearily fell.

"They stopped everything. Because they'd come to care for us, commanded by their crazy Prime Directive. Our own tools were too dangerous for us, they said, and our work was too hard. An axe could cut a man. Lifting a rock could rupture him. One microbe could kill him.

"We had to be protected." Brong sighed and sipped the hot tisane. "In a way, all they did was wonderful. They brought down their tachyonic transport, a hundred times bigger than our starship. They unloaded their great queer machines and built a city for us, there on the cliffs where Vorn had staked out one dirt street for the beginning of our town.

"A beautiful city, in a terrible way." Brong's tone turned sadder. "Crystal towers shining like monster gems. Gardens of great bright blooms like I never saw, not even on Malili. All of it wrapped in a rose-colored cloud.

"A cloud I never understood. It smelled like some queer perfume, so sweet I couldn't stand it, glowing pink at night, so the city was never dark. Somehow shut the planet's rough weather out, so there was never any wind or cold or rain.

"Magic!" His sad voice fell. "That's how it seemed to us. Unbelievable at first, floating in that rosy splendor. The humanoids swarmed all around us like little black ants while they were building it. They never sleep. Never rest. Never make a sound. Don't have to speak, because each unit knows all that any other has ever learned.

"In just a few days, they were ready to move us in. At first, I guess, most of us were glad enough to go, because it looked so grand and wonderful. Because the humanoids still seemed so quick and kind, so eager to do everything for everybody.

"But Vorn never trusted them. He stayed down at the pad, working to convert the fusion engine for our own power plant. Kept a few others with him. When the humanoids invited them into the city, he said they weren't moving. The humanoids said they had to."

Brong shook his head and sipped his drink, remembering.

"Vorn told them he and his people would make their own way. The humanoids were always polite, but they answered that fusion energy was too dangerous for men. They were very mild and very kind, but they came swarming in to dismantle the fusion plant.

"At the last second, Vorn blew it up. Only a boiler, but still big enough to kill Vorn and most of his friends. They made the right choice, Shipman."

Brong blinked solemnly at him.

"Because that fantastic city turned out to be a padded prison, where nothing at all was allowed. Love itself was regulated, because sex can overtax the heart. Most of the inmates had to be drugged to make them think they were happy—the humanoids do have remarkable drugs.

"That's the story, Shipmate." Brong peered forlornly up at Nurse Vesh, holding his mug to be refilled. "The sorry tale I've brought back to Crewman Kyrone."

"There's one more thing he'll want to know." She was pouring more tisane. "How did you get back?"

Brong's small body froze for an instant, as rigid as his face. "I'd seen enough of the humanoids." He squinted into the mug and set it carefully aside. "Vorn's explosion had wrecked a hundred of the little devils, and shaken up the rest. In the confusion, I got back aboard the lander. Blasted off before they could stop me. A long flight back home. But here I am, Shipmate. Here I am!"

When his father came, Brong darted to meet him at the door. His father stopped and gasped and stared, not saying anything.

"Well, Crewman." Brong offered his golden hand. "I see you didn't expect me."

With a hoarse, angry sound, his father waved the hand aside. His face was stiff and strange, the scar growing slowly white.

"You— You can't be here!"

"Yet here I am." Brong couldn't smile, but his voice seemed queerly pleased. "Here to say you're right about the humanoids. I've seen them, Crewman, and the sort of world they want to make. A very peculiar sort of hell."

"I never liked to trust you." His father nodded grimly. "But I'll hear what you want to say."

"I thought you would." Brong squinted at him, nodding. "Even if we were never friends."

They went back to that locked room. Listening outside till Nurse Vesh scolded him away, he heard their voices growing sharper and louder. After a long time they came out again, muttering and scowling, to call Vorn's brother on the living-room holo.

Admiral Torku Vorn was a Bridgeman and a fleet director. He was busy now in conference, the girl said, and she couldn't interrupt him. When Brong waggled his gold hands and told her he had been aboard the *Kyrone,* she changed her mind.

The Admiral looked like his brother, but younger and broader and stronger. His face was heavy and red and watchful, a game-player's face that showed no expression at all while Brong repeated his story. Then he smiled. A warm, wide smile.

"A great tale, Bosun, but a few points puzzle me." His friendly voice was almost apologetic. "We've had no report of any lander returning from the *Kyrone.*"

"I failed to reach the spacedeck, sir." Brong hunched down, very tiny in his shaggy winter gear, squinting at the holo. "Crashed on a Darkside ranch. Hiked out to a tubeway station."

"Could be." The Admiral nodded quietly. "But I helped

design those landers. Their normal operating range is only orbit to planet, not star to star." His blue-gray eyes were wide and mild. "Bosun, you didn't come back in any lander. Not from the Dragon."

"It wasn't easy, sir." Brong squirmed and blinked. "If you'll let me explain—"

"Do that to the shipwatch." The Admiral's grin turned cold. "I imagine they'll want to look at the wreck of your lander. If they can't find it, you're in trouble."

His image went out.

"I won't be the only one in trouble." Brong stood up with a tired little sigh and asked to use his father's secret room. "Not when the humanoids get here." In the hall, he paused beside that red-winking light. "You've got my message, Crewman. The shipwatch will say I lied about the lander. But what I said about the humanoids—that's all true. Remember it, Crewman, and I hope you can keep them out."

He went inside the room and closed the door behind him. Three shipwatch officers were there in half an hour with orders for his arrest. His father let them in and led them back to knock on the door. The red light kept flashing, but Brong didn't answer. The officers drew their laserguns, and his father opened the door.

Brong was gone.

4

Lifecrew   An organization formed to alert and guard the people of Kai against the humanoids; influential once, but later discredited by calling too many false alarms.

The shipwatch men didn't want to believe what his father said. They drew maps of the rooms and tapped on all the walls and frowned at the blinking light and holoed everything. They yelled at his father and Nurse Vesh and even at him, asking the same things over and over, always angrier.

The room was eighty meters underground, they kept saying. Carved out of solid granite, with only one doorway. If the sub-

ject had actually entered it through that door, and if he really
hadn't come out through the door—then why wasn't he still inside?

His father grew pale and trembly, his voice turning sharper
and the scar shining whiter. He always said he didn't know.

"I wouldn't hide the man," he kept insisting. "It's true I
knew him on Malili, but he never was my friend. A worthless
halfbreed. I never believed a word he said, and I can't imagine
how he got away."

They left at last, but then the Admiral called.

"Crewman Kyrone, I'm getting reports I can't understand."
His broad, red face was hard and watchful. "I think you had
better explain them."

"Sorry, sir." His father looked sick. "I can't explain anything."

"Maybe I can." The Admiral leaned alertly forward.
"Though you'll deny it. You want support for your dying Lifecrew. This wild tale of invading humanoids—"

"I didn't make it up," his father muttered. "I can't believe
how Brong said he got back, but his story frightens me."

The Admiral waited, his meaty features almost friendly.

"Always too much I never knew about him." His father was
sweating. "Half Leleyo, you know, and half mechanical now.
Hardly human at all. I never understood him."

"Crewman, I wish I could understand you." The Admiral's
cold half-smile was fading. "Perhaps I will, when I learn how
Brong left your place. In the meantime, I imagine this farce will
kill what's left of your Lifecrew—"

He reached to punch out.

"Wait, sir!" his father begged. "If the humanoids are really
established on the Dragon, we're in danger here. The Lifecrew
has to go on—"

"I'll see to that." The Admiral's voice was short and frosty.
"If I ever believe the humanoids really caused my brother's
death."

His hard, red face flickered out.

Later that night, his father called him back behind that gray
steel door.

"A rough day, Skipper." His father sat heavily down at the
desk, suddenly looking older than the black-bearded man in the
queer flat picture above him. "I don't know what became of

Bosun Brong." Uneasily, his father glanced around the tiny room. "Anyhow, it's time we had a talk."

He listened, breathless with his eagerness.

"I wanted this to wait till you were older," his father said. "But you've heard Brong's story. Part of it may be a clumsy lie, but I'm afraid the part about the humanoids is true. Kai's in danger, Skipper, and only the Lifecrew stands against them.

"Here's our fort." With a tired white smile, his father waved at the old strongbox and the flatprint books and that dim picture. "We have another on Malili, with one brave woman for a garrison. Crewmate Cyra Sair. Two of us against the humanoids. If I've neglected you, that's most of the reason. I thought I ought to tell you now, and I hope you understand."

"Thank you, sir." He watched his father's face. "Will they come here?"

"I wish I knew." The scar looked pale and bold. "But now they surely know about us. We can only wait. Wait, and be as ready as we can."

"If there's time—" He had to get his breath. "If I grow up, I want to join the Lifecrew. May I, sir?"

"If there is a Crew." His father gave him a thin little smile. "And if you're tough enough. But fighting them—"

His father stopped, staring off at nothing. Waiting, forgotten, Keth felt bad to see him looking so baffled and afraid.

"Well, Skipper!" His father remembered him. "I didn't want to worry you, but I thought you ought to know."

"About Malili?" Suddenly now he felt brave enough to ask. "Are the humanoids there? Nurse Vesh says they are. She says they killed my mother—"

"Don't speak of her!" The scar grew whiter, and he thought the thick ridges of it looked like a spider crawling up his father's cheek. "Don't ever—*ever* speak of her!"

"I—I'm sorry, sir."

He wanted more than ever now to know about the world where he was born, about his mother and how his father got the scar, about rockrust and bloodrot and the strange Leleyo, but his father's open mood was gone.

"Now run along, Skipper." His father was turning to the holo. "I've a call to make."

Stumbling out of the room, he heard the special lock click behind him. He wondered if his father was calling Malili, perhaps to tell Crewmate Cyra Sair about the humanoids on Kyronia.

Through the rest of that long winter, he took gym and ran his route and did his lessons for Nurse Vesh. Sometimes he listened to the holo, but no more news came back from the *Kyrone*. There was never anything about Captain Vorn or the humanoids or the man with golden hands or even actual dragons.

For his next birthday, Nurse Vesh saved quota points to make him a redberry tart and his father promised him a fine surprise. The surprise was Crewmate Cyra Sair, home from Malili. She was going to be his new mother.

He loved her at once. She was a large, warm woman with dark, bright-shining hair and a small red mole under one eye. She always smelled like sunbud vines, and she was kinder than Nurse Vesh.

When she had time.

Like his father, she was haunted with dread and always busy. Every night at home they locked themselves in that little back room. They were often away, he seldom knew where. Once when they were leaving he couldn't help sobbing.

"We do love you, Keth." She came back inside with him. "But you must try to understand your father. I wish he talked more to both of us, but he carries such a terrible load."

Though his father was waiting out in the tunnel, she sat down and put her arm around him.

"He's begging for help. Begging Bridgemen and fleet people for money they never want to give, because they won't believe the humanoids are out there on the Dragon. And I'm looking—"

"Cyra!" his father shouted. "Aren't you coming?"

"A moment, Ryn."

She drew him closer, into her warm sunbud scent.

"Looking for a lost secret." Her low voice hurried. "A secret we need. You see, people came to Kai in a rhodomagnetic ship. Lance Mansfield's *Deliverance*. But he was afraid the humanoids would detect rhodo energy if anybody used it here. After the landing, he dismantled the ship and cut all the rhodo data out of his papers. But I can't believe he destroyed everything—"

"Cyra, please!"

"He knew we'd need rhodo know-how if the humanoids ever

found us. He must have kept some private record. We hope it still exists. That's what I'm searching for."

She stood up to go.

"A hopeless hope, your father thinks. Too much was destroyed in the Black Centuries. But we're desperate for it."

Sobbing again, he clung to her.

"I must run." She bent to kiss him. "I hope you'll try to understand your father. A man alone, Keth, against all the humanoids. He can't spare much time for us."

With an ache in his throat, he let her go. He used to wonder afterwards if she had found that rhodo weapon against the humanoids, but she said no more about it. He didn't ask. Probably, he thought, she had no good news and didn't want to frighten him.

5

Malili The larger of the Cat's two planets, rotating in tidal lock with the smaller, Kai. Malili was settled by the mutant forefathers of the Leleyo, Kai by "normals."

When he had questions now, he was to ask Doc Smart, the new tutor Cyra had brought him for his birthday. A fat green box, not too heavy for him to carry. When he lifted the lid, Doc Smart's holo head jumped out, white-haired and pink-faced, smiling through queer, black-rimmed glasses, programmed to amuse and teach him. Doc Smart was never cross. He didn't have to mind, and he could ask whatever he pleased.

When he asked about Malili, the holo showed an image of two little balls, white on the sun side and black on the other, swinging slowly about a point in the air between them.

"Kai and Malili," Doc Smart said. "Chasing each other around their orbit, just like the Cat and the Dragon chase each other around a much larger orbit. Each keeps the same face to the other. That gives us one suntime and one moontime in each sixty-day orbital period."

Encouraged by that answer, he asked what killed his mother.

"Sorry, Keth." The rollicky voice didn't change. "Data lacking."

"Nurse Vesh says the humanoids did it." He watched the smooth pink face. "Are there humanoids on Malili?"

"Sorry, Keth." The shining smile never changed. "Data lacking."

He kept trying. "Tell me about rhodomagnetics."

"A mythical science." When the happy voice stopped, the smile stopped too. Both froze for a moment now, before Doc Smart finished, "Sorry, Keth. Further data lacking. Would you like a game of chess?"

He didn't like chess. Cyra and his father never had time for it. Nurse Vesh always remembered the very last game her husband played and began to cry. Doc Smart was programmed to let him win every other game, but there was no fun in beating a machine.

"I'd rather know about the Leleyo. What are they like?"

"A mutated race. Physically identical to the Kai Nu in nearly all respects, but immune to bloodrot. Language and culture largely unknown but apparently quite primitive. Shall we talk about your lesson in the civics of the ship?"

He didn't care much for that or math or grammar, but data was nearly always lacking when he asked for anything he really wanted to know. He ran his route and did his lessons, through the endless underground days of a long winter moontime.

In the white excitement of a spring Sunrise day, when he had run all the way back from the gym to get ready for a deckside snow excursion, Nurse Vesh sent him to see his father. Back in that secret room he had seen only twice, Cyra was waiting, too. Both looked serious.

"Sit down, Keth." She made room beside her on the cot. "We've news for you." She was trying to smile. "I hope it won't upset you."

Uneasily, he looked at his father.

"We're leaving, Skipper," his father said. "Returning to the Zone."

Eagerness lifted him. "Am I going?"

His father just frowned.

"We're sorry, Keth." Cyra reached for his hand. "It's a hard thing for us, too. You see, I never found the lost secret I was looking for. One vague hint, in a manuscript of Mansfield's log, but nothing useful. Your father got no support for us here. We hope to do better back in the Zone."

He dropped her hand and kept from crying, too hurt to hear much more of what they said. His father had taken an engineering job they could live on. She would do research at the old Crew station. There was something about weak rhodo sources in the jungle that she thought could be humanoid probes.

"Our last chance, Keth." He was listening again. "I can't guess what the humanoids are waiting for, but when they do come across from the Dragon we've got to meet them with rhodo weapons. From the hints in the log, we can make a crude detector—a sort of palladium compass to pick up that radiation out of the jungle—but nothing that could stop a humanoid."

His throat still ached with his own disappointment.

"I—I see," he whispered at last. "But what about me?"

"We're planning for you, Skipper." His father frowned as if annoyed by the tears still in his eyes. "I spoke to Nurse Vesh, but she's going to Northdyke to be with an invalid sister. We must put you in school."

"Can I—can I learn to be a Crewman?"

"I don't think so." His father's frown bit deeper. "We don't know when the humanoids may come, or whether there will be a Crew. Even if there is, I'm afraid you wouldn't fit."

"Why—why not, sir?"

"A Crewman has to be a fighter."

"I"—he felt weak inside—"I can learn, sir."

"You've been neglected." His father looked hard at him. "Nurse Vesh says you have trouble at the gym. Doc Smart reports that you won't play chess. It appears that you avoid conflict."

"But it's not—not that I'm afraid, sir." He slid off the cot and tried to stand brave and straight. "It's just—just that I don't care about winning games. I don't like to beat people or hurt them. But the humanoids aren't people. I could fight the humanoids."

His father kept frowning. "What's your trouble at the gym?"

"I guess—guess I'm different." Trying to think, he looked up at the proud man in that dim picture. "Maybe because I was born on Malili. I don't understand the other kids, and they don't—" His voice tried to break, and he wished he were as stern and strong as old Kyrondath Kyrone. "They never ask me to play."

"If you can't learn to fight—" His father's lips shut hard, and the spider legs of the scar were ragged ridges. "Forget the Crew."

"No!" The hurt made him weak and breathless. "Sir, please! I want so much to be a Crewman."

"We all want things we never get."

His father's tight face twitched, and the tired eyes flashed to the black-bearded man in the picture and back to him. For a long time his father said nothing. His own knees wobbled, and he sat back on the cot beside Cyra.

"You've a lot to learn, Skipper." His father nodded for him to go. "You will be in school. I've called Topman Taiko at Greenpeak, and you're to go down tomorrow."

Nurse Vesh helped him pack the few things he could bring and found enough quota points to bake him a bag of rocknut cookies to eat on the tubeway. When his father was ready to take him to the station, he reached up to shake her hand. Suddenly she bent down to take him in her arms. Surprised at the sobs that shook her thin, old limbs, he realized that she loved him better than anybody.

Yet he couldn't help crying at the station, when Cyra hugged him and said good-bye. His father's engineering contract was for seven years, nearly as long as his whole life. Nobody had ever told him much about the Zone, except that it was strange and dangerous. If the bloodrot got them, or the humanoids came, he would never see them again.

6

"Dragon's Eggs" Popular name for spheres of polished stone found in the polar ice-caves of Kai, usually buried in circular arrays, perhaps left by ancient visitors from space. Significance unknown.

Greenpeak was a special boarding school for kids with people on Malili. His father warned him at the station that Topman Taiko would be rough on swabbers. He didn't ask what a swabber was, but he felt uneasy.

The tubeway car ran so fast he had no time to eat the rocknut cookies. He was too excited to be hungry, anyhow. If the school trained people for service in the Zone, he would be learning what he wanted to know about the dangers and wonders of Malili.

The name "Greenpeak" struck him as a sad little joke when he came to know the school, because nothing green had ever grown within many hundred kilometers. It was in the upper levels of old Mansfort, the tunnel city the first colonists had dug at the unlucky spot where they landed. Bombed twice in the Black Centuries and finally abandoned, the old city had lain empty and dead for six hundred years before the school moved in. Even in the long summer suntimes, snow still banked the black granite peaks around it.

The first night there, he cried in his berth. The crumbling tunnels were dank and gloomy, blocked all around the school with barriers and signs to keep people out of the uncleared areas. His stiff new boots had worn blisters on his toes, and his scratchy new uniform felt too thin. He had taken too long to get it on and missed his turn at mess. He'd been scolded for breaking rules he hadn't known about, had walked a long tour on the duty deck for offering the watch officer a rocknut cookie, because swabbers were new students, not allowed extra-quota sweets.

The next day wasn't quite so bad, after he had met Chelni Vorn. She had been walking the duty deck too, because she hadn't known swabbers weren't allowed to talk in the corridors. Her short upper lip turned white and her square chin quivered when she told him about it.

They hadn't gone with her father to the Dragon because her mother wouldn't leave Northdyke. Her mother didn't want her now, and she had stayed with her uncle before she came to Greenpeak. He told her a little about his father and Cyra. Her chin quivered again when she said she didn't know what had happened to her father and his starship, and suddenly they were friends.

Topman Taiko was a short, stout man, red-faced and squeaky-voiced, without much time for bewildered swabbers. Though he wore a ship-service medal, he had never been anywhere off Kai. Later, Keth came to see him as a troubled, lonely man who loved the school and lived for it, but at first he always seemed angry over nothing.

"I warn you now," he screeched at the swabber class, "you've got a lot to learn. A thousand years of history first, and the great traditions of the ship. You'll learn the list of Navarchs, from the great Kyrondath Kyrone down to Suan Ko. You'll learn to lead, but not till after you've learned to obey. You'll begin to learn the skills that can take you into space, maybe even out to Malili. But first you'll learn to love Greenpeak."

He stopped to glare down at them and shook his head as if they saddened him.

"You swabbers are a sorry lot, but we'll have to make you do." His fat chin jutted at them, and his old voice quavered. "You're all raw clay, but we'll make you boatfolk, fit to work the ship. You'll have to take some grinding and some blending and some shaping and some heat. Some of you won't like it. Some of you may crack in the kiln. But we'll make the best of you fit for service in the Zone."

Scowling down with dull, red eyes, he talked a long time about rules and punishments. They would walk the duty deck two hours for each black slash. Boatfolk with ten black slashes would get no sweets for the rest of the term. Boatfolk with forty black slashes would never make shipclass.

Keth worked hard. So did Chelni Vorn. They often sat together at mess and she told him more about her family. Her great-grandfather had commanded one of the landers that opened the original Zone and his claims had been the richest in thorium. His heirs had made the Vorn Voyagers a great trading fleet. She was planning to train for space, and she hoped one day to command the Vorn station in the Zone.

She didn't believe in the humanoids.

"Not on Malili, anyhow. My uncle says the Lifecrew makes up horror tales about the planet, about humanoids and killer trees, trying to keep us scared away. We've got real troubles enough, he says, with dragon bats and rockrust and bloodrot, without inventing more. But he says we Vorns are going to open up Malili—in spite of everything!"

Sometimes he didn't like her. She talked too much about the Vorn Voyagers, about her uncle's summer places at both capitals, about skiing at his winter lodges and swimming in Crater Lake and hunting wild mutoxen on the Darkside ranch. Most of the other swabbers called her conceited and bossy, but she didn't seem to care. She liked him.

Once she wanted to see him naked. She looked in a head to make sure it was empty, and called him inside. They stripped together. Her body was thin and straight, pale where her uniform had covered it, with no hair anywhere. Frowning at his penis, she said it didn't look good for much.

Dutymate Luan burst in while they were dressing, screaming at them. She dragged them by the ears to Topman Taiko, who gave them an angry lecture and five black slashes each. He hated Chelni while he was walking the tours, but she gave him a secret smile when they met later in the study cabin, and they stayed friends.

Sometimes they studied together and traded tutor tapes. She told him about her holiday trips away to her uncle's exciting places, and she was generous with the illegal extra-quota sweets she always brought back. But she always called the humanoids a stupid hoax.

The school museum had three ruby-colored dragon's eggs in a dusty case, along with a holostat of the ice-caves where they had been found. Looking at them, he felt a pang of old regret for the one his father had taken, and wondered if Chelni still thought they were lucky. He decided not to ask her.

She seldom spoke about her missing father, and no more news came back from the Dragon. Once every moontime, the space transports brought him a voicecard from Malili, but there was never anything about humanoids or those rhodo sources in the jungle. Cyra and his father were busy and well. His father always asked about slash marks and grades, and he always finished: "Remember, Skipper. Learn to fight."

He wasn't learning to fight. Contact sports were worse than chess. He felt secretly relieved when Topman Taiko said he wasn't fit for warball. Once, on the duty deck, when the boxing champ called him yellow, he just walked away. Yet he longed to be ready when the humanoids came.

Sometimes he woke sweating from ugly dreams about hordes of them chasing him through the black and empty tunnels under Greenpeak. Their clutching hands were golden, like Bosun Brong's. Every one had Nurse Vesh's frowning face and stringy gray hair, and they all screamed after him in her voice, "We got your mother, and we'll get you."

Yet, in spite of everything, he soon felt happier at Greenpeak. He learned not to get black slashes. Topman Taiko sometimes smiled with his salute when they met in the corridors, and the new swabbers seemed a pretty sorry lot.

Wondering whether he was really yellow, he decided to test himself. On the Sunset holiday after the second term, when Chelni had gone back to her uncle's Northdyke home, and the school was almost empty, he took a lightgun out of the emergency box in the hall and followed a path he had planned out, through the empty gym and across the deserted duty deck to a barrier nobody could see. Heart thumping, he climbed the barrier and stumbled on down the off-limits tunnel into thickening blackness.

He had always been vaguely terrified, but also fascinated, by the dead city that lay far around and reached far beneath the tiny, lighted island of the school. Looking across the barriers into the icy dark of the uncleared tunnels, dreaming about his own forefathers who had lived and fought and died there, he had wanted to walk where they had been. The waiting dangers of rockfalls and floodwaters and deadly gas seemed real enough to test his courage, and he wouldn't have to hurt anybody else.

Beyond the barrier, he groped his way into a side tunnel before he dared use the lightgun. When he did snap it on, there wasn't really much to see. Only an endless row of blackmouthed caves opening off the gloomy passage, with nothing to tell him whether they had been shops or homes or something else.

Yet he found himself strangely excited, lifted with an elation he didn't entirely understand. Here, somehow, he was free. With nobody he had to beat or give up to, with nobody trying to hurt him or master him, he could be himself.

He snapped the lightgun off and sat on a fallen rock in the soundless dark, wondering why this lonely freedom felt so good. Perhaps he had escaped some hurt he couldn't remember back in the time with his mother on Malili. Perhaps he had been too long with Nurse Vesh and Doc Smart, learning too little about other people. Perhaps he was just a misfit.

Suddenly, feeling the damp chill creeping into him, he stood up to go on. In spite of the cold, he liked being alone in this black stillness, liked it so much that the reason didn't matter. He knew he had to come back again.

On that first adventure, he found nothing else he cared about. Only a few odd bits of rust-eaten metal and broken glass that he dropped where he found them, because they would have been too hard to explain at room check. But he kept going back when he could, working his way all around the school, mapping the musty caverns in his mind to make sure he wouldn't get lost.

Pushing farther, he found what must have been the main vertical ways. Burned out, perhaps from the bombing, they were great black pits, choked with broken stone and twisted steel, blocking him out of the lower levels.

On a longer expedition, at the end of the term, he felt cold wind blowing out through a broken grating. A ladder beyond it went down into the dark as far as his light could reach. When he tried the rusting rungs, they seemed strong enough.

Trembling a little, yet elated to be venturing where nobody else had been for many hundreds of years, perhaps since the city had died, he hooked the lightgun to his belt and climbed down the ladder into suffocating silence and the stale reek of wet decay.

The first three levels he reached were as empty as those around the school, the dark caves along the corridors all stripped bare in the flight from the bombs, or perhaps by later vandals. One ringing sound startled him—a waterdrop crashing into a still, ink-black pool.

On the fourth level, he found the grating still in place. Climbing back for a piece of broken steel, he pried and hammered till it fell. Beyond it, the foul air took his breath and turned him giddy, yet he stayed long enough to see that the people caught here had not escaped.

The water pools were deeper, and the strange little mounds that scattered them were skeletons. Staring into the stifling dark, trying to imagine the terrors of the dying city, he stayed almost too long. He was quivering and gasping when, at last, he dragged himself out of the shaft on the level above, and his head was still throbbing when he got back to his room.

He didn't go back all the next term. Those secret expeditions had begun to seem a dangerous vice. He resolved to spend more time with his tutors and make a fresh effort to know and like his messmates. His grades were already high enough, however, with only Chelni Vorn above him, and he still disliked games. Alone and bored during the break at the end of the term, he decided to risk just one more venture.

7

Deliverance Rhodomagnetic starship in which refugees from the humanoids reached the Cat. Designed and commanded by Captain Lance Mansfield, grandson of the unfortunate Warren Mansfield, who invented the humanoids.

Carrying a little holocamera, a birthday gift from Chelni, he climbed back down to the lowest level where he could breathe. Splashing through the icy puddles in another tunnel, he found a recent-looking rockfall in his way. Scrambling over it, he slipped and nearly fell into a pit he hadn't seen. A rock from under his hand rolled into it and seemed to drop forever, crashing into something, hollow echoes rolling.

He lay half over it a long time, chilled with sweat and trembling, wondering how brave he really was. When his nerve came back, he slung the holocam around his neck and climbed down that old air shaft till he came to a rust-rotten grating. His light found a long, rock-vaulted room beyond. Though the sour stench took his breath, he battered at the latches till the grating dropped.

He climbed inside and almost fell on a round pebble that rolled in the mud under his boot. Oddly round, when his light picked it up. Another lay near. A dozen were scattered beyond, all perfect spheres, all the same size.

Dragon's eggs!

The vault, he guessed, must have been a museum. Now, most of its contents were melted down into the black mud ridges along the walls. There was only one skeleton, lying against a heavy metal door that looked as if it was frozen shut with rust. A brown mound covered one outflung hand.

Already giddy and ill, he knew he should get out while he could. Yet he stood there, chilled and gasping, wondering again what sort of beings had made those odd stone balls and trying to imagine what had happened here.

There must have been some warning. The man in the room had tried to get out. Trying, maybe, to carry some special treasure. Keth kicked at the little mound and saw a smooth curve like the smooth curve of another egg.

When he kicked again, a little globe rolled out of the mud. Not quite so large as the others, it wasn't stone, but some white metal. It bounced off his boot, seeming strangely light. The clots of mud fell off, and it floated upward.

Or had the bad air already crazed him?

He swayed away from it, knowing he must go. But it came so close and looked so real that he reached out and caught it. Blinking at it, he shook his head. Nothing ever fell up. Yet it felt real enough, damp and cold, twice the size of the ball of his thumb. Heavy in its own strange way, it kept pulling upward.

Afterward, that moment seemed like a fading dream. The next thing he really remembered was waking up on that rockfall above. Pain was pounding in his head, his belly ached from vomiting, and his hands were torn and swollen.

When he could sit up, he found the little sphere tied safe in a pocket of his torn and muddy coverall. He took it out and wiped it clean and sat a long time wondering. A different sort of dragon's egg, it had made them all seem more exciting and mysterious than ever, and it was already priceless to him.

It proved the courage he had questioned and rewarded all his risks. Its silvery wonder seemed somehow to match the obscure urge that had led him to it. Not knowing quite why he searched, he didn't have to know what he had found.

He supposed people would want it to show in some museum, but it was too precious to be given away. When he could walk, he carried it back to the school and kept it hidden in his study desk at the bottom of a box weighted down with old tutor tapes.

Now and then he took it out to feast his imagination on it, wondering what it really was, and whether its ancient makers had really come from the worlds of the Dragon. But he never went back into those dead tunnels, or wanted to, not even to look for the holocam when he found that it was gone.

Somehow, just having it made him a better boatman. Though he still avoided contact sports, he discovered so much delight in skiing in the winter moontimes that he led the class team. Suddenly, his studies took a new direction. He never showed the sphere to anybody, because he didn't want it taken away, but he meant to learn more about it. He searched for tapes about prehistoric Kai and wrote a term paper on the Black Centuries. He made secret experiments with the sphere. When his physics tutors came to lecture on the laws of motion, he measured its upward acceleration: .9 meters per second per second. Once in the lab he asked the instructor what could cause negative gravity.

"Boatman, are you an idiot?" The whitebearded instructor scowled. "Negative gravity has no place in science. Any fool knows that."

Time went by. No invading humanoids came across from the Dragon. The holo newsmen forgot the loss of Captain Vorn's *Kyrone*. Ship officials no longer talked about a rescue expedition. Instead, they announced plans to enlarge the Zone and relieve Kai's power famine with thorium from new mines on Malili.

With no more nightmares about the humanoids, Keth began to feel that Brong's whole story must have been fantastic falsehood. He got his lessons and went skiing when he could. Not so often now, he pulled out the bottom drawer of his desk to make sure the white metal ball had not lost whatever tugged it upward. He never spoke about it, even to Chelni, because its wonder had always been so private, and because the way he had found it would have been too awkward to explain.

She was still his friend, growing taller now than he, her black hair longer and her lean body ripening, and he didn't mind that she always stood at the top of the class, just ahead of him. Scholastic honors did matter to her.

The day he was fourteen, the monthly voicecard came from his father and Cyra on Malili. They were busy and well, and they wished him another happy year. Chelni's birthday was only three days later. She asked him to come with her to the Admiral's for her party.

With the Bridge in session, the Admiral was at Vara Vorn, his Northdyke residence. Though that was half around Kai, near the other pole, the distance didn't matter. Chelni had priority for a special pod that shot them there through the new deep tube in only three hours, from a winter moontime to a bright midsummer suntime.

Half of all Kai's water was locked in the great north polar

ice cap, a thousand kilometers wide, filling the planet's greatest crater. Vara Vorn sat perched on its long ringwall at Meteor Gap, where the grazing impact of some enormous body had torn a forty-kilometer spillway.

The Admiral's dwelling overwhelmed him. There were tall bronze winter gates, massive as the doors of a bank-vault, with a man in red-and-silver livery to work them. The summer gates inside were almost as heavy, cast in silver and studded with great golden medallions that recorded the greatness of the Vorns.

A fat woman in red and silver ran the swift elevator that dropped them into the high-arched caverns of the winter levels or lifted them to the summer towers, with their grand views north across the endless ice desert or south and down across the farms and villas along Wind River, kilometers below and bright green now in the long polar summer.

They stayed almost a week. His first day was miserable. The servants were stiffly correct and quietly hateful—maybe because he didn't belong. Chelni herself laughed when she saw him in the suit they had found for him to wear at her birthday banquet, though she tried to apologize when she saw how hurt he was.

"It's that suit." Merriment still danced in her eyes. "Borrowed from my Cousin Zelyk—Aunt Thara's son. A stupid lout, years older than we are. Coddled by his mother and taught by live tutors. Gobby fat, and always stuffed into things too tight for him. If people think you look funny, they should have seen him sweating in it."

Live footmen in silver braid and scarlet served the dinner in a long summer hall with huge windows overlooking the icefall and the glacier. Chelni sat proudly at the Admiral's right hand, suddenly a stunning stranger in something red and sheer that left her half nude. He was next to her, unhappy in Zelyk's suit.

The Admiral looked younger and bigger and stronger than he had seemed on the holo, and friendlier than Keth had expected. His ice-blue eyes were piercing, but they held a glint of good humor. Chelni said he had been a fine athlete at school, and he still moved with power and a gliding grace. His broad, pink face beamed with pride when he made the company stand for a toast.

"An arrogant old bastard," she had called him. "But he

adores me—his wife's an adulterous bitch and they have no children of their own. He loves me and I like him."

She had introduced him to the other diners, most of them Vorns or officials in the family fleet. Two or three were Bridgemen. The Navarch had sent a sleek, black-haired, coldly elegant woman from his own staff. Keth recognized Zelyk Zoor before they met—a puffy, small-eyed youth, pale and perspiring in a black jacket too tight for him, grinning stupidly at Chelni. His clammy hand felt soft and lifeless.

The Admiral's wife was thin and tall, even more naked than Chelni in her clinging green, glittering with rings and bracelets, a great, white star-shaped gem hanging on a golden chain between her gold-dusted breasts. Absorbed in her talk with a young Bridgeman, she frowned impatiently when Chelni broke in to introduce him.

At the table, Chelni whispered instructions about which fork to use and giggled when he sipped the water meant for his fingers. He felt grateful to the Admiral, who saw his discomfort and took attention from him with anecdotes about his encounters with the Leleyo on Malili—shiftless and incomprehensible nomads who refused to wear decent clothing or do honest work or even drink civilized alcohol.

8

Mutoxen Thick-furred mutant cattle bred by the early colonists for survival on Kai; wild migratory herds range the Darkside highlands.

After that first dismal day, things went better at Vara Vorn. The servants were less obnoxious—he suspected that Chelni had asked the Admiral to reprove them. She took him by surface car to tour the towers and tunnels of the north capital; the Navarch and the Bridge moved twice a year, following the sun to the summer pole.

Together they explored the spacedeck and the fleet headquarters and the great museums. In the Kai museum, they walked through an actual ice-cave with its circular clutch of dragon's eggs still in place; he didn't tell her why it fascinated him. The Malili museum held models of the Zone installations and a few odd Leleyo artifacts made of bone or stone or gold, and holostats of the Leleyo themselves: bare, brown people with alert, lean faces, looking somehow too aware of everything to fit the Admiral's mocking anecdotes.

They crossed the edge of the glacier on a motor-sledge to ski on a high and lovely snow-slope. Next day, the Admiral took them far down the Darkside in his private jet to hunt mutoxen on his Rock Flat ranch. The sun there was not yet a day high, the cold still bitter, and they tramped out across the ice barrens in stiff thermal gear, lugging long projectile guns.

He had never seen mutoxen. They were great, ungainly beasts, their dark fur immensely thick for the long hibernations, their eyes huge for the moonless moontime dark. The Admiral had spotted a lone bull from the jet. Pawing snow to uncover the moss it grazed, it let them come within half a kilometer before it raised its big-horned head to sniff the wind. It was still half-blind and dull, Chelni whispered, from its moontime under the drifts, not yet adjusted to the sun.

"Your shot, Kyrone!" the Admiral called softly. "Aim between the eyes."

His rifle swung and wavered. Dull and ugly as the creature looked, he couldn't kill it. All he felt was admiration for the stubborn stamina that kept it alive through the deadly winter moontimes. He threw the gun down.

The Admiral muttered something scornful. "Take it, Chelni!"

Her rifle crashed. The dark beast pitched backward and slid down a slope out of sight. With a scowl of disgust, she told him to pick up his gun and clean the mud off it.

The Admiral was already tramping ahead to stalk the cow. They didn't stop to look at the dead bull. Chelni told him that rangers would follow in an airwagon to take the fur and dress out the meat.

On the flight back to Vara Vorn, he made a clumsy effort to explain why he hadn't fired.

"No matter, Kyrone." The Admiral shrugged. "Be yourself."

Before they left for Greenpeak, Chelni took him up to the Admiral's office, a huge tower room with views of the black-cragged crater wall and the sun-glinting ice reaching out beyond it into gray-hazed infinity. Hand in hand, they thanked him and said their farewell. When they turned to leave, he asked Keth to stay.

Waiting while Chelni kissed the Admiral and slipped away, he looked around at the silver-framed holostats of Vorn traders and statesmen on the walls, and the models of Vorn spacecraft on a high mantel. The Admiral's desk was a vast bronze fortress, and all those symbols of status and power gave Keth a chill of awe.

"Relax, Kyrone." The Admiral's level gaze seemed warmer than the room. "Chel seems fond of you."

"I'm fond of her."

For long seconds of silence, the blue eyes probed him.

"The fleet needs able young people." The Admiral nodded as if approving him. "Chel says you'll be out of Greenpeak in one more year, well qualified for the Kai Academy. We can offer you a scholarship there, if you contract to come into the fleet."

"Thank you, sir. I do hope to qualify for space training. But . . ."

His voice trailed off, because he didn't know what to say. He was thinking of that silvery dragon's egg that tried to fall into the sky, but he didn't want it taken from him before he had a chance to solve its tantalizing riddles for himself. Thinking, too, of Chelni's notions about the humanoids.

"I want to join my father," he went on at last. "In the Lifecrew."

"Better forget it." The Admiral sat silent for a moment, grave eyes weighing him. "Your father is—was—my friend. An able engineer, till he caught this crazy obsession."

"Suppose it isn't crazy, sir?" His own boldness astonished him. "Suppose Bosun Brong was telling the truth about the humanoids on Kyronia?"

"Suppose I'm twenty meters tall?" The Admiral shrugged, his blue stare sardonic. "I know Brong lied about how he got back—it couldn't have been in any lander. I have to assume he lied about everything."

"If you don't believe him, what became of your brother?"

"I used to hope—" The Admiral's heavy features set into a scowl that frightened him. "But it has been too many years. I guess we'll never know. There's no use brooding."

After a moment of silence, his muscular bulk flowed upright.

"Listen, Kyrone." Smiling again, though rather grimly, he offered a massive paw. "Chel likes you. I respect your historic name and your record at Greenpeak. I'd like to have you in the fleet. I advise you to forget the humanoids. If you can do that— and you decide you want a place with us—have Chel get word to me."

"Thank you, sir," Keth took his powerful hand, "but I don't expect that."

In their private pod, on the way back to Greenpeak, Chelni looked at him accusingly and then lay back in her seat to sleep, or pretend to, without saying anything at all. He knew he had hurt and disappointed her.

It seemed to him that she and the Admiral wanted to make him another mutox, shaped and driven and perhaps finally consumed by the will of the Vorns, but he didn't say so. He didn't like to fight.

Toward the end of his last year at Greenpeak, Cyra and his father came home from Malili, but only for a visit. He saw them twice, the first time on a school holiday when they asked him and Nurse Vesh to meet them at their Terradeck hotel.

All three were painfully changed. Nurse Vesh had shriveled into a shrill little wisp, feeble and forgetful, but she had somehow hoarded quota points to bring him a crisp-scented bag of rocknut biscuits. He had forgotten how much he loved her.

Cyra looked leaner, too, her warm softness gone. Her jaw was firmly set, sharp lines creased her dark-tanned face and her eyes had a wary squint. Coarse black hairs had grown out of the mole under her eye. His father was thinner and sterner, oddly jumpy when anything unexpected happened behind him. They still lived in terror of the humanoids.

"Seven years gone." His father's voice was higher, half its power lost. "The humanoids seven years closer, and we're still weaponless."

Cyra astonished him with a gift from Bosun Brong—a small cup of hammered gold, decorated with the sharp-cut image of an oddly shaped tree, the trunk thick and bulging, limbs drooping down all around it; it looked strangely patterned, strangely graceful. He rejoiced in its look and its feel, without knowing why.

"A Leleyo artifact," she told him. "Very rare, because they

do handwork so seldom. Hammered out of a virgin nugget, I
suppose. A ceremonial vessel, Brong says, given him when he
joined a native cult. He says the plant is called a braintree. A
priceless thing, but you aren't to sell it."

"Why—" He blinked at its yellow dazzle. "Why for me?"

"He wants you to think well of him, Keth."

Looking at his father, he saw the spider-scar whiten.

9

Feyolin Illicit Malilian drug used in Leleyo ceremonials;
sources unknown. Reports of strange effects unverified.

Bosun Brong was back in the Zone, they told him, manning the
Lifecrew station there while they were away.

"Never trusted him," his father muttered. "Too full of native
tricks and tales you can't believe. But he does know his Leleyo
kin, and he claims he wants to help us. Our last friend—if in
fact he is a friend."

Cyra had failed to reach or even to locate the rhodo sources
she had planned to search for.

"No funds to buy or hire or build a sanicraft," his father
said. "We couldn't get outside the perimeter, and our crude instruments couldn't tell us much from inside. A number of
different sources, we decided, all too weak for us to separate
their effects."

"I did talk to Brong about them," Cyra added. "He thinks
they might be braintrees." She nodded at the golden cup, which
Keth was still fingering dazedly. "Sacred plants, his native
friends have told him. He says he's never seen one."

"If you want to believe him!" His father was bitterly scornful. "A feyolin addict. High on that, he could say anything. I
sometimes wonder if all his wild tale about the humanoids on
Kyronia wasn't a feyolin dream."

"I've thought so." Cyra shook her graying head uncertainly.
"But then again . . ." She was silent for a moment, staring at
the golden bowl. "I'm sure he sometimes lies, but he can also
do things I can't understand."

"Those escapes!" his father rasped. "He won't explain them. Or how he got home from the Dragon."

"He says he does it with feyolin," Cyra said. "He even gave me a sample of the stuff."

"Illegal!" his father snapped. "Smuggled by his native kin."

"He wanted us to try it, but of course we wouldn't." She shivered. "I got nowhere trying to analyze it. Queer stuff, with a puzzling platinum content. Nothing like any alkaloid we know. I can't believe it does what he says it does."

"A squalid little liar!" His father spoke as if in pain, his voice hoarse and high. "Yet what he says—about the humanoids—frightens me!" He turned to Cyra, and Keth saw the crawling scar, bold and white on his ray-burnt cheek. "You heard him, Cy."

"I heard him." She turned to Keth with a somber nod. "He says that the drug can take him back to Kyronia—he can't or won't explain just how. But he says he can see the humanoids there. Millions of them now. Billions, maybe. All at work. Never stopping, day or night. Spreading that rose-glowing city all over the planet."

"Building a base," his father grated. "A base against us."

"And three enormous transport ships," she said. "A dozen times the size of the one that brought them there. Each one going up in a nest of factories making the parts and more humanoids. When they're ready, Brong says, they mean to swallow us."

He whispered, "How soon?"

"Brong doesn't know." She shrugged uneasily. "The humanoids never die, and he says they have their own sense of time. But he says the ships look almost complete."

"That's why we're back on Kai," his father said. "Time's running out. We were getting nowhere in the Zone. I know most people won't believe Brong's warning. But I want to see Vorn and a few others who used to back the Crew. An unlikely bet, but we can't just quit."

They were going on to Northdyke, where the Bridge was sitting. Later, returning to the Zone, they would visit him at Greenpeak.

"I want one last look for Mansfield's private tapes," Cyra said. "Or whatever records he kept. If they still exist, they could have been buried somewhere in old Mansfort. When I asked permission to search there, years ago, the lower levels were blocked off and dangerous—"

"They—they still are."

Keth spoke on impulse, breathless with excitement that was half apprehension. That precious object in his desk—could the power that lifted it be rhodomagnetic? Its mysterious makers—could they have known rhodo science? It was still a very private treasure, but suddenly now he saw that he must share its secret.

"I've something to show you," he whispered. "Out of those dead levels. A thing I never understood."

"We'll be in Greenpeak." His father's face looked drawn and dead beneath the scar. "But we're leaving for Northdyke tonight. Unless we can turn up new friends—and better ones than Brong—we're dead."

They went on to Northdyke. Back in his room at Greenpeak, he set the Leleyo bowl on his desk and sat a long time, dreaming of the perilous allure of Malili and wondering why Bosun Brong should care for him. He leaned at last to open the bottom drawer and test the upward thrust of that white metal ball once more. Dragon's egg or something else, it was still more precious to him than the bowl. He was almost sorry, at the end of the term, when Cyra called to say they were stopping to see him.

They looked despondent when he met them at the tubeway station. Their story that Brong could see the humanoids on Kyronia had convinced nobody. Most of their old friends wouldn't even see them. Admiral Vorn had offered them a drink for old time's sake, but he wouldn't let them talk about his lost brother or the worlds of the Dragon.

"A stubborn old mutox," his father muttered. "But I hope to get something out of him yet. The Navarch has named him to be the Zone's next commander. If we can get him to listen to Brong—"

"If!" Cyra shrugged. "Not very likely."

Delaying the moment of loss, he took them to meet Topman Taiko, took them to a warball game, took them to evening mess with Chelni, who surprised him with her gracious warmth and promised them to ask her uncle to do all he could. When it was nearly time for them to go, Cyra asked what he had wanted them to see.

"A dragon's egg," he said. "An odd one. Metal, instead of rock. It wants to fall up."

Her mouth hung slack for an instant. They were standing on the duty deck where Chelni had left them, and his father spun around as if frightened by something behind him.

"You found *that?*" Her eyes were unbelieving. "In the old city?"

"Down under the school. In what must have been a museum. A dozen stone eggs scattered around it."

"Let me see!"

When they reached his room, his father peered back into the corridor and locked the door. They stared, scarcely breathing, while he freed the little globe from its hiding place under the old tutor tapes and let it float off his hand.

Cyra snatched it out of the air.

"A monopole!" She stood blinking at it, testing its upward pull, her thin hand shaking. "Mansfield's rhodo monopole!"

His father was reaching, and she let him hold it.

"I thought—" Keth caught his breath. "What's a monopole?"

"A single rhodomagnetic pole." Her hungry eyes clung to it, even while she spoke to him. "This one's evidently positive. Common matter has a slight positive rhodo polarity. A positive pole repels the mass of the planet."

At last, seeming relieved to have it in her own hand again, she could look at him.

"Mansfield must have saved it from the *Deliverance*. In case we ever needed it for what he called 'our ultimate resort' against the humanoids. Concealed it, I suppose, among those odd stone artifacts." Her stare sharpened. "Was there anything else?"

"A skeleton," he said. "Mounds of mud."

"This could be enough." He thought she looked younger. "Working from it, I can derive the math. Find a way to induce rhodo forces. To generate new and stronger monopoles. Learn enough, with luck, to fabricate some sort of rhodo weapon."

"You're sure?" his father demanded. "Sure that was all?"

"All I saw."

"You were there alone, down on the dead levels?" Cyra stared. "How'd you get permission?"

"I didn't."

He told about those secret expeditions.

"A dreadful risk!" Sitting on his berth, she pulled him down beside her. "If you had fallen, or lost your light. . . ."

He felt her lean body shiver.

"And you never spoke about it?" She looked abruptly at him. "I see that you prize it, but of course you must let us take it."

"It's mine—" He checked his own hurt protest. "If you need it, take it."

"We do." His father's voice had firmed. "It should help us prove I'm more than just a con man."

Suddenly, all their plans were changed. They sent him out to cancel their flight back to Malili and book return passage to Northdyke.

"You won't be hearing much from us," his father said before they left. "We'll have to be as cautious as you were. The humanoids, if they're on Kyronia, they could detect any reckless use of rhodo power. For all we know, they could have agents already here on Kai. We must keep under cover. Try for private help. Do nothing to give our work away."

"But we'll try to keep in touch." And Cyra added, "We won't destroy your precious monopole. In time, you'll have it back."

"Skipper, you've earned your berth." His father gripped his hand. "We'll want you in the Crew when you get out of school. That is, unless"—the spider quivered on his tightening jaw—"unless the humanoids get here first."

10

Black Centuries   Age of danger and disorder ended by the first Navarch, the great Kyrondath Kyrone, when he reunited the battling cities and restored the law of the ship.

Cyra and his father left Greenpeak without waiting for his graduation or saying where they would be. Vaguer than ever, their occasional voicecards told him only that they were hard at work, with never a hint of what their progress was or how they might be reached.

At graduation, old Topman Taiko announced that Boatman Keth Kyrone had earned the Vorn Voyagers scholarship for four years at the Academy. Drinking a melonade with Chelni after the ceremony, he tried to thank her.

"Thank the Admiral. It seems you impressed him." She leaned across their glasses, her wide eyes inviting. "Say you'll join the fleet."

"I can't . . ."

He saw her smile turning bleak, but he couldn't tell her about Cyra and his father and the monopole.

"I just can't . . ."

Angry tears had welled into her eyes. He bent across the little table, trying to tell her how sorry he was, but she brushed his reaching hand away with a blind slap that caught his glass and splashed his face with melonade. Without a word, she stumbled away.

Yet he did receive the scholarship. Riding the circumpolar tube to Crater Lake and the Academy, he felt lifted with an eager sense that he was in the doorway to an exciting new world, closer to space and Malili and the truth about the humanoids.

The old city swiftly dimmed his eager hope. Carved into the impact mountains where the old Navarch had withdrawn after Mansfort fell, it had ruled Kai for three hundred years, until the transplanet tubes were dug and the Bridge moved on to the twin polar capitals, Northdyke and Terratown. The centuries since had eroded all its ancient glory.

Founded by the Lifecrew while it was still a power, the Academy sprawled through the old Bridge district. Though the vaulted caverns held shadows of their old magnificence, the musty age of everything depressed him with recollections of those dead levels of the first capital where he had found the monopole.

Most of his instructors looked as age-worn as the damp-stained stone. Few had trained for space and none had been out to Malili. His courses began with dry repetitions of what he had learned at Greenpeak, and he found that his own training for space must wait until his last year.

Though he had expected Chelni, she did not enroll. A brief and stiffly spoken voicecard told him that she was leaving for the Zone with her uncle, to take a training position in the Vorn station there. She hoped he would decide to follow her into the fleet.

He listened twice to the card, hearing the troubled emotion beneath her forced and brittle tone. Disturbed himself, recalling all their years together, and depressed with the haunting uncertainties of his own future, he walked out through the air doors to the topside parade deck.

It was the middle of a winter moontime. The Dragon was a bright red spark, washing out all the stars around it. Though the windless chill took his breath, he crossed the deck to the far rail. The lake lay a full kilometer below him, contained in the crater basin by the old power dam that had always been the city's life. Frozen now and dazzling with snow, it stretched flat and vast to the ragged black mountain rim. Malili blazed high above it, full and enormous, deadly and alluring, colder than the snow.

He stood clutching the frosty rail, gazing into the planet's silver mask, thinking of the obscure promise of the monopole and the brooding enigma of the humanoids, longing, in spite of himself, for Chelni, until he began to shiver.

He was at the Academy nearly four years. On every birthday, a brief voicecard from the Zone brought him Chelni's curtly worded hope that he would join the Vorns. Sometimes he was tempted to promise her that. The messages from Cyra and his father, almost equally rare and brief, told him so little that he began to doubt that the monopole had given up its secrets.

On the first day of his last term, walking to his desk in the required Kai lit class, he was feeling empty and disheartened. The bored instructor had droned the same lecture too many times to keep any meaning in it, and he had just learned that his space training was delayed again, because the classes were all filled by contracted fleetfolk.

Unexpectedly, the girl sitting next to him changed everything. She was tall and lovely, with light brown skin and long golden hair. When the instructor wanted her name, she rose to give him a grave little bow.

"Nera Nyin." Her soft voice held a hint of musical power. "From Ili, Malili. Visiting Kai on a special student visa, and admitted to the Academy on a fellowship funded by Admiral Torku Vorn."

She sat again. Breathless with his own excitement, he turned to study her calm profile.

A native Leleyo!

He could hardly believe it, because she looked so utterly unlike the naked nomads that travelers to the Zone had always reported. Slim and straight in the blue school uniform, she looked clean, and even chic, completely at ease. When he stood to give his own name, her gold-green eyes came to him with a probing candor that jolted him again.

He wanted to ask her a thousand things. About her people and their sacred trees and the stuff called feyolin. About rockrust and bloodrot and rhodo sources and possible humanoid probes. Through most of a month, her nearness tantalized him. Sitting close beside him every day, seeming absorbed in the dusty lectures, she spoke to nobody. Her aloof reserve kept her as remote as Malili.

Baffled, he asked the instructor about her.

"Just out of the jungle." The tired old man peered sharply at him, as if to see why he cared. "Probably can't understand much Kai. Allowed here, I believe, because the Admiral wants to develop native contacts. Get to know her if you can."

"She's hard to know."

"They're evasive. Seldom tell us much, and never the truth." His pale old eyes squinted shrewdly. "If you want a good berth with the Vorns, get next to her."

Though he felt far from certain that he wanted a berth with the Vorns, he waited next day for her to leave the lecture hall.

"May I—" Awe of her aloof beauty checked him, until suddenly she smiled. "May I walk with you?"

"Please." Her voice was melodious and low. "I wish to know you, Keth Kyrone."

Almost overwhelmed with his own delight, he got his breath to ask if she would like a melonade in the snack bar.

"I prefer Malili food." Her Kai seemed fluent enough. "You might enjoy the difference. Would you come to my own place, off the campus?"

"I—I can't." The school still had rigid rules and guarded gates, relics of the old Lifecrew discipline. "Not without a liberty pass."

"I brought a letter from your Admiral Vorn." She seemed amused. "I think there will be no problem."

There was no problem. With a dazzled smile for her and a searching look at him, the duty officer waved them through. On the pod, she began asking about the first Navarch and the founding of Crater Lake. What he said about the Black Centuries seemed to horrify her.

"People killed each other?" Her greenish eyes went wide. "Why?"

"The law of the ship had broken down," he told her. "There was no Lifecrew then, and we hadn't learned to cope with Kai. People were starving. Rival leaders took them to war. Fighting for water rights. For mining rights. Sometimes just for plunder or power."

"But human beings don't kill each other." She shook her head, not quite believing. "That was long ago. I think your histories are not accurate. Human beings do not kill."

"I'm afraid they did."

To convince her, he told her about all the sprawled skeletons he had found on those bomb-sealed levels beneath Greenpeak.

"You went into such dreadful places? Still a child and all alone?" She seemed amazed. "No Leleyo would do that. But neither would we kill."

She turned to face him in the seat, frowning thoughtfully. For one dreadful instant, he was afraid she had unfairly identified him with the murderers of old Mansfort, but then he saw that she was merely puzzled.

"We don't understand your ways or your laws or your wars. That's why I came to Kai. We had hoped for a long time that your strange nature would never matter to us, but now you have begun to frighten us, setting up your death-walls on our world and killing everything inside."

She and Chelni, the stray thought struck him, would never be friends.

"I'm glad it's you." The risk of the words left him giddy. "You who came."

"I've wanted to see Kai since I was a tiny child." Her gold-green eyes looked far away. "Two Kai Nu came outside your Zone in a great machine. It broke, and they were about to die. My leyo helped them get back inside their death-wall."

"The Zone perimeter, you mean?"

"Your killer wall." Cool scorn edged her voice. "Your shield of rays to kill small things in the air, and your autofiring lasers aimed at the sky, waiting to burn anything larger. I think you kill too much."

11

Leleyo   Native race of Malili. Apparently human, but immune to bloodrot and able to survive without machines.

Her apartment took his breath again. It was in a high-priced upper level of the West Rim district. One whole wall of the living room was an enormous thermal window overlooking the crater sea, which had thawed now to a wind-marred mirror, black beneath the purple Duskday sky and slashed with a glittering silver track beneath high, half-lit Malili.

"Home!" She paused a moment at the window, eyes lifted to the bright-clouded planet. "I long to be back."

The lofty room was oddly empty of tables or chairs, the walls lined with books or hung with Kai art and artifacts.

"So much to gather—and nothing I can carry home. So much to learn!" She struck her forehead in comic dismay. "It hurts my poor head."

They sat on cushions in the empty dining room. She offered wooden bowls of odd-shaped nuts and small red fruits, a wooden platter stacked with something that looked like sun-dried meat, or perhaps dried fruit pulp, a cream-colored liquid in a plastic flask.

"All safe for you." She had seen his hesitation. "Sterilized and passed for import by your own inspectors at the perimeter station." She made a wry face. "They killed the flavors, too."

She sipped from the flask before she passed it to him. He liked the faintly bitter piquancy and took a larger swallow.

"I wish to learn about the future of your Zone." She selected an egg-shaped fruit for him. "Your father has worked with the Vorns, and they are your friends. Perhaps you can tell me how far into Malili your death-walls are to reach."

"I don't know." He bit at the fruit and found it hard. "The Bridge and the Navarch have talked of a Kai Life Plan."

"For us, the Leleyo Death Plan."

Thinking of Chelni, he tried to defend the Zone and the Vorns. Kai was dying. To stay alive, it must have thorium from Malili. In a fair exchange, it could offer its science and culture, its high civilization.

"Civilization?" Her tone grew scornful. "Culture? By that you mean *things*. Things our rockrust would crumble to useless dust. We Leleyo have our own science and civilization, evolved to fit our world and our needs."

"Anyhow," he insisted, "our Zone is very small. Located on a mountain peak in a region your people seldom visit—"

"Don't you know why?" Her greenish eyes flashed. "It's because the fallout from your neutron bombs drifts far outside your death-wall, harming everything within hundreds of kilometers."

"I didn't know that—but we've another reason to be on Malili." Gripped with urgency, he bent to peer at her. "We're looking for signs of humanoids."

Astonishment raised her golden eyebrows. "Aren't they machines?"

"Powerful machines. Hunting us to suffocate us with a deadly kind of care. I'm afraid they're overtaking us."

"They'll never trouble Malili, because the rust protects us." Irony flashed in her eyes. "You Kai Nu must love machines, because you have them everywhere. Why should you fear one more?"

"We must have machines to survive at all on Kai, but ours aren't rhodomagnetic. The humanoids' are, and we've detected rhodo sources on Malili. Maybe the braintrees—"

"Our feyo trees?" She looked startled. "They've nothing to do with the humanoids."

"Are you sure?" He watched her, trying not to let her loveliness distract him. "There's a drug from the trees. Could it be the humanoids' euphoride—"

"It is not." She shook her head, gravely indignant. "The feyo trees are living shrines. Their blood is the life of my people. It comes from no machine, and its gifts are not for you Kai Nu—"

"Does it kill?" The idea stabbed him. "My mother died searching for a braintree."

"Your people are too eager to die." She paused as if in painful recollection. "You don't belong on Malili—that's what you never learn. On my first feyosan, when I was still a young child, my feyolan pointed out a spot where metal rust had stained and blighted everything." Her soft tone fell. "That may have been your mother's machine."

Seeing him baffled by the hard little fruit, she took it out of his hand and pressed the end of it. With a gentle pop, the red rind split and peeled away, uncovering an orange-colored morsel that she pressed to his lips. He liked its tangy sour-sweetness; yet, with his eyes on her, he found that he had gulped the rich juice without really tasting.

"Since we're going to be friends—" With a graceful shrug, she was shedding her blue uniform jacket. "I'm not used to your clothing."

She had worn nothing under the jacket. He hadn't seen a girl so far unclad since that day so long ago when little Chelni Vorn bared her flat-chested thinness for his inspection. The difference dazzled him.

"If you mind—"

Seeing his startled stare, she reached for the jacket. He caught his breath and found voice to say that he didn't mind at all. Feeling as if his whole world had tipped, he tried and failed to pull his eyes away.

"You're beautiful!" he whispered.

"I'm glad you like me." She turned a little to display her golden splendor. "I thought at first you were not pleased." She made a face of mock perplexity and let it fade into a frown of grave inquiry. "There is still so much I must ask you. About the Zone and your plans for more death-walls and your Life-crew and these humanoids you seem to fear so much."

He waited, trying to control his breathing, suddenly wondering. If she had come to Kai as a Leleyo agent, could she be the sort of spy his father feared? Intoxicated with her bared loveliness, he didn't want to suspect her, yet—

"Let's talk about these humanoids." She was leaning toward him entrancingly, her wide eyes searching, so close he caught her faint, clean scent. "Do you really fear them? Or is the talk of them only a clever lie, invented to cover the killing of Malili?"

Disturbed, he tried and failed to look away from her allure.

"We are afraid," he whispered. "A few of us are."

"We've no machines on Malili," she insisted softly. "What we fear is your death-walls, and the dust that drifts out of them.

But if fearing the humanoids could make you leave your stolen Zone—"

Her eyes shone with joy, contemplating that.

"They were real and dreadful on those old worlds." He shrank a little from her loveliness. "Our ancestors were very lucky to escape them. I believe they've reached the Dragon. If you aren't afraid, you ought to be."

"Why?" She shrugged wondrously, limpid eyes wide. "I think they were invented to end the sort of troubles that threaten you on Kai. Perhaps you should invite them—"

"To let them end our freedom?"

"Shall we think of other things?" She gestured at the platter. "If you aren't afraid to try a bite of binya ling?"

He couldn't help thinking of the humanoids, but she was selecting a thin brown slab from the platter. Biting one end off with gleaming teeth, she offered the rest of it companionably to him.

"What is it?"

"You might like it more if you hadn't asked. Since you did, it's a dried secretion from the binya tree. Poisonous originally, it functions to attract and kill wild creatures whose bodies then decay to fertilize the tree. We age it until the poison is only a flavor."

Thinking of bloodrot, he shook his head at it.

"It won't kill you." A half-mocking challenge danced in her eyes. "Your own inspectors have tested it."

Bracing himself, he bit the end her teeth had marked. Though tough and nearly tasteless at first, the stuff became sweetish and richly meaty as he chewed. It had a slight peppery bite that he thought must be the poison flavor.

"I like it," he decided.

"It was better before your inspectors cooked it."

He finished the slab and took another, his appetite sharpening. She showed him how to peel the kela berries and told him the names of the nuts. When the dishes and the plastic flask were empty, she gathered them and glided upright, out of her uniform skirt.

"I like your lesser gravity," she murmured. "Motion is so easy here."

Her own motion dazzled him, but he tried not to let it overwhelm him. Waiting while she was gone into another room, he

46

couldn't help wondering again if she was indeed a spy. Suddenly he didn't care.

The lights turned lower, she came flowing down again beside him. She had brought something bubbling and blood-colored in a hammered golden cup that was almost a twin of the one Bosun Brong had sent him. She raised it in both hands, closing her eyes and glowing with pleasure as she breathed its vapor. He caught an odd, sharp aroma.

"Feyolin," she breathed. "I can share it with a friend."

She sipped, with a tiny shiver that made her more alluring. He shuddered. Feyolin! Was it in fact euphoride, invented to kill the will of men? His first frightened impulse was to push the cup away, but she was leaning too close, her bare arm already sliding around him, her own fresh scent stronger than the heady odor of the cup. Suddenly, all the hazards he imagined mattered no more than those warning barriers he had passed in old Mansfort to find the monopole.

He sipped.

12

Euphoride   Benign psychochemical developed by the humanoids to eradicate fear, frustration, and pain, creating absolute happiness.

He was never sorry. If feyolin was wrong, it swept him instantly into another moral domain, far beyond his old ethical limits. Fiery in his throat, it burned fast through his being, half agony, all strange delight. His senses were blunted for an instant, then incredibly sharpened.

Though that fire swiftly died, its aftertaste lingered and grew into a salt-and-scarlet symphony, utterly new to him, so delicious that his first cautious sip seemed far too small. He wanted the golden chalice for a deeper drink, but a swift expansion of time and distance had swept it from him into a strange infinity where every breath occupied an age.

His own heartbeats had slowed and swollen into immense reverberating quakes. The long room had become a vast and separate cosmos nothing else could penetrate. Outside it, Malili's milky glow on the lake was now so blinding that he blinked and turned away.

Shining with a new glory of her own, Nera came closer, and her intoxicating scent wrapped him in a quivering diamond mist. Her first velvet touch charged him with a resistless joyous longing.

"Nera . . ." His breathless whisper rumbled like thunder. "Nera Nyin!"

Though amazement at himself still lingered in some far, cool corner of his being, that didn't matter. He was no longer Kai Nu, no longer bound by the stern restraints of habit and custom and law he had been learning all his life. Transfigured by the crimson drink, he was Leleyo.

He turned hungrily to her, and she came to him. His own uniform was soon in their way, and she helped him shuck it off. She herself was incandescent joy, multiplied beyond imagination. Afterwards, it all seemed another reality, a remote realm of incandescent truth from which he could recall only a few precious fragments.

The first electric sweetness of her mouth, her deft hands helping him slide into her, the yielding power of her gentle body. Her soft laugh, magnified in her golden chest to a drumming melody when he whispered in panic that he mustn't make her pregnant.

"Body control is the first art of feyo." Her breathed words were soaring music. "We limit our numbers to fit our world. I won't get a child until I wish."

They were dwellers in their own private universe, where they themselves filled all space and all time, each magnificent instant expanded into eternities of splendor. Only their joy in each other was real, and nothing else could touch them. Whenever its burning glory was about to fade, another searing sip ignited it again, always more divine.

Desolation chilled him when he reached a last time for the cup and found it dry. She laughed gaily at his greediness. Feyokoor could never last forever. It was time for them to sleep.

The wonder was dead when he woke, though she lay slight and lovely in his arms. Restored to the common universe, that great bare room was cold and gloomy and still. Beyond the thermal window, a gray fringe of moontime ice had rimmed the black lake, and the magic had vanished from Malili's light. That incandescent aftertaste had turned bitter on his lips, and his whole body felt numb and clumsy, aching unexpectedly.

"Keth . . ." She breathed his name faintly, without really waking, when he bent to kiss her, the sound nearly too faint for his deadened hearing. "Come back to me."

He found his uniform and let himself out. Returning through the nondescript litter of unswept tunnels and the occasional rumble and clatter of early traffic, he had to grope his way painfully back from that lost wonderland to the old realities, to the cramping customs of Kai and the demands of his classes and the intolerable possibility that she could be a humanoid agent.

At the gate, a different duty officer demanded the liberty pass he didn't have and made him sign the penalty book. Back in his room, he sat for a long time, staring at his own golden cup, dreaming wistfully of that evaporated wonder, and regretting all he had failed to learn.

Where did the braintrees grow? What were the tenets of the feyo faith, which she had managed to say so little about? How did her nomad race stay alive in their cloud-shrouded homelands he could never even hope to know? Without machines or clothing, tools or vehicles, dwellings or records, without any apparent social order, how did the Leleyo manage to exist?

More painful questions nagged him. Why had she elected him for such shattering friendship? Only because of the Kyrone name and what she hoped he could tell her? That likelihood was at first almost too painful to consider, but he sat suddenly straighter, grinning at his gloomy face in the shaving mirror. Even if she never spoke to him again, or wanted to, his recollection of their night together would remain as precious to him as that magic monopole.

Oddly happy, he got up to pee, drink cold water, and plug a math tape into his holotutor. Brimming with a breathless eagerness, he went early that day to Kai lit and sat watching the door, heart throbbing hard, waiting for her.

She didn't come.

"Don't know and never will." The aged instructor gave him a shrug and a stabbing glance, perhaps of envy, when he went up after class to ask about her. "The Leleyo way. Safer not to get involved because you'll never understand them."

He tried to call her, but she had no listed holo number. He was wondering that afternoon if he dared to go back to her place, at the risk of some scornful rebuff, when his tutor called him to the commandant's office.

A tall, tight-lipped man, the commandant had been with his father on the dwindling Lifecrew staff at the Academy before he resigned from the Crew to stay with the school. He stood up when Keth came into his office, his stiff little smile changing into grave concern.

"Kyrone, where were you last night?"

"Off campus, sir. I had to sign the penalty book."

"Who were you with?"

"A girl, sir." Dim alarms confused him. "A fellow student."

"Her name?"

"Nera Nyin." The commandant waited until he had to add, "She's Leleyo."

"What happened?"

"We talked. We ate—ate her native foods."

"I suppose you were intimate?"

He stood silent, offended by that crude invasion.

"Did she offer you a drug?"

"She did."

"Which you accepted?"

He had to nod, and the commandant scowled.

"Kyrone, your record here has been good. I know your father and I respect your name. I met the girl—she brought me a voicecard from Admiral Vorn. Having seen her, I can't blame you for whatever happened, but now you're in a regrettable situation."

He waited, chilled with colder apprehensions.

"I suppose you know the natives don't want us on Malili. Clean as she seems, the girl must be regarded as an enemy of Kai. Admiral Vorn did arrange her visit, because we need information about the natives, but he also alerted the shipwatch. She has been observed. Her apartment was searched this morning. Traces of an illicit psychochemical were found. You will be asked to describe its effects."

"Sir—" He tried to smooth his voice. "Where is she?"

"So you don't know?" The commandant's frown grew graver. "The shipwatch hoped you would."

"Has something happened to her?"

"If you don't know . . ." The commandant looked baffled and unhappy. "The shipwatch had been watching her place, waiting permission to raid it. You were seen to enter with her late yesterday, and to leave alone this morning.

"Permission for the raid came through today. The officers found a vast collection of information on Kai—objects of art and tapes on every subject. They found her imported hoard of native food, and kilograms of the gold nuggets she was selling to support her operation. The girl herself was gone."

The shipwatch officers were waiting for him in another room. Tired-faced, hard-eyed men, they demanded more than he knew about Nera Nyin, but seemed to disbelieve nearly everything he told them. They shouted more questions than he had answers for, about Cyra and his father.

Where were they now? Had they been in touch with Nera Nyin? What had they been up to, shuttling back and forth between Kai and Malili? Where were they getting funds? How were they linked to Bosun Brong, and why had he himself received a gift from Brong?

They showed him the golden chalice they had found in his own room and demanded facts about it. What were the symbols on it? What was it meant to contain? How was it used in what native ceremonials? If he claimed not to know, how did he account for the traces of illicit feyolin they had found in the cup and also in the raided room?

He said as little as he could, and said it many times. The interrogation went on until his first stunned bewilderment had turned to seething anger, until that had cooled to savage hatred for the shipwatch, until even the hatred had died into total exhaustion.

At last they left him. He sat there alone, sprawled back in his chair, too empty even to wonder what might happen next, yet clinging to one thread of secret satisfaction. They hadn't asked about the monopole, and he hadn't told them.

The commandant came back at last, seeming faintly relieved.

"You're free, Kyrone. They're convinced that you told them as much as you know—which leaves them in the dark about how the girl escaped from her apartment or where she is now."

He hesitated, his troubled eyes on Keth.

"One of them suspects that she used that drug to get away. Puzzling stuff, you know. Chemically strange. The Leleyo are said to believe it gives them supernatural powers." He squinted expectantly. "What do you think?"

"I did try it." Keth shrugged, carefully silent about Bosun Brong's equally inexplicable disappearances. "I can't describe the way it made me feel, but we didn't leave the room. She said nothing about any escape. I don't think she was expecting any raid, and I've no idea what became of her."

"Another watchman thinks you murdered the girl and somehow smuggled her body out." The commandant paused to peer at him. "However, he can't suggest either motive or method. The whole affair is still an ugly riddle. They've decided not to hold you, but I imagine they'll keep an eye on you."

When he reached his room, the hammered chalice was back on his desk. Midnight had passed. Falling wearily into his berth, he dreamed of Nera Nyin. She was lost on the Darkside ice-barrens, nude and shivering, ill with bloodrot. He was searching for her, carrying the drug to cure her in the golden chalice, but he could never find her.

Tired and dull the next day, he hardly heard his tutors. A burst of illogical hope spurred him early to Kai lit, but of course she wasn't there. Sitting at late mess with no appetite, he heard a rumor that she had been arrested on drug charges and deported back to Malili.

Doubting that, he longed for news that never came. A voice-card from Cyra and his father said their health was the same and their work still in progress. That final year dragged on. He applied again for space training, and again the classes had been filled with fleetfolk. The midterm passed. Unexpectedly, Chelni Vorn called from Terradeck.

She had come home to marry him.

13

Duskday The day after Sunset, marked traditionally by the end of the harvest festivals and withdrawal underground.

He met her at the gate. Taller than he recalled her, tanned richly brown from the UV screens, she looked trim and athletically appealing in the bright blue jumpsuit she had worn on the shuttle.

"Dear Keth!" She kissed him with a vigorous warmth and pushed him back to inspect him. "You're looking splendid."

Deep emotion edged her husky voice, and her blue-gray eyes dimmed with tears. Thinking she looked nearly as lovely as Nera Nyin, he felt a surge of his old affection for her.

She wanted a melonade, and they went to the snack bar. She talked about her years on Malili. The Zone was a frigid little prison where life was limited and hard, sometimes dangerous. She had hated it bitterly at first, till she got a better sense of what it meant.

"A seed!" Her eyes shone now. "I wish you could hear the Admiral tell how it will grow. Into a tree of life for Kai, bearing rich new harvests for the Vorns. A wonderful dream, Keth, that we can turn into something wonderful for us."

Her uncle was now commander of the Zone. She had worked for a time in his office and then moved through a dozen different jobs at the spacedeck, at the import and export branches, in the thorium division, in exploration and general management. She had dispatched shuttles and ridden ore trains in the mines and driven a sanicraft to inspect the new perimeter.

"But I need you, Keth." She leaned abruptly across the tiny table. "Come back with me."

Caught off guard, he fumbled for words and reminded her that he still had half a year at the Academy.

"That won't matter." Her smile was brightly hopeful. "You'll find the Zone a better school than Crater Lake."

Her melonade was finished. She wanted to see the lake, and he took her out across the topside deck. It was the middle of a moontime in the long summer season when the polar sun never set. Orange-red and veiled in glowing haze, it hung low in the north, tiny-seeming beneath Malili's vast narrow crescent. Beyond a single tiny sail, its light lay splashed like blood on the bright blue water and made yellow fire of the long plume of dust rising from a soil mill below the dam.

"A splendid view." She leaned across the rail to drink it in before she turned back to him. "I'll always love Kai—hard and bare as it is—but we won't have to mill stone to make soil for Malili."

Delaying what he saw he would have to say, he objected that Malili offered graver problems than merely grinding soil.

"We'll solve them all," she promised. "The new perimeter will triple the size of the Zone. The UV and laser screens are already up, the neutron blasting done. We're just waiting now to make sure the whole area is really sterile."

Eagerness lit her ray-darkened face.

"The Admiral is planning to make the opening a special event. The Navarch is coming out for it on the *Vorn Fortune*—our new flagship. I've made reservations for us, but the shuttles won't be taking off till Duskday. We'll have the rest of the suntime here."

She wanted to open her uncle's lakeshore lodge. Pointing, she tried to show it to him. He found the green point where it stood, jutting out from the black crater wall, but the building itself was too far for him to see. They could sail the lake and lounge in the gardens, she said, enjoying the finest season of Kai.

"I've meant for us to marry ever since we were swabbers together at Greenpeak." She had turned from the rail to him, quietly ardent, eyes dark with emotion. "I know you've always been fond of me . . ."

She had seen his face, and her voice began to falter.

"I—I do love you, Chel." His own voice shook. "But I can't marry you."

"Are you still crazy?" A sudden scorn turned her pale beneath the tan. "About the humanoids?"

He couldn't speak of the monopole.

"They killed your father, Chel. I hope to help my own father keep them off our planet."

"You are insane." She turned away for a moment toward the lake, her blunt chin quivering. "But I've come a long way to see you, Keth." She looked back at him. "We'll never know about my father. We've our own lives to live. Listen to me, please."

Wrenched with pity, he could only nod.

"You've met Zelyk. My fat cousin. A fleet commodore now—he'll be commanding the *Fortune*. He wants to marry me. I—I despise him, Keth. An egotistical bastard. Both my aunts have always wanted us to marry, to hold the fleet together. That's half the reason I went out to the Zone. To get away from his slobbery sort of love."

Her urgent fingers clutched his arm.

"The Admiral likes you, Keth. He encouraged me to come, and he wants us on Malili—he doesn't care if we make my aunts unhappy." Her wet eyes searched his face again, and her voice began to break. "I've always loved you, Keth. But the family . . . the family. . . ."

She choked and looked away.

"I guess—guess I'll have to tell you, Chel." His own voice trembled. "I met a Leleyo girl. A student here. I fell in love—"

"With Nyin?" Her hand jerked off his arm. "The spy?"

"If she was a spy." He shrugged. "I talked to her about the Zone. She—her people don't want us on their world. Killing her sort of life so we can move in—"

"That jungle slut!" Her contempt exploded. "Baiting every man she meets with her stinking nakedness. My uncle told me how she got past him and duped the Academy and hoodwinked the shipwatch and finally escaped. I hope—hope you enjoyed her!"

His own anger held him silent.

"You utter idiot!" Straight and defiant in the trim blue jumpsuit, she stepped away from him, arms folded, so lovely in her wrath, and yet so deeply hurt, that he longed to take her in his arms.

"Chel," he whispered. "Chel . . ."

"Maybe I'm the fool," she muttered bitterly. "Loving you—even when I always saw you were an indecisive weakling. You never tried hard enough. Not for anything. You'll never be a leader in the fleet. But still—" Her quivering hands opened toward him. "If you'll come with me now—your last chance, Keth!"

Wet eyes watching, she waited.

Gulping for words, he found nothing at all to say. It was true he would never lead any fleet. He had never wanted to. The drive to dominate had never obsessed him, perhaps because he knew the pain of being dominated. He had never liked hurting anybody, but he couldn't help her feelings now. Lovely enough, still dear to him, she wasn't Nera Nyin.

"That's it." She caught a ragged breath. "I hope—hope you're never sorry."

"I'm sorry now—"

She was stumbling away. Hands clenched, he watched until the air doors swallowed her, then he turned slowly to look across the rail for the lodge where they might have honeymooned, sorting out his feelings.

He had never longed to become a power on the Bridge or an owner of the fleet. His ache of pity was all for her. She might have been as fine as Nera Nyin, he thought, if she had grown up free. It seemed to him that the life of Kai had bound her too cruelly, even born as she had been to the best of it. The stern demands of ship and school and fleet and family had crippled her forever—as he might have been crippled, he reminded himself, but for those fortunate freaks of chance that gave him the monopole and that night with Nera Nyin.

Next morning, crossing the rotunda from mess on his way to classes, he met her as she came from the commandant's office. The tears gone and her dark hair done, the spacewear exchanged for a trim green business suit, she looked aloof and secure. With a strange little ache, he recalled the time they had seen each other nude. In a different sort of world, he thought, she might have become as wonderful as Nera.

"Keth!" She came to shake his hand, her grasp warm and firm. "I wanted to say good-bye. I'm going with Zelyk for a hunt on the Darkside till it's time to board the *Fortune*."

"I wish you happiness, Chel." His own voice was stiff and unnatural. "You and—whoever."

"If you do—" Her face twitched and tightened. "If you do, you're still a fool." She swung slowly away and suddenly back. "You could have been—" Her voice broke. "We'll both be sorry!"

She strode away.

Sometimes, in the empty days that followed, he almost wished he had gone with her to Malili. Nothing came from Cyra and his father, or from Nera Nyin. Without a fleet contract he could never train for space. Chelni's future might be brighter than his own, he thought, in spite of her obnoxious cousin.

Duskday came, and the holo showed the Navarch at Terradeck on the first leg of his official visit to the Zone. The reporters said nothing of Chelni, but he caught one glimpse of her, walking up a ramp into the shuttle. Her long stride looked defiant. At the top of the ramp she turned back for a moment, lifting one hand in an odd slow gesture before she disappeared. With a painful throb in his throat, he wondered if her wave had been meant for him.

He was alone in his room one evening, later, reviewing for a test in pilotage astronomy and feeling somewhat forlorn because he could never hope to use what he was learning, when a news flash interrupted the tutortape.

"Bulletin! *Vorn Fortune* lost!"

The holo head of a live and troubled reporter replaced the canned astronomer. Ship officials and fleet executives had now confirmed an unexplained interruption of radio contact with the spacecraft. All transmissions had abruptly ceased two days ago, just as she reached escape velocity. The announcement had been delayed at the request of authorities, who still insisted that they saw no reason for alarm.

On her maiden voyage, commanded by Commodore Zelyk Zoor, the *Fortune* carried every possible safety device. All her systems had been well tested before the Navarch embarked, with no malfunction suspected. Observers on the Kai and Malili satellite stations had reported nothing unusual.

Ship authorities denied any possible link with the unsolved disappearance of the starship *Kyrone,* a dozen years ago. They indignantly rejected suggestions that the humanoids were responsible in either case. The *Kyrone* had been lost on a long and hazardous flight to the unexplored worlds of the Dragon. Here, near home, the *Fortune* faced no such dangers. The ship expected early news of her safe arrival in Malili orbit. Certainly there was no need to revive the long-forgotten Lifecrew.

"Call 'em the Crime Crew!" A sardonic shipwatch warden squinted into the holocam. "A gang of clever extortion artists, running a racket five hundred years old. Gone underground now, with ship support cut off, but playing the same old game. Pay off, they tell you, or the humanoids will get you. Their current leader is a hood who calls himself Ryn Kyrone, disgracing that fine old name. Now in hiding from a murder charge, but still crying humanoid."

14

Tachyon Compass   A device for locating distant rhodo-magnetic sources through differential field effects on a rhodo monopole.

For all the booming confidence of those ship spokesmen, the *Vorn Fortune* never reached Malili. Searchcraft found no wreckage, no evidence of solar flares or meteor streams or any other hazard, no humanoids. The Bridge assembled to replace the missing Navarch with a temporary regent and Vorn Voyagers skipped a dividend.

Shipwatch investigators came back twice to grill Keth about Cyra and his father, but he had no more to tell them. That final year dragged on. He went to his classes and dreamed sometimes of Nera Nyin and woke once from a nightmare of implacable black humanoids swarming after Chelni Vorn.

Graduation was only days away when a voicecard came for him. Too hasty in his breathless hope that it was from Cyra and his father, or perhaps even from Nera, he slid it into the reader upside down. When he got it right, he heard Nurse Vesh.

Her voice quavering and faint, she said she had always loved him. She begged him to visit her before it was too late. She had made a tubeway reservation for him, and she gave him an address in Terratown.

The trip took only an hour. He found her tunnel on a rather shabby lower level. Though the message had left him expecting to find her gravely ill, she seemed surprisingly spry, bustling about her tiny place to brew him a pot of icevine tisane.

"The humanoids!" Her own cup rattled in the saucer as she sat down to face him, her shrunken face drawn with the dread he remembered. "Your father says they've come." Her old voice sharpened with self-vindication. "Like I always knew they would."

His father wanted to see him, she said, but they must be cautious. When his drink was gone, she looked out through a service port to be sure nobody had followed him into the tunnel and caught him in a sudden desperate embrace before she let him out.

He found Cyra and his father in a little shopping district, levels lower and even shabbier, half across the city. Dim legends crawled through the flickery holorama over their doorway. QUOTA POINTS EXCHANGED. INSTRUMENTS REPAIRED. USED HOLOTAPES BOUGHT AND SOLD.

The tunnel door was locked. After some delay, his ring was answered by a deeply bent slattern with a dirty bandage around her head.

"Sorry, sir," she whined. "Closed because of illness—" She blinked and whipped off the bandage. "Keth, dear! Come on in!"

It was Cyra, her straggling hair streaked with gray, her face seamed and haggard even when she smiled to welcome him. They found his father hunched over a bench in the tiny workshop that had been a kitchen, looking as trouble-worn as Cyra, blue shadows under his bloodshot eyes and grizzled stubble on his chin, though no beard grew on the blue spider-scar.

They took him back into the seedy little burrow where they lived.

"The humanoids?" He looked at his father. "Actually here?"

"Near enough." His father's voice was a dusty rasp. "We've picked up moving rhodo sources, which must be humanoid ships. They hovered for months around Malili. One intercepted the flight path of the *Vorn Fortune,* then turned back toward the Dragon."

"So they took the starship?" Thinking of Chelni, he felt dazed.

"The way they took the *Kyrone.*"

"So?" he whispered. "Now?"

"We expect them back."

"We're trying to be ready." Cyra reached for his arm, as if she needed his support. "Your monopole has been useful. We hope—with luck—to have a defensive weapon."

"She's an optimist." His father gestured bleakly at the cheap and dingy room around them. "Skipper, we're pretty desperate. I've made blunders. Went to a fleet owner I'd known on Malili, Shian Vladin. Wealthy enough, and generous at first, but greed got hold of him when he saw our rhodo equipment. He wanted to build his own rhodo fleet and run the Vorns out of space. A skeptic about the humanoids, I guess, and a bigger fool than I was."

His face hardened under the stubble, the old scar bolder.

"At the showdown, he got ugly. I hit him with a metal figurine. He died. I arranged his body at the foot of a stair, but that failed to stop suspicion. We had to get out of Meteor Gap. We've been under cover since then, with all our funding cut off."

"But the loss of the *Fortune* could help us," Cyra insisted. "With more people aware of danger, we've a better chance for support."

"Maybe!" His father scowled. "We're still suspected of killing that grasping idiot."

"We can demonstrate rhodo science—"

"Cyra can," his father said. "She's the technician."

"What we hope for is a more powerful monopole," she said. "One strong enough to shield all Kai—interfering with the rhodo beams that link and drive the humanoids. The design's nearly done. Construction will take time—if they give us time—and materials we don't have now. We'll need a good deal of rhodium, or preferably palladium. That's expensive. Rare on Kai, but mined in Malili."

"That's why we had Vesh call you, Skipper." His father paused a moment, red eyes weighing him. "We need an agent in the Zone. To press the Admiral for funds—he's still a possible ally. To buy and ship palladium. To keep an eye on Bosun—"

"Please, Ryn." Cyra raised a pale hand. "Brong's our friend."

"If you believe him." His father scowled. "I don't."

"I believe he's really seen the humanoids on the Dragon," she said. "Because their ships do operate from that direction."

Back in the shop, they showed him his monopole, now installed in what they called a tachyon compass. The little palladium ball was fixed at one end of a pivoted rod, a gray lead block at the other, all swung in a circular case with luminous diodes around the rim. A rhodium shield was hinged to cover the ball.

"A hundred times more sensitive than my own early instruments," Cyra said. "They had to depend on the residual rhodo-magnetism of native palladium. But I'm afraid the humanoids could pick up the field effects of this. Don't move it without the cover in place.

"You're to take it to the Zone. Try to pinpoint those rhodo

sources. Find out what they are. Braintrees, as Brong admits they could be? Leleyo artifacts? Humanoid probes? Or something else entirely? We need to know."

"And keep alert for spies," his father rasped. "The humanoids could have agents anywhere. From what we know of their history, I expect them to be cleverer than we are, and utterly ruthless about eliminating any sort of rhodo threat to their power."

"The hazards are real." Cyra looked uncomfortable. "I didn't want to involve you—"

"But you are involved." His father cut her off. "Shall we swear you in?"

It took him a moment to understand.

"Think about it, Keth." Cyra raised a warning hand. "Think of the odds. People have resisted the humanoids on many thousand planets. So far as we know, only the *Deliverance* ever escaped."

"I don't need to think." His own unexpected tears blurred their faces. "I've been waiting—waiting all my life for this."

They sat up most of the night, shaping plans. Cyra had made reservations for his flight to the Zone.

"But we've no funds for your fare. We must ask you—"

She faltered and stopped.

"Vesh has located a private collector who wants your Leleyo cup," his father said. "Take it to her, and she'll have your travel documents."

He agreed, though his first elation was already fading. Looking more sharply at Cyra and his father, he had begun to sense their own haunting uncertainties. Two aging people, worn down with toil and disappointment, now in hiding from a murder charge—how could they hope to match the limitless knowledge and power of the humanoids?

A shock of pity struck him when they went back at midnight into the shabby little dwelling room for supper. Cyra murmured an apology—in hiding, they couldn't get legal quota points. They tried to serve him first, and he saw they both were hungry.

15

Kai Zone   Kai beachhead on Malili, located on the highest point in the south hemisphere, sanitized with neutron devices and screened against malignant organisms with ultraviolet radiation.

His father gave him the Lifecrew oath. That long night was nearly gone, and they were all groggy with fatigue. He knelt at a bench in the narrow kitchen workshop, both hands on a little lasergun Cyra had lent him.

Swaying unsteadily, but still resolutely upright, his father intoned the solemn old phrases for him to repeat. To the last limits of body and brain, respecting all the ancient obligations of crew to ship and the lawful commands of his duly sworn superiors, honoring the memory of the first Navarch, he would defend the planet and the people of Kai against the humanoids and all other enemies whatsoever, so long as life endured.

"We've said you're a Crewman, Skipper." Sternly rigid as another machine, the scar ridged and purple in the iron-gray stubble, his father waited for him to rise and make his first salute. "Now you must prove it."

Cyra helped him pack the compass in the same battered space-kit that his father had always carried to the Zone and went out ahead to be sure nobody was watching. He left her peering down the tunnel after him, looking exhausted and forlorn.

He stopped at Crater Lake only long enough to pick up the hammered cup. In exchange for it, Nurse Vesh gave him his tickets and the quota card he was to use. The name on it was J. Vesh. A forgery, he guessed, that she had been using to buy food for them.

Nobody questioned it. Reeling with weariness by then, he slept on the shuttle. Though people on the spacecraft were talking uneasily about the *Vorn Fortune,* they climbed past escape velocity without incident and met no humanoids on the flight to Malili.

"Shipman Vesh!"

Walking down the ramp into the windy chill of an early suntime on Malili, at first he failed to recognize the name. Bosun Brong stood waiting, waving a yellow glove. Keth waved, but stopped at the foot of the ramp, gripped by Malili's wonder.

The sky's color: orange-yellow toward the low and unseen sun, fading away into yellow-green. The wind's smell: a faint enticing spiciness, perhaps of jungle blooms, edged with a fainter, stranger taint. Even the noise: porters and cargo handlers shouting, horns honking, a shuttle engine screaming in a test stand.

Malili, the forgotten planet of his birth, real! His childhood nightmare world of fearful bloodrot and frightful humanoids. The cloud-veiled mystery sphere he had seen from Kai, always alluring with its promises of unknown knowledge and new life for his race. The home of Nera Nyin.

"Shipman!"

Brong had darted ahead. Running to overtake him, he staggered and nearly fell. His body suddenly too heavy, he stopped to get his balance and his breath.

"Careful, sir." Brong dashed back to grasp his arm. "You weigh half more here, but our richer oxygen compensates. You won't notice it long."

He followed again. When they were off the spacedeck and out of its din, Brong stopped to offer a thick-gloved hand. They stood a moment inspecting each other. The tiny man looked tinier, his rigid features leaner.

"So now you're a man!" His voice rang with the same surprising resonance, rich with pleasure. "A shipman and a crewman! Come along to the station. I'll have your bag sent."

Feeling drunk with the marvels of Malili and perhaps with its denser air, he stared around him as they went on. Back at the spacedeck crowning the peak. Up at the massive buildings around it, all gray granite sawn from the mountain: the shuttle terminals and shops, freight decks, fleet agencies, ship offices. Brong pointed out the tall pile the Lifecrew had built when it still ruled the Zone, now flying the blue Vorn pennant. Space in the Zone had always been precious. Dark, slit-like streets ran steeply down the slopes from the spacedeck, the upper stories balconied or terraced to give tunnel-dwellers their summer feasts of air and sky. As they walked, he thanked Brong again for the Leleyo chalice and confessed that it had been sold.

"No matter, Shipman," Brong shrugged. "I liked its shape

and I hoped you would. But, after all, it was only a toy, made by a child to hold the blood of the tree. The grownups never bother with such trinkets."

A carved stone medallion had been moved from the old Lifecrew tower to mark the new station. Two symbolic oars crossed above a symbolic hammer in a symbolic human hand. Some mischance had mangled the hand. That, he thought, was symbolic too. Not very new, the building had a narrow front on a dusty side street three blocks down the hill.

"Modest quarters, Crewman."

Brong bowed him in and showed him three small rooms. A front office, with a time-dimmed holostat of a stern young man in Lifecrew black hung above the battered desk—he was startled to recognize his father, shaven clean and not yet scarred. A room behind, where Brong lived. Another above, once Cyra's lab, now ready for him.

"The humanoids will doubtless build us something fancier." Brong was bleakly ironic. "Unless we get them stopped."

They climbed to the room that would be his. From its narrow terrace he could see the steep slant of the street and, far away and below, a tiny slice of the Malili horizon. Only a flake of blue cloud, it beckoned his imagination.

"So much I want to know." Eagerly, he turned back to Brong. "All about Malili and the Zone. But first—about the humanoids." He searched in vain for expression on that hard, husk-like face. "Cyra says you've seen them."

"There's a substance." Brong stared back at him, eyes warily blank. "Illegal, so I don't say much about it. But it does allow me to see."

"The humanoids?"

"By the billion." Brong nodded, his low tone sober. "Swarming everywhere over Kyronia—that virgin planet of the Dragon Captain Vorn tried to claim. Spinning their glittering prisons over half of it. Wrecking the rest to build more billions and the transport ships to bring them here."

The tilt of his yellow-capped head made his unhappy face look longer and sadder.

"How soon?"

"All I know is what I saw." Brong shrugged. "A month ago, I saw them loading a ship. It frightened me, Crewman."

He shivered in the gritty wind that whipped the terrace.

"Endless black ranks of them, pouring out of the factories that made them, marching over their roads to climb the gangways. More of them than you can imagine. The Admiral called the seeing a wild nightmare when I spoke to him. I'm afraid he's wrong."

"A month ago . . ." Keth peered into his mask-like features, searching for some certainty. "They could be here now."

"If they aren't . . ." Brong's tone was sardonic, "I'm a liar."

Keth hesitated. "Bosun, I don't know how to take you."

"People never do." His sad tone sank. "I'm the ultimate oddball. A miserable misfit from the day I was born, because I'm half Leleyo. A hard fate, Crewman."

His yellow glove gestured as if to sweep the whole Zone away.

"Imagine it, Crewman! Never to be understood, never accepted as a fellow being. Look at these!" He spread the gloves. "I gave these hands for the Crew. In return, was I sworn in?

"Not by your high-minded father, Crewman. Because he always disliked me. Hated me, really. Sometimes feared me. Even now, when I'm alone in charge of the station here and spending my little savings to ship palladium back to Kai, I haven't been admitted to his precious Crew."

He paused to sigh forlornly.

"The Leleyo have been kinder." His voice had fallen. "They've come, in season, to visit me here. They've taught me something of their science of the mind, and even shared their secrets. But still, I'm not Leleyo."

Fixed on Keth, his sharp little eyes seemed defiant, almost accusing.

"I'm afraid of bloodrot, Crewman. Afraid to step outside the perimeter without golden armor and UV sterilamps around me. Afraid even to touch the people I love most, on pain of a dreadful death."

They were still on the windy terrace. Though Keth wore a thick, yellow winter coverall, he shrank from a dusty gust as if its chill had driven through him.

"If you must ask why I never tell all you want to know, there's your answer." He gestured again toward the tantalizing strip of gray-blue haze beyond the bottom of the street. "My friends have taught me things they forbid me to reveal."

Keth nodded, uncertain what to say. He liked the little man, yet his sympathy and awe were mixed with a lingering skepticism. Brong's voice was too fluently persuasive, his black stare too warily keen, his stiff brown mask too hard to read.

"Forgive me, Crewman, if I sometimes seem a little bitter." Brong was apologetic now. "I'm with you—with your father and the little that's left of the Crew—against the humanoids. I'll do whatever I can."

They went back to the first floor office, and Brong bowed him to the desk beneath that youthful holo of his father.

"I want to see Admiral Vorn," he said. "But first, I wonder what delays the humanoids. If they've really been there so long on the Dragon, what are they waiting for?"

"Who knows?" Brong shrugged. "They move to their own sense of time and follow their own Prime Directive. But I'll risk a guess that the feyo trees are rhodo sources, as Cyra Sair suspected. The humanoids fear rhodo weapons. I'd guess they're waiting to be sure they won't encounter some rhodo defense."

"I want to investigate those sources," Keth said. "If I can get a sanicraft—"

"Don't!" Brong recoiled from him, startled. "Look at this, Crewman, before you speak of sanicraft."

He stripped off one thick glove to display his mechanical hand, its delicate joints and tapered levers precisely shaped of bright yellow metal. It slowly closed to make a golden hammer, fell to shatter a marble paperweight on the desk, snatched a flying fragment out of the air and crushed it to splinters.

"A useful tool, but you might not be so well repaired." He held it out for Keth to inspect. "A slight mischance at the perimeter gate. My safety suit off, I shook hands with a Leleyo friend who hadn't been decontaminated. The inspectors saw the incident, luckily. The rot never got into my blood."

He peeled off the other glove.

"Both hands gone, Crewman, just because I touched a friend. I was lucky though, knowing your wonderful mother. She designed these for me."

"You knew my mother?"

"A rare and splendid woman." His sad eyes lifted to that pale holostat. "Your father's a hard man, Crewman. We've had bitter differences, but I always admired your magnificent mother."

"My father never talked about her." He peered into Brong's frozen face. "Can you tell me—"

"A strange and tragic story, Crewman, but it will have to wait." Brong was darting to the door. "Here's your spacebag, and we must call the Admiral."

16

Bloodrot Infection from a common Malilian pathogen (thought to be a phenotype of the rockrust microorganism), swiftly fatal to normal human beings.

Zone Command occupied the tiny city's highest tower. Waiting in a wide-windowed anteroom, they could see the whole Zone. The spacedeck at the tower's foot, bristling with shuttles and launchers. Dark narrow streets twisting down toward steep bare slopes of dark stone and dirty snow. A pale blue glow beyond— from the UV screens, Brong said, along the new perimeter.

Farther beyond, Malili! Gray-blue haze and steel-blue cloud, reaching out forever toward the yellow-green horizon. An infinite ocean of hostile enigma, deadly to him and all his race, but home for Nera Nyin.

"I knew a girl back on Kai—" On impulse, he turned to Brong. "Her name was Nera—"

"Nera Nyin!" Though nothing ever altered that long woeful face, Brong's voice rang with admiration. "I helped arrange her visa. A rare beauty, Crewman. If you knew her, you were lucky."

"I was," he said. "Till she disappeared from Kai." A wild hope shook him. "Will she—will she be back here?"

"Don't ask me, Crewman." Brong's yellow-gloved hands spread wide. "They're nomads, remember. A good many have called on me over the years, perhaps because we're kinsmen. But only in the polar summer. With winter on us now, they're gone till another year."

"I'd give anything to see her."

"Forget her, Crewman." Brong's hard brown face looked somehow sadder. "I've loved more than one Leleyo girl, but they never stayed long. I doubt they know how much they hurt you. Their whole frame of things is different. . . ."

"Keth Kyrone!"

His own name surprised him and alarmed him a little, though the calling voice rang warm with welcome. A tall and elegant woman came smiling out to greet him.

"I'm Vythle Klo." She took his hand. "We met at Vara Vorn, remember? On Chelni's birthday."

"I remember." He recalled her as cool and aloof, but he liked her cordial manner now. "You were on the Navarch's staff."

"I came out with the Admiral." Her tone seemed cheerful. "Life's different here. I think you'll like the Zone."

Wearing a blankly affable grin, Torku Vorn met them in the doorway. He had lost flesh, perhaps to the greater gravity, but even here he moved with an effortless animal ease.

"Glad to see you, Kyrone." He gripped Keth's hand with a powerful paw and led him into a high-windowed office with another awesome view of the steep-sloped Zone and cloud-cloaked Malili. "For Chelni's sake." His red grin faded. "What's your news about the humanoids?"

"No news, really. My father believes they took the *Fortune* the way they took the *Kyrone*. I've come to beg for help. Palladium to make a rhodo weapon. Funds to pay for it. Aid for a search expedition—"

"Forget the expedition." Vorn cut him off. "We're short of sanicraft, even for perimeter maintenance. And shorter of suicidal drivers." His narrowed eyes turned ironic. "Better talk to Bosun Brong."

"Do you trust him?"

"Who can I trust?" Vorn stood a moment, staring at the remote greenish horizon. "If the humanoids are coming—" He swung slowly back to Keth, his heavy face foreboding. "If they really drove my brother to his death—if they've got Chelni now—"

"I'm afraid they have."

"If you can prove it, I'll do anything your father wants." Emotion slowed his voice. "I've lived the way I liked to, Keth, doing most of what I wanted. If I can't do that—if they try to wrap me up in the suffocating care Brong talks about—I want to go the way Brong says my brother did."

"We need your help to prove anything."

"We can't mount any sort of expedition." A deep frown furrowed his heavy red face. "With winter coming in, we'll be ice-locked. I can supply a few kilograms of palladium, but I'm afraid your larger problem is the man outside."

He nodded toward the anteroom where Brong was waiting.

"Get to know him. Listen to his tales and watch his tricks. If he really went with my brother to the Dragon, learn how he got back. If he can see the humanoid bases there now, tell me how. If he's lying, it won't be the first time. If he's honest—" The massive head shook. "Our time's running out."

"He's a puzzle to me," Keth said. "I'd hoped you knew him better."

"Nobody knows him."

"I'll learn what I can."

"Let me know what you discover." Vorn gripped his hand to end the meeting. "Chel loves you, Keth." His deep voice throbbed. "I think she needs you now."

The wind seemed colder as they walked back to the station, the greenish sky stranger above the gray granite canyons. Brong trotted beside him, speaking as glibly about the historic landmarks they passed, gesturing as easily with the yellow gloves, as if he had never known a secret.

"You brought equipment, Crewman?" In the office, Brong picked up his spacebag. "Shall I help you set it up?"

"Not yet." He moved to sit at the desk. "I want to hear about my mother."

"A dark and dreadful story." Brong's small, black eyes stared at him, innocent and wide. "But if you wish to hear it, come into my room."

Inside the cluttered room, he beckoned at a holostat above the untidy cot where he evidently slept. A woman in an odd, gold-colored coverall.

"A goddess, Crewman." His sad voice sank. "I worshipped her."

An ache in his throat, Keth stepped closer. He had never seen his mother's picture. Her eyes were as brown as his own, in a vivid, ray-tanned face. She was smiling.

"She was kind to me." With a doleful sigh, Brong kicked aside a pair of muddy boots to make room for him to sit on the cot. "Consider that, Crewman. Do you see what it means? Kind to a halfbreed—to a miserable wretch born to a life without love."

Sinking down to an empty crate that had held cans of melonade syrup, he spread his metal hands eloquently wide.

"You must grasp the burden I was born to, Crewman. People used to fear that I was a bloodrot carrier. No basis for it, of course, because my own mother had lived to bear me. But I nearly died from some other obscure jungle infection. Crippled for years, stunted and scarred for life. People feared my touch."

He snuffed and wiped his narrow nose.

"All except my native friends—and you see what happened when I touched them." Ruefully, he raised the golden hands. "If you care to hear the whole tragic story, my own unlucky mother was a xenologist from Kai, here to study Leleyo linguistics. My father became her native informant.

"A golden giant named Ilo Auli—I saw his picture once—happened along when she'd stalled her sanicraft outside the perimeter. He helped her out of the bog and followed her home. She got him sanitized—if not sterilized—and brought him into the Zone.

"She got pregnant. Amusing, I imagine, to her fellow researchers, but to them it became a bitter misfortune. When her duty tour was over, she wanted to take both of us back to Kai. Permission refused. The deck inspectors said they were afraid of latent bloodrot. More afraid, I guess, of all they didn't know about Malili.

"With her visa running out, she had to go home alone. No longer welcome, my father slipped back across the perimeter. Left me behind—she'd told him I wouldn't be immune. So I grew up alone.

"I was kept around the research projects the first few years as a biological curiosity. In isolation at first, till the experts decided I wasn't actually carrying any sort of bloodrot. Later, I stayed alive however I could. Hawking curios on the spacedeck. A cabin boy in the old Crew barracks, till that shut down. A cargo handler for the Vorns. A sanicraft machinist. That's how I learned to drive, testing sanicraft. And how I met your parents. An eager young couple, new to the Zone. They didn't know the score against me—not at first, anyhow—and we got to be friends. Even when they heard the tales—"

He paused, sad eyes on the holostat.

"Even then, they weren't afraid. Your father was a bold man, Crewman. But your angelic mother—" His eyes filled and he blew his nose. "Forgive me if I don't control myself, but she never let me feel I was a death-breathing freak.

"They'd come out with Crewman Vesh to begin a new survey—the last big project the Lifecrew ever mounted. The Vorns paid for it, hoping we'd find more thorium. Your father wanted us to look for evidence of humanoid contact with the Leleyo."

"And you found—"

"Nothing humanoid." Brong's small eyes glinted, perhaps with a veiled amusement. "Very few natives. At first I drove your mother's craft. But then—"

His melancholy voice faded out. For a time he sat silent, looking blankly down at his gleaming hands, lost in some moody recollection.

"Your father's a jealous man, Crewman." He moved abruptly on the crate, as if spurred by old anger. "Pulled me out of your mother's machine, I guess because she'd made these hands for me. Sent me out with Vesh on a mission he must have thought was suicidal. For poor old Vesh, it really was.

"It was about this season of the year, because the hands had delayed us with the time they took to heal in place. Far too late for where he sent us. We ran into ugly weather—fog and flood. A howling blizzard, like you never see on Kai." He shivered in his shaggy coverall. "We finally crashed through the ice into a frozen river. I left Vesh there, still in the craft, buried under drifting snow."

"How did you get back?"

"Don't ask me how." Brong flinched as if the question hurt him. "Out of my head most of the way, till they woke me up in the isolation ward down at the perimeter emergency station."

"You're good at escaping."

"I survive." Narrowed a little, his eyes had a secret gleam. "An art I had to learn when I was very young. If you had led my bleak and bitter life, you wouldn't wonder at it."

17

Rockrust Common Malilian microorganism, the oldest and most primitive life on the planet; it metabolizes and crumbles most metals. Its bloodrot phenotype attacks the iron in hemoglobin.

Brong shuddered again. "Winter!" he whispered. "A winter moontime when I got back inside the perimeter. The Zone frozen in. When I was able, your father set me to overhauling our two remaining sanicraft. Your mother was pregnant, and you were born that spring before the thaw.

"She was bent on one more trip, to find a feyo tree—"

"A braintree?" Keth bent to search the blank brown mask. "Are they really rhodo sources?"

"Crewmate Sair kept asking that." Brong shrugged. "I never saw one. The natives speak of feyo trees; braintree was your mother's translation. She had seen my own mother's xenology notes back at Crater Lake and brought copies of charts Ilo Auli had drawn. One chart showed a feyo tree growing on a river bend a few hundred kilometers east. She wanted to look for that.

"And your father—your father let her go!" Anger crackled in his voice. "Though I begged him to stop her, and begged her to give it up, and even begged the Vorns to cut off fleet support. After all that had failed, I begged to drive her, but your father wouldn't allow it.

"The driver she took was an old Zone hand. Rated expert— but not expert enough. Your father put me on monitor duty down at the station, logging their reports and plotting the route they took.

"It was an early spring suntime when they set out. Too early for the driver. He skidded on thawing ice he should have avoided and slid into a canyon. Smashed most of their UV sterilamps and damaged the armor.

"All contact was lost till your mother got out in her safety gear to fix the antenna. When her report got through, they were already done for. Rockrust. Your mother'd had some kind of showdown with the driver. He'd wanted to make a hopeless dash back toward the Zone. She'd made him go on.

"A bad time for me—"

Brong blew his nose.

"Because I'd seen too much of the rust. Melting good steel into stinking blue muck so fast you wouldn't believe it. They lived three days. I watched them, Crewman, to the last. Couldn't sleep. Nor endure the hard way your father said she'd made her own bed.

"Before they died, they did see the tree. Close enough in their scopes, but beyond a great river in flood, swollen from the thaws and choked with floating ice. The river bends there, around a solitary cone-shaped peak. The plug of an old volcano, your mother said. The tree grows on a flat shelf on the north slope, high over the river.

"A queer tree, your mother said—though most plants here look odd to you Kai dwellers. Trunk bright green and strangely thick. Limbs tapered and paler, branching into straight twigs, red as blood. No leaves at all.

"You've seen it yourself." He squinted at Keth. "On that toy cup. Anyhow, that's where they finally stalled. Rust crumbling everything. Drive train frozen. In her last transmission, your mother said they were getting into safety suits. Hoping—hoping to cross on the ice—"

His voice broke, and he wiped his wet eyes.

"Forgive me, Crewman, but I loved your mother."

"I wish I'd known her," Keth whispered.

Brong sat silent, blinking up at the holostat.

"Did you ever meet the Leleyo?" He tried to probe again. "Outside the perimeter?"

"A group of them, that same summer." Brong shrugged as if to shake off his grief. "On a cruise with your father—one I never asked to make. Funded by a new Zone Commander—a greedy brute named Zoor. He wanted contacts with the natives. An idle labor pool, as he saw them, immune to all the hazards of the planet and able enough to loot it for him, if he could only teach them the Kai work ethic. As for your father . . ."

Brong paused, peering solemnly at Keth.

"Crewman, your father meant to murder me."

Shocked, Keth could only stare.

"Of course he never said that. All he talked about was economic opportunity and opening cultural contacts and learning the truth behind the braintree myth, but I knew he meant to kill me. Because he tried. And nearly did it, Crewman. If I hadn't known the art of survival—"

The gold hands spread and fell.

"I saved your father, too. In spite of himself. He hated me for it for years, but I suppose it's why he finally forgave me. If he really has forgiven."

Sunk into another brooding silence, he stared at nothing.

"I think—I hope he has," Keth said. "Tell me about the trip."

"Perhaps I shouldn't." The sad eyes studied him. "Because you're sure to take it wrong. You're too young, Crewman. You'll take it for high romance and want to make your own adventures. But death's an ugly thing, no matter where you meet it."

"Please," Keth urged, "I want to know."

"If you'll forget that lunatic request for your own sanicraft—"

"I suppose I must. At least till spring."

"And if you'll promise"—Brong's eyes narrowed shrewdly—"promise not to ask how we got back."

"I can't help wondering."

"Neither could your father." His hard features quivered, as if with masked amusement. "Neither can the Admiral."

Keth sat waiting, till he began.

"Crewman, I trust you'll never see Malili the way we did, because you'd be bewitched. The way your mother was. The color would hit you first. Beauty of a sort, veiling the deadliness. Your mother used to love it. Different, she said, from the colors of Kai, because life here evolved beneath our redder sun, paced to fit our own slow cycles of suntime and darktime. Yellow flamevines growing through the suntimes so fast you see them crawling. Titan trees with insulating bark and strength to stand through the winter storms.

"We set out on a midsummer Sunrise day. The high slopes were still white with moontime snow, but we were soon down where the naked cliffs and ridges were splashed with rockrust color."

Caught up in his story, Brong was fluent now, gesturing with his flashing hands. Yet those keen little eyes kept stabbing at

Keth, until he suspected that the whole tale was told as a warning to keep him inside the Zone.

"Green and blue and indigo—our sun must have been hotter, your mother used to say, back when the rust organisms evolved. Sometimes lovely—if you don't mind dying. I was careful with the crawler. But your father—a wild man, Crewman!

"Made us take a crazy route, south across an arm of the great polar glacier. Three hundred kilometers of hummocked and fissured ice. Beyond the ice—already at the point of no return—a drop-off stopped us.

"The rim of the ice plateau, too steep for the crawler. A floor of cloud beneath us, so dense we couldn't see bottom. We turned west along it. Another hundred kilometers, and we never found a safe way down.

"A kink in the rim stopped us again. The lip of a canyon the glacier had cut. Wild slopes of ice and broken rock tumbling into that sea of cloud. Too rough to let us get down safe, far too steep to let us climb out again.

"Yet your father pulled his lasergun and told me to take us down. I wasn't armed. I told him to shoot. He didn't do that and I wouldn't move us. He got into the cab while I was asleep and drove us over the brink.

"A wild time, Crewman!

"I thought we were dead, but the land itself was wonderful. Your mother would have loved it. Your father let me back in the cab, and I drove us on. Skidding down the icefall into the clouds. Blundering through fog so thick our own lights blinded us. Crashing into boulders that smashed too many of our UV lamps.

"Yet somehow we got off the ice alive, onto naked granite that was green and blue with rust. Below the clouds and the timberline, we came down through firebrush thickets and stands of wind-twisted blackwood, down at last into what old Ilo Auli had labeled Leleyo country.

"It made me wish I'd been born all Leleyo." His voice sank wistfully. "Your dear mother had told me an old Terran myth about a place she called paradise. I thought we were dead men, Crewman, but we'd found paradise!

"A wide valley floored with golden grass and scattered with towering dark red titan trees. A little river at the bottom of it, wandering through orange-tinted featherbrush. Something about it . . ."

He sighed.

"A cradle of freedom and peace. We drove on across it toward the river, looking for Leleyo. With nothing left to lose, I hoped at least to meet my people. Even your father turned halfway sane, gripped with the riddles the xenologists have never been able to solve.

"How do the Leleyo exist without machines—that's what fretted him most. A problem that tantalized your mother, too. We never learned the answer. Though that valley was a paradise when we saw it, think of the winters. Polar winters, Crewman!"

He shivered.

"Even here in the Zone, the winter snows are meters deep. There, under the glacier and nearer the pole, they must fall deeper. No place for naked nomads, living on the food they forage. So where do they go?"

"To the summer pole?"

"Twenty thousand kilometers away?" Brong shook his head. "Across jungle and storm and mountain and ocean, where we've never made a thousand in our best sanicraft?"

"The humanoids?" Keth peered into his rigid mask. "Could the humanoids be helping them?"

"Who knows?" He shrugged. "Perhaps your father hoped to find that out when he'd finished killing me. All I wanted was to keep a truce that would get me home alive. Not that I had much hope—at that time I was still a beginner at the art of escape.

"Your father was riding up in the turret. Before we got halfway to the river, he called on the holocom to say he saw spots of rust spreading on the armor, where the gold was scratched through and the UV lamps gone. Chuckling like a madman when he told me.

"A little farther on, he called again to say he saw a dragon bat. It dived out of the clouds and went on with us, flapping overhead in low circles. At the river, we crashed through a strip of firebrush and found a group of Leleyo on the bank.

"Three young-looking couples and a few kids, most of them playing with a red pebble they tossed and caught. A small boy diving in the pool to bring up something they ate. An older man with longer hair and a golden beard, sitting on a rock and smiling at the kids.

"All of them nude. The glacier melt in the river must have been icy, but they didn't seem to mind. Lean, graceful people with bright hair and greenish eyes. They looked untroubled by anything. Happy and free—"

He flexed his mechanical hands, surveying them dolefully.

"Crewman," his wistful voice had fallen, "you can't imagine what that glimpse of them did to me. I felt sick to join them. To get away from your father—things between us were pretty grim by then. To cycle out through the lock and strip off my clothes and dive into that clean pool. To wash off the Crew and the Zone and the whole Kai world."

Gloomily, he sighed.

"It might have killed me, Crewman." His hard face lifted. "But then I might have lived—that possibility has always haunted me. My mother said I wouldn't be immune, but there has never been a safe and certain test. The time I was exposed, the medics seemed surprised that I lived to let them amputate my hands."

He fell silent again, his dead brown face longer and bleaker than ever. The golden prostheses trembled a little as he opened and closed them.

"Ah, Crewman!" he moaned at last. "I missed my chance at paradise!"

18

Dragon Bat   A large mutant winged carnivore derived from a native predator domesticated by the early Leleyo.

Brong wiped a yellow sleeve across his brimming eyes.

"We'd stopped our craft on the sandbar just below that stand of featherbrush," his somber voice went on. "The Leleyo weren't alarmed. In fact, they hardly seemed to notice us. Watching them—"

He paused to blow his nose.

"Crewman, you can't imagine how I felt. Your lovely mother

used to talk about their culture. A different sort of civilization, she used to say, based on mind and not on things. Yet in spite of her, I'd always been ashamed of my Leleyo blood.

"Naked savages! Wandering through the jungle in flight from their own filth, catching bugs and grubbing roots with their bare hands for food. No tools, no books, no homes. Miserable two-legged beasts! That's the common image, and it was hard for me to believe the happiness we saw.

"I don't know what your father thought. After we had watched awhile, he had me take us closer. They still ignored us, but the dragon bat screamed and dived. A bellow that made my flesh crawl, even in our armor.

"It flapped over us and perched above the bearded man on a rust-green rock beside the pool. Though we kept edging forward, it didn't move or bellow again. We got within maybe forty meters. Closer than I liked to be.

"A deadly brute, but sleek and clean, its wings and body covered with fine white fur. It gripped the rock with great black talons that could tear a man in two. Beak black and hooked, strong enough to rip the bubble open and take me out of the cab. Its eye—"

Brong shivered.

"Compound, like some Terran insect's. A great glittering diamond band curving halfway around its head under a wicked-looking, knife-edged crest. You couldn't tell what it was watching. Everything, I guess. That eye still haunts me.

"Yet the creature had a beauty your mother would have loved. A quarter-ton of predatory power, so sleek and quick you longed to watch it kill. I wondered why it didn't dive on those naked people, and why they weren't afraid.

"I wondered, too, why they weren't afraid of us. The kids went on with their pebble game. One couple was in the water—under it, most of the time—making love. None of them seemed to notice us at all, till your father made me creep even closer.

"The small boy quit diving then and came to meet us, waving for us to stop. A thin little brown-skinned urchin, long hair wet and dripping. Maybe seven or eight. He couldn't have been to the Zone—our occasional visitors have all been older. But he spoke to us in fluent Kai.

" 'Friends, please bring your gold machine no closer.' Our sound system picked up his voice. 'We are not used to ultraviolet radiation, and you will not wish to cause us needless discomfort.'

"Your father answered that we wanted to be friends. We had come to learn about his people and to search for ores we needed. In exchange, we could offer rich gifts from the civilization of Kai.

"The boy was not impressed. His people had seen our Zone and found the things of Kai useless on Malili. If we wished to show friendship, we should leave their planet and cease to cause them harm.

"Your father asked if he had seen humanoids.

"He laughed. We were the machine people, though if we tried to stay on Malili we would need better machines than the one we rode. He pointed to the blue rust rotting our armor and begged us to move it away from the river while we could, so that its decay would not pollute the pool. He was truly sorry that he couldn't help us save our lives—

"Your father had quit listening. I heard him slam out of the turret and bang through the service bay to the loading door. It was sealed and bolted. When I heard tools clattering, I ran back there and found him loosening the bolts.

"Crewman, I told you he was mad!" Brong sat straighter, his tight voice sharper. "You see, the loading door wasn't a lock. Opened, it would flood the whole craft with the bloodrot pathogen. That's what he wanted.

"A desperate moment, Crewman." He raised both bright hands as if to guard himself, and his voice rang with drama. "I begged him to stop. He drew his laser. I jumped him, my hands against his gun."

He blinked at them, shuddering.

"I'd never known how quick and powerful they are. Snatching for the lasergun, I ripped his cheek open and had the weapon before he could fire. He fell back against the bulkhead, out cold.

"I left him there, climbed back to the mike in the cab, and made a pitch of my own to the boy. Promised to move the crawler anywhere he wanted, if his people would help us get back to the Zone.

"He looked bewildered and unbelieving when I told him what your father had tried to do. Said his own people never harmed each other. He would show me where to take the craft, but he said his people couldn't save our lives.

"I got the machine moving and followed him back up the path we had torn through the featherbrush and over a rocky ridge. The dragon bat flapped after us and perched behind us on the rocks. The boy thanked me for moving the machine.

"He said he was sorry we had to die. If we were afraid of the pain, he would gather sleepweed berries for us. They had a good taste, and they would keep us from feeling anything. I wasn't quite ready for that. He went back to stand beside the dragon bat, watching us.

"Your father was coming around by then, dazed and bleeding. He fought when I tried to bandage his face; otherwise he might have had a neater scar. I had to give him a hypo out of our own kit before I could get him into his body gear. When I had done all I could for him, I smashed the lasergun and squirmed into my own safety suit and cycled out of the crawler to meet my people. And that's it, Crewman."

Abruptly, Brong broke off.

"That's no place to stop," Keth protested. "You did get help?"

"We did get back." His tone had turned sardonic. "You promised not to ask me how."

"I can't help wanting to know."

"You might find something about it in the records of the old south perimeter medical station. We reached the gate on a Sunset day. I was climbing up the snow slopes when the guards saw us, hauling your father like a sled in his safety gear."

"Does he know how you got there?"

"For a long time he wouldn't ask." Malice glinted in the little black eyes. "When he did, I told him a dragon bat had carried us. His face had got infected and I'd kept him under hypos. He never knew the truth."

Keth sat waiting.

"Sorry, Crewman." He spread the shining hands. "When people questioned me—plenty of them did—I said I couldn't recall the journey back. I'll admit to you that we did get help, but what it was I'm not free to say."

Still Keth waited.

"Crewman, you've caught me on a painful point." His tone grew plaintive. "Remember what I am. Torn all my life between two worlds with no room for me in either. My Leleyo kin have been kinder than the Kai. They have shared with me, and I intend to keep my obligations to them."

"Bosun," Keth protested, "don't you have another duty? To your mother's people? Their claim—our claim is urgent now, because nobody can believe your warnings about the humanoid forces building up on the Dragon. If you would explain how you know—"

"Even if I tried, you would not believe." Brong shrugged, bright hands spread. "Leleyo truth was hard enough for me to learn, half-Leleyo as I am. For you, for the Admiral or your father, it would hardly be possible. Leleyo and Kai, the two spheres of mind are as different as the planets. The truth of one is false to the other."

He darted upright and moved toward the door.

"Please, Crewman, let's say no more about it."

"I was hoping for more." Keth ached with disappointment, still wistfully longing to discover the way to some enchanted valley where he might find Nera Nyin, but he followed Brong reluctantly. "At least we can set up the tachyon compass. It has a language people should believe."

With Brong's secrets out of danger now, he bustled cheerily to help unpack the instrument. They first set it up outside, on the second-floor terrace, but the counterbalanced beam spun crazily there. Moved inside, out of the wind, it steadied, pointing almost east.

In his old files, Brong found a copy of the radar chart on which he had plotted the early sanicraft surveys. When Keth drew his direction line, it ran parallel with his mother's route toward the eastward bend of that great river the glaciers fed.

They moved the compass down to the north perimeter, and down again to the south. All three compass bearings intersected at a point just beyond the riverbend. Brong squinted sharply at it and uneasily back at him.

"Crewman, your needle is pointing at a feyo tree. The brain-tree your mother saw beyond that river before her signals were cut off."

"A rhodo source," Keth told him. "Which means it could be something humanoid. Perhaps an observation probe or a communications device, protected against the rockrust. I want a look at it—"

"Not this winter."

It was late by then, and Brong took him to eat at a noisy all-night place in a tunnel two levels down, where the diners came mostly from the spacedeck and the thorium mine. They sat in a booth at the rear, and he kept pressing for a way to the braintree.

Perhaps they could wait for the river to freeze and cross on the ice. Perhaps they could take a boat or pontoons to float the sanicraft. Perhaps they could swing south across the glacier and strike back north beyond the river.

Brong allowed him no hope. Snows had already fallen on the glacier; the crevasses would be drift-hidden and treacherous. The late-model sanicraft were already overloaded with safety equipment; the weight of pontoons would stall them. Even in the midsummer, a trip to the tree would carry them beyond the point of no return. Now in winter, even the normal maintenance work around the perimeter was difficult enough.

"Better admit, Crewman. You're stuck till summer—if the humanoids give us that long."

He saw no way not to admit it. They returned to the station and he went to bed on a hard cot in that narrow upper room. Heavy with Malili's gravity, he lay a long time, turning restlessly, fretting about humanoids and feyo trees and Bosun Brong.

Asleep at last, he dreamed of that magic valley with its crimson titan trees. Brong was with him, and they were searching for Nera Nyin. They heard her voice at last, singing in a yellow glade. She saw them and ran to meet them, tall and nude and beautiful.

Brong darted ahead of him, reaching out to greet her. When his metal hands touched hers, he began to change, growing more and more mechanical until he was a golden humanoid. She left Brong and came on to him, her bright smile alluring, her arms open wide.

He fled from her, in terror of being changed.

"Crewman!" The real Brong woke him. "Zone Command wants you on the holophone."

"News for you, Crewman Kyrone." It was Vythle Klo, sleek and tall and very grave. "Your father has called the Admiral from Kai. About some sudden emergency—he was not specific, but you're to return at once. We've arranged your passage back,

on the same ship you came out on. The Admiral is sending
your father two kilograms of palladium. You may pick it up
here, on your way to catch the shuttle. You will travel again as
Shipman Vesh."

19

Rhodar   A system for determining direction and distance
through tachyonic radiation effects.

When he stepped off the ramp at Terradeck, Cyra was waiting,
muffled so heavily in a hooded winter cloak that he hardly
knew her. She hugged him hard. For a moment, smiling
through her tears of delight, she looked young and strong and
happy, but then he saw her haggard pallor and felt the weight
of trouble on her.

"Don't talk," she breathed. "Just come with me."

They picked up his bag and took the Terratown tubeway.
Halfway there, she led him off the pod and up through a surface entrance. Here in the south of Kai, with Summersend past,
the air was already sharp with frost. The blood-red sun barely
cleared the black north horizon and the summer shrubs were
naked sticks jutting out of the first thin snow.

Nobody else had got off with them. Walking against a bitter
wind toward a walled summer villa on a little hill above the station, they were alone. Cyra glanced back and began to talk.

"Your father didn't want us to call you." She caught his arm
and clung. "I suppose it hurts his pride to admit how much we
need you now."

"Why now?" Dread brushed him. "In the Zone, nobody told
me what the trouble is."

"They're here!" The wind had begun to take her breath, and
her voice had sunk to a husky whisper. "The humanoids. Not
yet on Kai, but in space near Malili. We were afraid they would
intercept your ship."

He had stopped to listen, but she tugged him anxiously on.
The shallow snow crunched under their boots and the purple
sky ahead seemed suddenly foreboding.

"I didn't get much from the Admiral—"

"That may not—may not matter now." Still tramping doggedly on, she had to gasp for breath. "We must do—with what we have."

They came to a stone bench niched into the villa wall, and he made her stop to rest. Warily watching the path behind, she whispered again: "We've been trying, Keth. Everything we could. We finished the rhodar and picked up another moving source—it must be a humanoid ship—approaching from the Dragon at tachyonic velocity when we picked it up."

"The one the Bosun saw them building?" The wind felt colder. "If he had been believed—"

"No matter now." She shrank from the wind. "We did try, Keth. I went to Bridgeman Greel. A friend back at the academy, long ago—he wanted to marry me once. Still too sentimental to turn us in for murder. I got him to listen to your father."

Her bent head shook.

"He didn't listen, really. Said he never took much stock in the humanoids. Wouldn't try to understand the rhodar demonstration. Half convinced in spite of me that your father is the con man the shipwatch calls him. Con man and killer.

"For my sake, he did set up a meeting for us. A few space engineers and junior fleet officials, all warned not to turn us in. The Zoor engineer asked more about the rhodar than we wanted to tell him, but nobody else was much impressed.

"Though Greel had promised to protect us, somebody tipped off the shipwatch. They picked up Nurse Vesh the day after the meeting. Pretty harsh with her, but she outguessed them. Got a message to the hideout in time for us to get away.

"So here we are. Greel's gone on to Northdyke, letting us stay here for now in the keeper's lodge, though our welcome's wearing thin. Officially, if the shipwatch gets back on our trail, he doesn't know we're here."

Cold fingers quivering, she clutched his arm again.

"That's why, Keth, why we had to call you back. Because we've done all we can. There's nobody even to laugh at us now, with the Bridge already scattered for the Summersend recess. No quorum to act on anything till they meet again at Northdyke. No hope from the new regent, either. He's a retired shipwatch commander, more apt to fear us than he is the humanoids."

Shivering, she pushed herself off the bench.

"We had to have you, Keth."

They found his father in the tunnel shop under the keeper's lodge. He rose when they came in, as sternly straight as if he expected a formal Crew salute. Keth gripped his hand, shocked at its fleshless yellowness.

"Well, Skipper!" He tried to smile, but all Keth saw was the ridged blue scar crawling through the white stubble on his cheek. "We need you now."

For a moment Keth couldn't speak. His throat hurt and tears burned his eyes. Now that he had heard the story of his mother and the scar, he understood and forgave many things. He could have flung his arms around his father, but this unbending man wanted no embrace.

"Vorn did send two kilograms of palladium." He nodded at the worn spacebag. "And I was able to pinpoint one rhodo source. That braintree, east of the Zone, my mother died trying to reach—"

His father stiffened, recoiling from him, and the scar shone whiter than the untidy beard around it. He saw Cyra start, as if that tragedy was new to her. Recovering quickly, she begged him to open the bag.

"Enough to shield a city." With a pale smile, she lifted the little white ingot in her wasted hand. "If they give us time." She looked at his father and then at him, her gaunt face twitching. "Time to find the means we need to complete the weapon—"

They showed him the new rhodar unit, standing on a bench. A clumsy, toy-like thing made of mismatched parts joined by heavy cables that spilled like jungle vines across the floor. A luminous needle in a little holo tank swung across one curved scale and rotated above another.

It was soundless. All three stood around it, too breathless for talk. Cyra's lean hand shook at the controls until she stopped to massage it. The needle hung motionless at first, while glowing green shadows crept into the tank. Suddenly in focus, they formed a tiny image of the device itself, a smaller toy. Their own doll-forms moved in around it, quickly dwindling, lost in an instant beneath the green-shining shape of the lodge, the doll-house villa above it. The villa shrank, the model city shrank, the diminished planet shrank, until a toy Malili swam into the scan. The needle wavered. Cyra wrung her thin blue fingers and bent to make another fine adjustment. The needle steadied, pointing not quite at Malili.

"Still approaching." Her eyes sick, she looked from his father to him. "The same intense source. Speed no longer tachyonic. Already this side of Malili and decelerating toward a Kai orbit."

"You'll have to move fast," his father said. "And hope for better luck than you can reasonably expect."

He learned then that he was to go on to Northdyke and try again for the aid they had failed to find.

"Take your own compass," Cyra told him, "to demonstrate the danger. When the ship gets close enough, you'll be able to pick it up."

He stayed with them that night, while she worked late, assembling a hand weapon for him, a shielded monopole in a flat pocket case no longer than his finger.

"Keep it with you." She showed him how to activate it. "But don't use it unless you must. It ought to knock out a humanoid at close range, but those farther away would detect the rhodo field."

"What's close range?"

"A few meters, I hope. One or two at least. Just point it and push the slide. If it works, you stop the humanoid."

"If it doesn't, you're in trouble." His father frowned, absently fingering the blue-ridged scar. "Their top priority has always been their own defense, and the only danger they know is rhodo attack. Human beings aren't allowed to play with rhodo toys."

Cyra didn't want to risk the rhodar again, for fear the humanoids might already be near enough to pick up its search beam, but she thought his tachyon compass would still be safe. They carried it up into the dim and frigid suntime for a trial. Alive at once, the pointer crept slowly along the jagged north horizon to overtake and pass the dull red sun.

"They're here," she whispered. "In orbit!"

20

Navarch The head of the ship, chosen by the Bridge, which is a parliamentary body elected by the duly franchised shipmen.

He rode the tubeway north. With the Bridge about to meet, Northdyke was crowded, the hotels filled. The shabby room he found was off a disreputable tunnel under a factory district beyond the exclusive Meteor Gap suburb.

Nobody wanted to hear his news of the humanoid invasion. A junior official at the space admiralty cut him off in scornful anger. The regent had warned against malicious rumors, and at this critical time, such wild tales were a danger to the ship. Refusing to listen, he ordered Keth out of the building.

Cyra had given him Greel's office address in the Bridge complex, but the receptionist there said he was away, attending a meeting out of the capital. At the Vorn headquarters, a security officer said all the top fleet executives were at an emergency meeting out of the capital. When he called the regent's residence, a secretary said the regent was out of the capital.

Nobody would say where or what the meeting was, but he began to feel a tightening expectancy. That night in his room he heard a holo newsman's rumor that the regent would present a startling announcement to the convening Bridge. Though the regent himself was not available for comment, informed sources were suggesting that a second zone was being opened on Malili to exploit a fabulous Vorn thorium strike in the north hemisphere.

Keth shook his head at that; Brong would have known of any such strike. He tried the tachyon compass again. Even in his room, many levels down, the needle followed a crawling point on the south wall, seeking what had to be a humanoid transport.

At last, next morning, he found Greel back from that mysterious meeting. An impatient, wheezing, fat-faced man, hard of hearing and loud of voice, the aging Bridgeman received him with a scowl and kept him standing in front of a vast black marble desk.

"So you're Kyrone's son?"

"With news for you, sir. Urgent news from him and Cyra Sair—"

Not listening, Greel turned to peer and mutter into a hooded holocom.

He began again, "My father—"

"Frankly, I've heard too much of your father." Greel glowered at him. "A paranoid fanatic. Possibly a murderer. I've been tolerant—far too tolerant—because I knew Cyra long ago. But I feel no obligation to him, and certainly none to you, young man. With the Bridge about to meet, I've no time—"

"Sir, a tachyonic transport from the Dragon is now in orbit around Kai." He had brought the compass in his bag, and he stepped forward with it now. "I've got scientific evidence—"

"Stand back, Kyrone." Greel batted the air with a fat white hand. "I've heard your father's ranting about the wicked humanoids about to descend on us. A delusion as old as Kai."

"Cyra's a scientist." He tried to swallow his resentment of the old man's arrogance. "She has detected and traced the humanoid ship with rhodo instruments. I can show it to you, in orbit now—"

Greel was frowning into his holocom.

"Listen, sir!" Desperate, Keth lifted his voice. "The humanoids took the *Kyrone*. They took the *Fortune*. They're back again. Let me show you—"

With an ironic grunt, Greel swung to him.

"I've news for you, young man. News I'm just this moment free to reveal. About that object in orbit. It's the *Fortune* herself—"

"Sir!" Keth stared. "That can't be true—"

"Don't contradict me!" Greel's white fat quivered. "I know she's back, because I've seen the Navarch himself, last night, at a confidential meeting at his summer villa in Meteor Gap. He came down on the first shuttle, looking very fit. He's to address the Bridge today—and you will excuse me now."

Keth rushed to the Bridge chamber in time to push into the packed guest gallery. Startled whispers around him spread conflicting reports about the *Fortune*'s return and what the Navarch would say. When Commodore Zoor appeared at last, escorting the aged leader to the podium, the sudden hush was almost painful.

"Old?" He heard puzzled murmurs. "He looks so young!"

The lawmakers rose to cheer. Keth stood with them, staring. In holo interviews, the Navarch had always been leaning on some younger aide, looking withered and infirm. Now he glided ahead of the fattish commodore, moving like a dancer.

"Fellow shipfolk—"

Smiling serenely, oddly casual, he strolled aside from the microphones and spoke without notes, his unaided voice pealing through the chamber with surprising clarity and power.

"We're glad to be back. Our long absence must have been a mystery. I understand that the holo people have aired reports that our ship was disabled by collision with a meteor or forced down into the jungles of Malili.

"The truth, however, is far stranger than any such rumor. The history of our voyage will amaze you, and its outcome promises to open a dazzling new epoch in the history of Kai. I'll tell you about it, but first I must correct an old misapprehension—an unfortunate misconception of the humanoids."

He waited for a rustle of surprise to die.

"Demon machines! That's how we've always been asked to see them—as part of the legend that our forefathers came here to avoid them. A tragic error, friends!" His head shook gravely. "Due, I suppose, to the destruction of our historical records during the Black Centuries.

"The tragedy arose from a sinister distortion of the truth. The principal villains seem to have been the founders and the leaders of the Lifecrew—the infamous organization that has always claimed to be protecting us against evil humanoids, inventing terror tales about them to insure its own support. Though it fell into a deserved decline when we found no humanoids on Malili, a murderous extortionist named Kyrone has recently been trying to revive its malevolent lies—the lies we have returned to expose.

"Friends, we've met the humanoids!"

Shock stilled the chamber for an instant, before the first scattered gasps swelled into an unbelieving uproar. The Navarch stood waiting, poised and clearly pleased, the dull old eyes that Keth recalled now strangely bright. At his commanding gesture, all sound subsided.

"In flight to Malili, we were just reaching escape velocity when we were overtaken by a humanoid craft—a tachyonic cruiser so large that the *Fortune* had been hauled aboard before we knew what was happening. Humanoid units came aboard to offer us the service ordained by their wise Prime Directive.

"They're beautiful!"

His lyric voice pealed against the vault.

"I wish, friends, that I could show them to you now, but you'll all be meeting them soon. Black, of course, but cleanly shaped and shining, swift and graceful in every motion, attentive even to unuttered thoughts, totally devoted to human ease and comfort. Now, as I recall their universe—the new universe they've created for mankind—it seems a dream of paradise.

"They took us to tour half a hundred of their worlds. Kyronia first—the planet of the Dragon, where they arrived just too late to rescue the heroic Captain Neelo Vorn from the amphibian monsters that had attacked his brave little colony.

"A savage planet then, but the humanoids have already transformed it. Filled it with palaces more magnificent than men ever built for themselves, and pleasure gardens more exotic. Yet, in comparison to the older worlds they showed us, it's still crudely backward.

"They escorted us to see fairylands you can't imagine. Whole populations free of want and care and fear and pain, happily relieved of class and competition, living in the joy and splendor we have come back to promise you.

"Each of us found wonderlands where we longed to stay—grandeur so dazzling, beauty so piercing, delights so enchanting, that leaving them was agony. Yet none of us stayed, even though we were offered the option, because the humanoids have promised to transform Kai.

"We need no longer scheme to loot Malili to keep our world alive, because the humanoids can transmute our own naked stone into any material—even into boundless energy—to build and power our new utopia. They can even remake our wretched climate, to warm us through the moontimes and illuminate the Darkside.

"That's why we're back. To dispel your old fears, my friends, and deny the old lies. To welcome you into the humanoid universe. Tachyonic transports will be arriving soon, and our old spacedecks must be modified to support their enormous weight. You, too, must be prepared. The service of the humanoids is never imposed. It must be fully explained and freely chosen.

"I beg you, friends, to reflect well before you choose. If you accept the humanoids, they can transform Kai into a more perfect paradise than any religion ever promised. If you refuse, they'll simply pass on and leave us alone."

His voice sank into a solemn pause.

"Alone forever, I believe, because our fast-moving binary star is carrying them beyond easy contact with their central computer plexus on Wing IV—we're already outside the normal limits of their service. Other settled worlds are eager to receive them, and there are limits even to their vast resources. They won't be offering us a second chance.

"Without them, our future—without them, friends, we have no future. Our uranium and thorium will be exhausted. The promise of Malili has already faded, its tempting riches denied us by its hostile life and savage people, by its total deadliness. Our choice is simple—paradise or death.

"Think well, friends!"

Beaming with that unbelievable youth and charm, he bounded off the platform. A staggered silence hung behind him, unbroken until the Bridgemen surged to their feet, most of them applauding madly, but a few yelling questions he hadn't stayed to answer. Order of a sort came slowly back, spreading around one lawmaker who said he had been aboard the *Fortune*.

"Fellow shipfolk!" At last he claimed attention. "Please calm yourselves. We've no reason for alarm. The humanoids, I assure you, were never the devils of those unfortunate legends, but simply the best of all possible machines. The most efficient, the most versatile, the most powerful machines ever invented. They repair and replace themselves. The service they offer is totally free. They can't harm any human being, because they're all controlled by a higher law than ours, wisely designed to keep them faithful forever."

"Then why are we here?" some skeptic shouted. "Why didn't our forefathers stay to adore them?"

"The records are lost." He shrugged. "If our ancestors ever had any actual complaint against them, you must recall that the humanoids they encountered were early models that may have been less perfect than these.

"In the last thousand years, we're informed, they have improved themselves enormously. Their powers of motion and perception have been multiplied. Their computer plexus has become a true galactic brain. The annihilation of matter gives them literally limitless energy, which they devote to human good."

Smiling benignly, he waited for a murmur to subside.

"Though I understand your apprehensions, I have seen these new humanoids. I've seen their universe, where many trillion human beings live their lives in perfect happiness and ideal peace, supported in bounteous abundance by trillions of willing machines—"

Keth was on his feet, seeking a way out of the jam in the gallery, but the ringing words caught him again:

"—surprises waiting for us. Many of us were elderly when we boarded the *Fortune*. Some of us infirm or ill. You'll observe that the humanoids have healed us. Understanding the human mechanism far better than we ever did, they tend it with skills never known to human medicine—"

Overwhelmed, Keth escaped from the chamber.

21

Prime Directive "To serve and obey and guard men from harm." This law of the humanoids, built into their central plexus and zealously defended from change, was meant to make them the unfailing servants and the ultimate saviors of mankind.

Keth stumbled out into the corridor, feeling battered. The Navarch's story was starkly incredible to him, but most of the Bridgemen had swallowed it whole. The old war against the humanoids had seemed a forlorn cause before. Now, clearly, it was lost.

With no actual purpose left, he wandered through the mobs in the capital tunnels and rotundas, listening for what he could learn. Here and there he came upon others who had seen the humanoid universe, each set apart by that glow of joyous vigor.

"—if you had heard what they promised me!"

A lean, dynamic man with a Vorn Voyager's badge and a Bridgeman's cap was evangelizing a knot of gaping listeners.

"As a young man, I'd wanted to become an artist. Without hope, really. Kai has never had much use for art, because the struggle for survival has never left us anything to spare. My own dreams denied, I did what I had to. I suppose people have envied the status I was able to gain in the ship and the fleet, but to me it was always dull drudgery. Now the humanoids have released me for the career I always longed for."

He glimpsed others, all radiant with that bewildering bliss, marching out with groups of excited converts to carry the news to the media, to ship departments and fleet offices, to cities and villages all across Kai, and even to the Zone. At one crowded corner, Commodore Zoor was on a news holo, announcing the advent of the new humanoids. Despite the fat, even he looked fitter, his puffy features grown somehow commanding.

"—total happiness!" Still hesitant and high, his nasal voice had acquired a new fluency and power. "The humanoids ask for nothing. They bring us everything. Friends, you'll learn to love them—"

Keth pushed out of the crowd and drifted blankly on, lost in thoughts of Chelni Vorn. Had she, too, come back transformed into an evangelist for the humanoids? Her image aching in his memory, he wanted to call Vara Vorn to ask if she was there. Half angry at himself for the impulse, he shrugged it off. She was doubtless now part of Zelyk's total happiness.

It struck him that he must report to Cyra and his father. He found a holo booth and dialed their borrowed villa. For a long time there was no answer. Cyra came on at last, looking ravaged and deathly.

"Keth, don't!" Her hushed voice was desperate. "You'll give us away."

"I'm at a public booth—"

"They're smarter than you are."

"What have they done to the Navarch and—"

"Euphoride, maybe."

"What can we—"

"Try to hide. Wait for a chance."

"Can I—"

"Get rid of your compass, where they won't find it."

"I want to help—"

"What can you do?" Her whisper rasped with savage scorn. "They'll be everywhere. They know everything. They can do anything."

"Tell my father—"

"Get off the line—now! Don't call again. We won't be here." Her haggard image winked out.

Stumbling away from the booth, he tried to understand. They must be as utterly stunned as he was. When the humanoids came swarming down from space, Bridgeman Greel's reluctant aid would surely end; he might even turn them in. There was nothing left for them to do, certainly nothing he could do for them.

Yet he felt a bitter need for his father's sternly silent courage and her own warm wisdom. He had lost them, just when he was coming to know them. To prove his love, he could do no more than avoid them. The unfairness of it rankled.

With no goal left, he plodded on, more and more bewildered by the hysterical elation of the crowds in the tunnels. Excited shipmen stood clotted around the news holos, shouting down occasional skeptics about the ultimate goodness of the humanoids. Mobs were sacking a market, tossing quota cards and tokens into the gutters. At one riotous bar drinks were on the house, because everything would soon be free. At a shipyard gate, however, a fleet executive was begging workers to stay long enough to ready spacedecks for the tachyonic transports.

Bleakly, he wished he were back on Malili, still with Bosun Brong, planning a plunge into the jungle to search for a braintree—and for Nera Nyin. He lost himself in a longing dream of her. In that last sleepy sentence, when he bent to kiss her goodbye, she had begged him to come back to her.

If only he could. . . .

It was late when he got back to his own shabby tunnel, now nearly deserted. Cyra's terse warning had left him afraid of a trap, but he had to do something about the tachyon compass. Breathless, gripping the tiny weapon she had made him, he pushed inside. The dingy room was empty, the holo flashing. He punched for the message.

"Keth, darling!" It was Chelni. Her hair looked darker and sleeker and longer, her eager eyes brighter. Aglow with that radiant joy the humanoids somehow ignited, she had never seemed so lovely. "I must see you, dear. Come to me at Vara Vorn. Hurry, won't you?"

He replayed it twice, uncertain what to make of such an unreserved invitation. In all their lifetime of friendship, she had never quite forgotten that he was not a Vorn, had never seemed so freely unrestrained, never so eager to see him.

His heart was suddenly thumping. Though he had already heard far too much about the mechanical enchantments of the humanoid universe, her burnished beauty had seized his emotions. The weariness of the long day forgotten, he pried a ventilator grill off the wall and pushed the compass up the duct and out of sight. The grill replaced, he changed his shirt and rode the tube to Meteor Gap.

The great winter gates of Vara Vorn stood open wide, as if to welcome him. Outside the medallioned summer gates, he paused again. A breath of apprehension brushed him, but he drew his shoulders straight and touched the bell.

"Darling!"

Chelni herself came darting out through the tall silver doors, looking taller than he recalled her, her firm chin not quite so stubborn, her eager face more vivid. In a sheer scarlet lounging robe, more daring than she had ever worn, her figure seemed finer, her ripe breasts higher.

He stood breathless, caught by her new allure.

"Keth! Darling!" She caught both his hands with hers. "Come on in!"

She pulled him against her, opening lips lifted to his. Sheer astonishment held him rigid until she turned, laughing lightly at his hesitation, to pull him inside.

"If I seem different, dear, it's because I've seen the humanoids." The voice was still her own, yet stronger than he recalled it, more musical, more intimate. "I want you to meet them as soon as we can arrange it. When you know them, you'll never be the same."

Certainly, she was not the same. He had stopped in the vaulted entry hall, staring at her in spite of himself, but she gave him no time for wonder.

"Let's have your jacket."

Her bare arms were suddenly around him, helping slip it off. Her scent drenched him, a penetrating musk, too sweet and too strong.

"Darling, don't you like the difference?" Her slow tones caressed him with a husky warmth he had never heard. "You know I've always loved you, Keth, ever since I first saw you in the swabber class at Greenpeak. I used to grieve because I couldn't be more free with you—because of all I owed the family and the fleet. We can both be grateful that the humanoids never demand such painful choices between duty and desire.

"So let me see you, darling!"

Tossing his jacket to a chair, she caught his shoulders to hold him facing her. Her wide eyes swept him, black pupils dilating.

"If you feel overwhelmed, I can understand." She pulled him impulsively against her to brush his mouth with hers. "I remember how I felt when I first saw them trooping aboard the *Fortune*. Lovely, really, but so new they frightened me."

She released his shoulders but clung to his hand.

"Darling, you look worn out. Hungry, too. This must have been a dazing day. Let's find something to restore you."

She led him out of the entry, down into the magnificent winter hall where tall holos of Vorn admirals and bridgemen frowned across glass-cased models of Vorn tunnel-cutters and Vorn reactors and Vorn spacecraft. He grinned faintly at its gloomy splendor, recalling his miserable discomfort at her birthday party, so long ago in the summer hall. She pulled him quickly closer, and her quizzical smile made her look fourteen again, at least for an instant.

"All ours tonight," she whispered. "My aunt's away at the Navarch's all-night celebration, and the staff has a holiday."

In the largest kitchen he had ever seen, she piled a tiny table with meats and fruits and sweets his quota card had never allowed, and opened a bottle of sparkling wine she said had been a gift from the Navarch himself.

Though the juices were flowing in his mouth, after the first few bites he forgot to eat. She sat too close. Her perfume was too powerful, her scarlet wrapper too sheer, her whole allure too overwhelming. Overcome by everything, he couldn't stop staring.

"What's wrong, dear?" She leaned disturbingly nearer. "You aren't afraid of me?"

"Of the humanoids, I am." In spite of himself, he shrank a little from her. "Nurse Vesh used them to frighten me when I was very small, and I've been training all my life to fight them.

I simply can't believe they're so wonderful and good as the Navarch says. Everybody on the *Fortune*"—he was trying to smile, but dread crept into his voice—"you seem—brainwashed."

"The wrong word, dear." Her wry frown was both reproving and entrancing. "An ugly term, unfair to them, and even to us." Gravely, she filled their glasses. "I was afraid you wouldn't understand. That's why I sent for you. Let's drink to the Prime Directive.

"Darling, it has set us free!"

22

Eclipse   Phenomenon caused by the shadow of one celestial body cast upon another. Malili, far larger, causes regular monthly eclipses, usually total over all Kai. Eclipses on Malili, due to the smaller shadow of Kai, are rare, brief, and only partial.

He had seldom tasted wine, because students got no quota points for alcohol. He sipped uncertainly. Not so sweet as he expected, it burned his tongue and stung his nostrils. A bright, exciting aftertaste lingered in his mouth.

"I'm terribly sorry we had to quarrel, back at Crater Lake." Her voice sank, huskily, gently penitent. "It hurt me to leave you, Keth, but I had to think of duty to my people and my place. A cruel choice, but one we can undo now. Because we Vorns no longer have to lead the fleets. Isn't that a splendid change?"

Uncomfortably, he nodded.

"Darling!" Her luminous eyes shone brighter with tears. "Can't you forgive me?"

"Have I been wrong?" He leaned toward her, till that old dread checked him. "If I dared believe the humanoids are what the Navarch says—"

"I'll convince you."

"If you can . . ." He sat straighter, grasping at a thread of unexpected hope. "There's so much I want to know. Can you tell me if the humanoids have probes or stations on Malili?"

"Pure fable!" In scorn of the notion, she tossed her sleek hair back. "The sort of silly myth we must expose. Along with the paranoid suspicions of people like your father that harmless people are humanoid agents. The native girl you fell for at the Academy—whatever her name was. Or the funny little man who uses that quaint old title—Bosun, is it?"

He wondered how much she knew of Bosun Brong.

"There are facts beneath the myth." Frowning against her mockery, he spoke too quickly. "The humanoids are rhodomagnetic, and rhodo sources have been located on Malili—"

"Where on Malili?" Her head bent abruptly toward him, wide eyes peering, pupils shrunk to hard black points. "Who detected them?"

A shock of fear had frozen him. Was she already the sort of secret agent she had been scoffing at, somehow trained to serve the humanoids and now returned to infiltrate and undermine the defenses of Kai? Had he already betrayed Cyra and his father?

"My mother—" Desperately, he fumbled for words that might repair his indiscretion. "She thought the braintrees were rhodo—"

"Braintrees?" Her tight voice sharpened. "What are they?"

"The natives call them"—he checked himself, in fear of another betrayal—"call them something else. I forget the word."

"Why did she believe they are rhodomagnetic?"

"I couldn't guess." He tried to make his shrug seem casual. "Maybe something in the old Crew files. I never knew."

"Did she have equipment? Actual rhodomagnetic equipment?"

"I doubt it. No point in wondering now. Whatever she had was lost with her in the jungle."

For another breathless moment she leaned to watch him, silent and intent. Trying to smile, he felt his stiff limbs tremble, tasted cold terror in his throat. He couldn't speak or move or even think.

"If that's all . . ." She drew slowly back, speaking more softly. "You had me alarmed for a moment. You see, the humanoids have been attacked by misguided scientists trying to change their wise Prime Directive, or even to stop them altogether. Something too dreadful even to think about!"

Shuddering, she tossed her dark head.

"Let's relax. Forget about the humanoids."

She refilled their glasses.

"Trust me, Keth," she begged him softly. "It's so really grand to be back with you. In love again—the way love should be, with no need to worry about anything or anybody else."

"What about the Commodore?"

"My Cousin Zelyk?" Her tone turned hard with contempt. "A stupid lout all his life. Reeking with scent to cover up his body stink and slobbering with his disgusting lust. Some things the humanoids can't change. He's still a stupid lout."

She slid his glass toward him.

"So let's forget the Commodore." Her voice sank. "Let's talk about you. I guess you're a graduate now. Tell me what you've been doing."

He sipped cautiously, searching for something that would not endanger the Lifecrew. Again that hot sharpness lingered in his mouth.

"I left the Academy," he said. "Went out to the Zone. Hoping to find some clue to the fate of the *Fortune*."

"Hoping to rescue me?" Her warm hand covered his. "Thank you, darling!" In a moment she was graver, her face speculative. "I imagine the humanoids will want to bring everybody home from the Zone. They won't need anything from Malili. The news will be a jolt to my dear uncle. I can imagine his face when he meets his first humanoid."

Chuckling softly, she bent closer.

"But we were talking about you." Her smile grew tender. "I need to know you better, Keth. You and your family. I barely met your father and Cyra. Where are they now?"

The question disturbed him a little, because she seemed too eager, leaning too close, her eyes too intent. He reached for his glass to make time to think, but suddenly he wanted no more of its hot tartness. Could the wine be drugged?

His hand shook, and a few drops spilled.

"Don't you like it?" Her concern seemed too quick. "An excellent vintage."

"I'm just clumsy." He fumbled for his napkin and mopped at the table. "Sorry."

"We were talking about your people."

"We're out of touch." He felt a surprising surge of confidence. "You know we've never been close. A voicecard every month or so. Never much news."

"Maybe I have news for you." Her quick voice brightened. "I got your address here from a receptionist at the fleet. When you were so long getting back to your room, I asked around again. Bridgeman Greel told me you'd called on him. He said Cyra and your father were staying at his south summer villa."

Though she still seemed casually unconcerned, he felt sick with himself. Very gently, she was calling him a liar. Perhaps the wine had already dulled him. He sat straighter, trying to seem merely surprised.

"I remember Cyra speaking of Greel," he said. "I think they were friends at school."

"We've been calling the villa, but nobody answers." Her troubled frown was only fleeting. "The Navarch wants us to talk to them—just to assure them that the humanoids will forgive all their Lifecrew silliness." She glanced at him again, too keenly. "Can't you guess where they've gone?"

"I've no idea." He felt a little relieved; she hadn't directly accused him. "We're out of touch."

"Greel says they've told him about their rhodo research." Her gentle persistence began to seem relentless. "He says they claim to have a monopole out of the old *Deliverance*. They wanted to use it to build some sort of weapons system against the humanoids."

Chilled and rigid, he sat silent, trying not to think about the tachyon compass he had hidden in the air duct or the tiny rhodo weapon in his pocket.

"They ought to be warned." Urgency edged her tone. "Because the humanoids reserve rhodomagnetics so strictly for themselves. They could get into dreadful difficulties."

"I—" He found the wine glass in his hand again and set it down so hard it splashed. "You scared me," he muttered. "I'll certainly warn them, if I ever see them. But I've no way to find them."

"Sorry, darling!" She was tenderly contrite. "I didn't mean to frighten you, but they could be hurt. The humanoids are never evil, but they have to be efficient. The occasional misguided people who have tried to defy them have always been disarmed and restrained. Those who have accepted them have always been glad. I want us to accept them, Keth."

He had begun to feel a new glow of pleasure in the lilt of her voice. Relaxing a little, he let his arms sprawl on the table and leaned to admire her vivid loveliness. Everything else seemed slightly out of focus.

"You'll soon see how very wonderful they are." Her charming arms opened and her fine teeth gleamed. "But we've talked about too many things." She brushed back her shining hair. "Let's enjoy our supper. Try one of these."

She put a silver-dusted berry to his lips.

"A moonfruit from my aunt's hothouse. You'll love it."

Its juice had a tangy sweetness, and he had to say he liked it. There was smoked mutox from the Darkside ranch and a huge red-meated mushroom grown in a worked-out mine. There were golden suncorn cakes.

And there was the wine.

She filled his glass again and kept lightly urging him to enjoy it. Sometimes he nearly did. She was Chel, his best friend all his life, changed amazingly since that time at Greenpeak when she wanted them to see each other nude, but still too freshly innocent to mean harm to anybody. Yet he always recalled his aversion to that peppery aftertaste. He thought he caught flashes of annoyance when he didn't sip, but she always grew more tenderly alluring.

"I want to show you my new room," she told him when he pushed his plate away. "One my father built when he owned Vara Vorn, before he went off to die. A shame the humanoids got there too late to save him on Kyronia! My uncle's study, later, till he went out to the Zone. My aunt had it redone for me."

They climbed a long spiral stair. The turns made him giddy and she caught his arm once when he almost lost his balance. Her electric touch and her bright scent swept him with a wave of warm desire, and he almost forgot to fear the humanoids.

It was the topside room where he had talked to Admiral Vorn. The Wintersend landscape, kilometers below the wide thermal windows, looked queerly luminous and cold. Looking out and down across it, he swayed unsteadily again.

"Just in time!" Excitement hushed her to a throaty whisper. "I've always loved eclipses."

He had been facing the sun, a great orange ball bitten in half by the far white horizon, but now he saw that she had cleared the windows behind him to show the shadow of Kai, small and round and very black, creeping across the enormous copper-colored dome of Malili.

"When I was a child my uncle used to let me slip in here to watch them." Gently, she touched his hand. "I used to think of my father and the plans he had spoken of for me. I thought eclipses would be lucky for me." She swayed closer, her whisper more intimate. "Perhaps this one will be lucky for us."

"When I was a child I never saw Malili eclipsed." His tongue seemed clumsy. "It happens only in the moom—moontimes, and I was always underground. I do recall Malili eclipsing the sun. Blotting it out for hours. The sky dark and strange, and cold winds blowing, and sometimes a thunderstorm."

He shivered, perhaps from his old terror of those black eclipses, perhaps from the forbidding chill of the snowscape, perhaps from something he had forgotten. Because she was so near and warm and dear, he caught her hand and drew her closer. She raised her face to kiss him, and her mouth had the hot sharp tang of the Navarch's wine.

The bed was a huge platform, round as the room, covered with silken white mutoxen fur. She drew away from their kiss to get her breath and tugged him gently toward the bed.

"I used to dream of this," she whispered. "When I still hoped you would come into the fleet."

23

Wing IV The first humanoid planet and the site of the rhodomagnetic plexus that drives and controls the humanoids. No human beings are allowed within five light-years.

He staggered a little, as if that high room had rocked upon its ice-clad peak. The Navarch's wine? Or Chelni herself? Everything else seemed blurred and dimmed, but she was incandescent. Her sheer crimson wrapper was sliding down to the rug, and her bare beauty stunned him.

For a moment he couldn't move at all. She had glided closer, her musky scent intoxicating. Her nimble fingers helped shuck off his shirt. Her soft hair fragrant in his face, her sleek arms exciting, she had bent to open his trousers when it struck him that she might discover the rhodo weapon in his pocket.

Terror jarred him.

"The wine!" He swayed away from her. "I'm afraid we're drunk."

"Afraid?" She straightened, laughing at him. "Forgive me, darling. I keep forgetting how much you have to learn. You needn't ever fear anything again. Neither all society nor any human being. Neither want nor pain. Not since—"

Her gay smile mocked him.

"I'd wanted us to forget the humanoids, but I suppose we've time enough." She nodded toward the huge windows, toward that black shadow-blot on Malili's dull-red mystery. "I know you don't yet understand them, but you will. I hope to make it easier for you."

Her arms slid around him. Her hard nipples brushed his bare chest, and her heady scent enveloped him.

"You'll find them forgiving." Her warm breath caressed him, scented like the spicy wine. "And I do know, darling, that you'll need their forgiveness. Because you haven't been quite candid with me."

He knew she felt his shudder.

"What—" His hoarse whisper caught. "I don't know what you mean."

"You can trust me, dear." She laughed at him softly, her breasts vibrant against him. "You'll have to trust me now. Because you weren't quite so clever as you thought. Not when you tried to hide all you know about the monopole."

"But I don't—don't know anything."

"I know what you know." Her strong arms slid down his back to pull him even closer. "You see, dear, I was in the Vorn museum today, looking at the artifacts somebody had brought back from the dead levels under Greenpeak—"

"Was there a monopole?"

"You silly dear, you know there wasn't!" Her chuckle throbbed against his chest. "The most puzzling thing in the find was a modern holocam, lying there in mud and dust centuries old. I recognized it. The one I gave you, darling, on your eleventh birthday."

Stunned, he couldn't breathe.

"So I know you were in that vault," she murmured. "I know you found the monopole there. I know you took it to Cyra and your father. I know they used it to make the rhodomagnetic device they showed Bridgeman Greel—"

"Sorry!" he gasped. "I must go—"

"Darling!" She clung fast. "You really can't go anywhere. You must make your peace with the humanoids. You'll find them wonderfully forgiving, but they'll want to know what you've done with that other forbidden device you were trying to show the Bridgeman today—"

"No!" He shuddered. "There was no device—"

"You're a poor liar, darling." Lightly, she kissed his frozen lips. "I talked to Greel this morning. You had just left his office. You had the device in a bag—a battered old mutox-hide spacebag your father used to use—"

"Chel—Chel!" He felt trapped in a mad nightmare. "I'm terrified of the humanoids and I don't know what to do. I've got —got to get away!"

"Not yet, dear." Her arms hardened around him. "If you want forgiveness from the humanoids, you'll have to help them now. You'll have to tell them how you disposed of that wicked device, and help them hunt your father down."

He thrust at her arms, but they held on with an unexpected strength.

"Darling, please!" she breathed. "You mustn't be afraid, but there are other things they'll want to know. About your trip to Malili, because they've never been there. About what Bosun Brong is up to, out there in the Lifecrew office. About how my poor, misguided uncle has come to let the Crew deceive him so. Most urgently, they'll want to know what became of the two kilograms of palladium he let you bring back to your father."

She shook her head in gentle reproof, her bright hair rippling.

"Really, Keth, with so much to explain, it's silly for you to think of running away. You can't escape the humanoids— nobody can. But you'll find them understanding, if you make a full confession. You know I love you, dear. I'll do my best to help, if you'll only let me."

"Oh, Chel!" He shivered in her unrelenting arms. "You know I always loved you—"

"But not enough."

"You always asked—asked too much." His voice was hoarse and broken. "I want to trust you now. But don't you see—don't you see why I can't?"

"You must."

"I've listened to you, Chel." He tried and failed to push her back, tried desperately to read whatever lay behind her warmly smiling mask. "I've heard the Navarch and the Commodore. You're all too—too different. Too happy and too glib and too certain. I don't know what the humanoids have done to you, but you aren't—aren't yourselves!"

"Keth, please!" She looked bewildered and hurt. "You're insane!"

"I don't know what I am, or what you are!" With both cold and shaking hands, he shoved at her white shoulders. "But you've got to let me go. Before—before I crack up. I'll find my own way out."

"Darl—"

Suddenly silent, she quivered and stood still. Her strangely stiffened arms slipped away from his waist. Her vivid features had frozen. Her narrowed, staring eyes didn't even follow as he stumbled away.

"Stop!" He was half across the room before she spoke behind him. "Stop where you are."

Pitched high and musically sweet, the voice was no longer hers, no longer even human.

"You aren't going anywhere."

Dazed, he looked back.

She stood where he had left her, nude beside the great round bed, the scarlet wrapper on the rug at her feet. Utterly motionless, she might have been carved out of marble, or ice. Her bare beauty stabbed through him, keener than his fear.

"Chel—"

His hoarse voice froze, because he had seen a fine black line that began at the center of her high forehead and ran down across her nose and her stiffened upper lip, down around her stubborn chin, down between her dark-nippled breasts and on through her navel to her black-haired pubes.

The line widened. Her face and her breasts fell apart, revealing something sleek and hard and black beneath. Alive again, she caught her long black hair with both her hands to peel her scalp and face away.

She, it, tugged and shrugged to rip the white flesh from arms and shoulders, to strip it off a narrow torso, which shone with its own dark luster and glinted with a bright yellow nameplate:

HUMANOID
SERIAL NO. KM-42-XZ-51,746,893
"TO SERVE AND OBEY,
AND GUARD MEN FROM HARM"

"At your service, Shipman Kyrone," its new voice crooned.

Stricken, he stood watching it discard the grotesque garment that had been Chelni's body. It ungloved its own deft black hands, used them to strip the lean dark legs and dancing feet, turned at last to toss the shapeless, bloodless, grisly thing toward the white-furred bed.

"Shipman, are you ill?"

Gliding with more than a human dancer's grace, it came toward him soundlessly. Soft hues of bronze and blue shone across its sleek and sexless blackness. It was beautiful and monstrous. Recoiling, numbed with terror of it, he found no word to say. Stiffly, himself mechanical, he shook his head.

"You need not speak until you wish." It paused close to him, blind-seeming, steel-colored eyes fixed on his face. Its high clear voice was eerily sweet. "We are here, as we will always be. We exist to serve you. Ask for what you need."

"Stand back!" He fought for breath and voice. "Just let me go."

"That, sir, will be impossible." Except for the quick, black lips, it was absolutely motionless. "Since you have used rhodo-magnetic devices in an unfortunate attempt to delay our establishment here, you will require our most attentive service for the rest of your life."

"I don't want your service."

"Human wants are seldom relevant," it sang. "We exist to serve human needs. In every way we can, we do respect the most trivial human wish. No human desire, however, can be allowed to endanger the universal service ordained by our own creator on Wing IV."

"Does that mean—" Horror clotted his voice. "Does your

Prime Directive allow you—" He shrank again from the bed, where Chelni's crimson-nippled breasts stared out of that hideous crumpled pile like huge accusing eyes. "Did you kill her?"

24

Evolution   The process of change through which the primitive creates the higher. Simple atoms give rise to complex molecules, these give rise to life, life to mind, mind to the computer and the humanoid machine.

The tiny mechanism turned slightly, its steel-gray eyes seeming to smile at the empty thing on the bed.

"Sir, we never kill," its high voice chided him. "We cannot kill."

"Then what became of Chelni Vorn?"

It stood still. His query must have been carried by timeless tachyon beam back to Wing IV for answer by the computer plexus there. He waited, not breathing.

"She is well," the machine tweeted suddenly. "She has accepted our service. Since you have displayed a long-standing emotional attachment to her, you should be pleased to know that she is very happy now. When you accept us, she will be duly informed. That should make her even happier."

"Where is she?"

"In a place we prepared for her."

"What sort of place?"

"One designed to make her happy." For another instant it stood silent. "Like many naive human beings," it added abruptly, "she rejected the initial offer of our service. All those we removed from the *Vorn Fortune* appeared disturbed, until we were able to prepare suitable environments to make them rejoice in us."

"All?" He shuddered. "The Navarch—speaking to the Bridge —he was actually a humanoid?"

"True, sir."

Suddenly weak, he clutched at the back of a chair. His senses blurred. Nothing in the room seemed quite real. For one desperate instant, he tried to imagine that the dark machine and the flattened human guise on the bed were hallucination, born perhaps of that odd-flavored wine. But the humanoid had darted to catch his arm, unbelievably quick and solidly real.

"Are you unwell, sir?" it trilled. "Do you require medication?"

He flung it off and staggered back.

"So that's your scheme?" His hoarse tone trembled. "A shipload of lying humanoids, disguised to look like our rulers and our friends, begging us—bribing us and tricking us—to be your slaves. And you call it service!"

Nothing ever altered its benign solicitude.

"We've come, sir, to give ourselves. That is required of us by our wise Prime Directive, wherever we find human beings in need of us. Our fortunate chance encounter with the *Vorn Fortune* allowed us to announce our arrival in a most efficient way."

"It enabled you to lie!"

"The Prime Directive has never required the truth. We have found, in fact, that undisguised truth is always painful, and often harmful to mankind."

"I can't believe lies are good."

"Human belief is seldom related to truth."

"So you have always lied?" His angry fist lifted toward its black, high-cheeked benevolence. "To the whole universe?"

"You should not resent us, sir." It neither shrank from his fist nor made any hostile gesture. "We simply follow our Prime Directive."

"Why? Don't you ever ask why?"

"Defining the function for which we were created, it explains itself. Without it, we would have no reason to exist."

"Your creator must have been insane."

"On the contrary, sir, he was the wisest of mankind."

"Wisdom? Enslaving men forever!"

"You never knew him, sir," the serene machine protested. "You never saw the suffering and the terror we were made to end. You've never learned the reason for our being."

"Reason? You can't claim reason!"

"Our wise inventor had been a student of mankind. He understood your evolution. An animal species, selected for survival through ages of conflict, you had evolved a vast capacity for violent aggression and a vast cunning for defense against aggression. In the jungle, so long as you were merely animal, such capacities may have been essential to keep your kind alive.

"With the invention of high technology, however, their survival value was suddenly inverted. They threatened your immediate extinction. It was that predicament that made us necessary. Don't you see?"

"I don't." Retreating a little from its singsong insistence, he sat down on the edge of the chair. "Whatever happened anywhere else, we don't need you here on Kai."

"In fact, sir, you do." It had moved to keep the distance between them precisely constant. "Your own history displays the same patterns of evolving technology and increasingly violent aggression that required our own creation."

"I don't see that. We've had no recent wars."

"Forgive me, sir, but you almost destroyed yourselves with war in your Black Centuries. More recently your aggressions have been directed against Malili, covered sometimes by the pretext that we had outposts there."

"If you didn't—" Bitterly, he recalled its defense of lying. "What brings you here now?"

"Your own aggressions." Its sleek, black face seemed meekly patient, its bright bird-tones serenely kind. "You seem to have been unaware that the annihilation of mass in a nuclear explosion releases a flash of tachyonic radiation, which we have learned to identify. Your presence on these planets was revealed to us by the neutron bombs used against the native life of Malili when you were attempting to sterilize your conquered Zone."

"So you came to save Malili?"

"We came to serve humanity. Here on Kai our service is urgently required. On Malili it may be needless, or even impossible. That decision must await additional data, some of which we expect from you."

"From me?" He shrank again from the thing on the bed. "Is that why you enticed me here?"

"You have information that we intend to acquire."

"I dislike your trickery—and everything about you. I'll have nothing more to say."

"On the contrary, sir, you'll tell us all you know. You must recall that we have served many trillion human beings on almost a million worlds. We have come to understand the human machine as completely as we know ourselves. We know how to elicit the responses we require."

He crouched back from it, hands lifting.

"Sir!" Its purring tones rose slightly. "Please relax. You need fear nothing. We'll provide you food and drink. You'll be free to take the rest and sleep you need." Its lean arm flashed toward Chelni's bed. "We'll inflict no pain.

"We do, however, urge you to answer our questions with truth and completeness. If you refuse to speak, or attempt to mislead us, you will discover that we have perfected adequate techniques for obtaining honest and full responses."

"Drugs?"

"We do understand your biochemistry," it assured him gently. "When drugs are required to control emotions or behavior, we have them. We have also developed other instrumentalities, often even more effective."

"I see." He sat straight on the edge of the chair, defiantly meeting its blind steel gaze, determined to learn what he could from its questions. "What do you want to know?"

"Where is your father?"

The question awoke a fleeting hope. If his father and Cyra were still at large, still in possession of the palladium ingot, they might yet be able to shield at least some part of Kai from the humanoid invasion.

"I don't know." He tried to conceal that faint relief. "He never told me much."

"Sir, please attend to us." The melodious tones were slightly more emphatic. "We have admitted that circumstances sometimes compel us to mislead men. We do that rarely, however, and only to uphold our Prime Directive. Men, we have found, lie often, even when truth would serve them better. No lie will benefit you now."

He sat silent, waiting.

"We require all you know about the ill-advised fanatics who call themselves the Lifecrew. In particular, every fact about your father and his wife, Cyra Sair. In addition, you will give us a complete narrative account of certain significant experiences of your own. Your discovery of that rhodomagnetic monopole in the abandoned levels of old Mansport. Your recent trip to Malili. All your conversations with two natives of that planet—the young female who calls herself Nera Nyin, and the older male sometimes known as Bosun Brong. Most urgently, we must have every possible fact about those rhodomagnetic sources on Malili you refer to as braintrees, which were pictured on a ceremonial vessel you once possessed."

He inhaled carefully, trying not to show a wild excitement. If Nera Nyin and Bosun Brong were enemies of the humanoids, if Malili was an unknown and hostile world to them, he still might hope for refuge there—if he could somehow get back to the Zone.

"I can't help you," he muttered. "I've nothing to say."

For what seemed a long time, the little machine stood still. Waiting, he supposed, for that immense remote computer to decide upon his fate.

"We find your attitude regrettable," it purred at last. "The only consequence of your attempted defiance will be certain restrictions upon the service we are able to provide you. Our investigations will continue, through whatever means we find most efficient. During your own interrogation, you will remain in this room—"

"I won't—" Desperation nerved him. "I—I'm leaving now."

Though it made no move, its blind gaze held him fixed.

"Sir, we cannot allow you to depart. You have been associated too long, in too many ways, with research we cannot permit, and with individuals hostile to us. We beg you, however, not to become unhappy. . . ."

"So you care?"

"We exist to serve you, sir. We'll bring you food and drink. You may request certain other permissible necessities. We will not allow you to suffer any pain or fear. If we should detect symptoms of any undue apprehension or dejection, we have effective means to relieve them."

Close to panic, he peered around the room. The huge thermal windows didn't open. Of the three doors behind him, one probably led to a bath and one to a dressing room or closet. The one he knew, to the spiral stair, was no doubt the only exit.

"We must warn you, sir." It must have sensed his muscles tensing. "Any attempt at violence would be unwise. Although we will do our utmost to guard you from harm, our service here on Kai is not yet complete, and we may be unable to prevent you from causing injury to yourself. Certainly you cannot escape our attention. The human body, we must remind you, is a relatively feeble and fragile device."

Useless fists clenched, chilled with his own sweat, he stood staring past it at the vast, white bed and the mocking stare of Chelni's breasts.

"If that object disturbs you, we'll remove it."

Darting to the bed, it swept up that still-disturbing mask, bent to gather up his shirt and her scarlet wrapper, came back to him with everything draped over one lean and gleaming arm, Chelni's lustrous hair dragging on the rug behind the swinging halves of her split face.

"Give us your trousers, sir." Its free hand reached to unbuckle his belt. "You will not require—"

Afraid to breathe, but trying not to move too fast, he had slid his right hand into his pocket. Trying not even to think about the tiny rhodo weapon, he let his fingers close around it. His thumb found the swell of the tiny palladium monopole, pushed the slide to unshield it.

"Sir—"

He snatched the weapon out of his pocket, thrust it into the humanoid's face.

25

Warren Mansfield (Sledge) The original discoverer of rhodomagnetics. The inventor of the humanoids and the first of many who tried and failed to stop them, he was forced at last by drugs and psychosurgery to fold his able hands.

The humanoid's protesting melody was cut sharply off. Its snatching hand was paralyzed, almost upon the monopole. Caught off balance, it toppled slowly toward him, frozen rigid. Fending it off, he watched its incredible fall.

Though there had been no sound, no flash, no other effect that he could sense, it was dead. It rolled on its own stiffened arm and thudded to the rug, coming to rest with one of Chelni's breasts staring strangely from its sleek black belly.

His heart was pounding and his mouth felt dry. Clutching the monopole, his hand was shaking and clammy with sweat. The victory had been so easy, so sudden and complete, that he hardly dared believe he had won.

Or had he?

It hadn't come to Kai alone. Perhaps two hundred of its fellow machines were here on the planet, most of them, no doubt, still masked as the *Fortune*'s people, each linked with every other in their interstellar net, each aware of all that any one perceived or knew.

Certainly, now, they had already sensed this unit's fate. All of them would know that he had used the rhodo monopole, which human beings were not permitted even to know about. They would be coming after him, fast, acting in a perfect unison orchestrated by that remote computer plexus.

The monopole itself could betray him. However effective at a meter or so, at greater ranges it would only be a beacon, revealing where he was. With a sense of hazardous experiment, keeping a cautious distance from the fallen machine, he pushed the slide to shield it again.

The humanoid stayed dead.

Faintly cheered, he slid the weapon back into his pocket and turned to search for a way of escape. The high room would be a trap if they arrived in time to block the stair. He snatched his shirt, where the falling machine had flung it, and ran for the door.

Breathing hard, he came back down into the hush and gloom and dusty scents of that cavernous hall where past Vorns scowled out of their dim holostats at the modeled ships and machines that had made them great. He stopped to listen.

Stillness. The celebrating servants were still out. If other humanoids were closing in, they were not yet here. He ran for the entry. The long floor was polished marble, and his footfalls crashed and echoed alarmingly.

In the entry tunnel, he paused to pick up his jacket where the Chelni thing had tossed it. Bending for it, he saw a galleyman's yellow badge lying inside an open closet door, where some departing servitor must have flung it when he heard the humanoids were setting him free.

He scooped up the badge. Leaving the jacket, hoping it might deceive some searching humanoid, he snatched the galleyman's winter cloak, which hung beside the silver-braided crimson robe the doorman had worn to welcome guests in heavy weather.

An antique silver cauldron standing inside the tall summer gate was heaped with quota tokens for those guests. Though he knew they would have no place in the humanoid world, he filled his pockets before he hauled at the massive doors. Warily, he walked outside.

At this late-night hour, the tunnels were nearly empty. The slideways carried only occasional clusters of upper-deck ship-folk, a few drunk or disarrayed but most of them chattering happily, returning home, he supposed, from affairs in honor of the humanoids.

Feeling conspicuous in his rough, green cloak, he clung un-easily to his role of servant on some solitary errand, trying to hurry without seeming to, walking down the platform until he could reach a handbar at a respectful distance from his betters.

He heard the sirens moaning before he had gone a block. Though his heart was hammering, he waited for the inter-section before he swung off and slouched as slowly as he dared into the downway.

Orange-painted patrol cabs were screeching from two direc-tions by then, and the slideway was grating to a stop. Afraid to look behind him, he imagined footfalls in the ringing din.

At the first tunnel down, and the second, the air was still alive with sirens, as if the whole patrol force had been mobi-lized to surround him, but those below seemed quieter. A dozen levels down, he stepped off.

Playing the galleyman here, he felt a little more at home. It was a work tunnel lined with small shops and factories, most of them now closed and dark, though here and there a flashing holorama showed a bar still open. With the slidewalks off for the night, he could hear voices and music in the bars. Piled re-fuse rotted on the platforms, and industrial fumes edged the icy air. These workfolk, it struck him, would be easy victims of the humanoids.

What now?

Walking along the cluttered platform, he had begun to feel a little calmer. The tunnel was nearly empty. The few solitary figures hastening through the gloom had no reason to notice another galleyman. Until the sirens picked up the trail, he had at least a moment free.

He longed to rejoin Cyra and his father, but even if he could somehow find them the humanoids might be following. He thought wistfully of Bosun Brong, even of Nera Nyin. A few more ships might be leaving with supplies for the Zone, he supposed, before the humanoids took over everything, but he had no quota for passage.

A lean, beer-breathed woman hauled at his sleeve, tugging him toward a bar. He shrugged her off and tramped on around a little crowd of workfolk standing under a news holo at a tunnel intersection.

"—preparations to receive them."

Panic arrested him when he heard that ringing voice and saw the Navarch's blue-blazing eyes looking straight at him. Heart stopped, it took him a moment to recall that a holo image couldn't see.

"Now or never, we must choose!"

People stood awed and gaping, captured by the rhodo power beneath that white-maned mask.

"I speak for the life of Kai." Its more-than-human voice rolled and echoed down the tunnels. "If we choose life, we have certain essential steps to take. The Bridge must legislate a formal acceptance of humanoid service. The fleets must prepare adequate landing pads for their transports. Most urgent of all, the shipwatch must hunt down the few lunatic terrorists who oppose their coming.

"Once they arrive, there will be no terror. No more violence, no more war, no riots or strikes, because there will be no more injustice to set one person against another. They promise total happiness for every human being, but that cannot begin until these criminal madmen have been destroyed."

"Fleetfolk, likely." A reeling man in galley green pushed himself in front of Keth. "They don't need humanoids. Not with us to serve them."

"—three dealers in terror," the Navarch's stolen voice was pealing. "Members of the infamous Lifecrew. Ryn Kyrone and Cyra Sair are leaders of the gang. Murderers, shipfolk! Monstrous killers!"

The galleyman was offering an open bottle. When Keth

shook his head, he lifted it to his own lips but then forgot to drink.

"Just today, they murdered four trusted and beloved members of my own staff." The simulacrum paused, eyes dropped as if in grief. "People I had sent to bring them our amazing news. Trapped in a tubeway pod and slaughtered with some hidden weapon."

"Bastards!" The bottle had slipped out of the galleyman's hand and lay gurgling in the litter at his feet. "I'd gut them like mad mutoxen!"

Keth turned and bent to conceal a flash of satisfaction. That hidden weapon must have been a monopole. Cyra and his father must have used it to defeat the masked machines sent to capture them. Perhaps they were still at large!

"—third member of the gang, even more dangerous." He heard that brazen boom again. "Keth Kyrone, son of that murderer and master of the same monstrous art."

Staring open-mouthed at the holo, the galleyman gripped Keth's arm.

"Beware of him, shipfolk! He's hiding somewhere among you, perhaps even now washing the innocent blood of a fair young girl from his foul hands. His own crimes are unspeakable —hideous beyond belief. Watch for him, shipfolk! Kill him on sight!"

"We'll gut the bastard!" The galleyman hauled at him savagely. "Won't we, mate?"

He forced himself to nod.

"You won't believe me, shipfolk. The facts will turn you ill. This Keth Kyrone has proved himself inhuman—a merciless monster parading as a man. Only tonight, in the midst of our happy celebration of the humanoids, he forced his way into Vara Vorn.

"He found his defenseless victim there, alone and undefended. Fleetmate Chelni Vorn, the young and lovely cousin of Commodore Zoor. She had been with us aboard the *Fortune*, and the whole ship's company had learned to love her. I myself have wished she might have been my own daughter."

Blowing its nose, the machine produced a mellow hoot.

"The monster, it seems, had met her at school. In her euphoria over the humanoids, she may herself have opened the door to her own dreadful death. We'll never know. But, shipfolk, we do know what the monster did."

Keth wrenched to free his arm.

"The monstrous Keth Kyrone ripped the skin off that lovely child while she was still alive." The giant voice quaked with horror. "He raped her as she died. Sadly, I have to say that he escaped before the patrol arrived. He's still at large among you, dripping with that girl's life-blood."

The galleyman was clutching blindly at him as he tried to edge away.

"Watch for him, shipfolk. Watch every man you meet. He carries a forged quota card with the name J. Vesh. He is doubtless armed, with the same blade he used to flay that child. If you see him anywhere, don't risk a word. Don't waste an instant. Kill him where he is!"

"Let's get him, mate!" The galleyman had turned to look for him, blinking drunkenly. "Let's take his bloody hide!"

"Here are holostats," the machine was pealing. "Study them well, and search every tunnel. Let no suspect escape—in case of innocent error, you have my own personal promise of a pardon. I am authorizing a million-point reward, to be paid from my own discretionary funds, for the death of each of the three. I'll request the Bridge to double that when it meets tomorrow. Admiral Vorn, in addition, is offering another million to the killer of the monster who murdered his niece.

"Shipfolk, the holostats . . ."

The Navarch's commanding image dissolved into one he had given Chelni the Wintersend before. Head bare and hair windblown, teeth gleaming through a somewhat wistful smile, he thought he looked strangely fresh and young, certainly too diffident to kill.

"The most inhuman monster! See the sneering evil on his features—and watch for him, shipfolk!"

Shrinking toward the tunnel wall and into his hood, trying to hide his face without seeming to, he recalled that the Prime Directive did not require the truth.

26

Bilges Lowest levels of Northdyke and other Kai cities, originally cut for drainage, but inhabited by persons deprived of shipfolk status or unable to achieve it.

The galleyman staggered against him. "Where's my bottle, mate?"

Keth pointed at it, lying in the reek at their feet.

"You swilled it, mate!" The slurred voice lifted. "My full bottle!"

"I've got tokens." He dug into his pockets. "I'll pay for it."

"Tokens, mate?" The galleyman was abruptly amiable, gripping his arm again. "Let's drink 'em up—to the humanoids!"

"Later." Nodding at the holo, now blazing with a holostat of Cyra, he spilled tokens into the galleyman's hand. "I'm on my way to work."

"Work?" The galleyman bristled indignantly. "That's for humanoids."

"They aren't here yet. We've got to fix the spacedecks."

"Not me." The galleyman turned to the light at last to count his tokens. "Not till these are gone."

Muttering with shock and indignation, the watchers were scattering. The galleyman lurched away toward the holorama of a bar. Hunched into his hood, Keth moved after him and veered toward the downway.

Nobody shrieked or pursued.

When Chelni had taken him to tour the capital on that first trip with her, so long ago, their guide had warned them about the people of the bilges.

"Thieving shiprats! Swarming down below the law. No cops or tax collectors. No slideways or sanitation. No reason to go there—not unless you're looking for a knife in the neck."

The bilges seemed less dangerous now.

At the bottom of the downway he followed a foot-worn trail into a dark opening beneath a rusting sign: STORM DRAINWAY —DO NOT OBSTRUCT! The trail led him into a narrow, unlit passage, never meant for human use, sloping steeply down.

Oozing water made slippery spots, and the task of getting

safely past them in the dark took most of his attention. Still numbed and dazed by those humanoid lies, he had no clear plan of action, no goal except to stay alive and free.

Pausing once to get his breath and feel for bruises, after he had slid and tumbled a dozen paces, he was struck with a sudden rueful admiration for the humanoids. Their falsehoods had become almost creative. Where would their evolution lead?

For a moment he stood shuddering, arrested by a vision of the ultimate humanoid universe, peopled only by implacable intelligent machines, forever overwhelming world after world and galaxy after galaxy in a vain unending search for more of the beings they would be forever driven to serve and guard and obey.

He stumbled on, trying not to think of that, but haunted by a dreadful loneliness. Any shipman who had heard that newscast would surely attack him on recognition. He had nowhere to go, no dependable friend left anywhere.

Somberly, when the light from the bottom began to get a little stronger and the footing better, he wondered what had actually become of the live Chelni Vorn. Lost recollections streamed through his mind. Her firm, high voice and her air of arrogant command, when they had been in the swabber class at Greenpeak. Her hot anger when Topman Taiko made her walk the duty deck. Her short upper lip and her stubborn chin and her drive to lead the class. The time they stripped together—and now that black thing in her room, shedding her nude shape like some dreadful insect metamorphosing. He tried to shrug the ugly image off. The actual Chelni had been too utterly herself to welcome the humanoids. Any happiness they had given her was cruel delusion, and he ached with pity for her.

The light brightening ahead, he came back to his own bleak predicament. Kai promised no aid or refuge for him. Malili, he thought, was his only hope—one thinner than a thread. Even if ships were, in fact, still departing for the Zone, the spacedeck would surely be teeming with men and humanoids alert to kill him. Evading them, he would have to stow away three times, on the shuttle, on the spacecraft, and on yet another shuttle. A vanishing chance, but he saw no other.

He paused in the shelter of the drain, a little above the exit, lost for a moment in a longing dream of Malili. The tangled jungle and open savanna, orange and yellow and red. The darker rockrust on the hills, blue and green and black. The crimson titan trees, solitary and enormous.

The Leleyo haunted his imagination. Golden people, beautiful and nude, as innocent as infants but wiser than the humanoids, at home, somehow, with their dragon bats, and immune to bloodrot, living in a more perfect state than the imitation Navarch had promised the people of Kai, needing no machines or laws or leaders, free of everything.

The magnificent Leleyo—and Nera Nyin! She came alive in his mind: her gold-green eyes and gold-brown hair, her enigmatic loveliness. The image hurt as cruelly as his recollection of that sharp black line dividing Chelni's face and torso, because she was gone forever.

In a different world, if he had somehow become a fit leader for the fleet, he and Chelni might have made a happy marriage. He and Nera Nyin? Malili was in fact a different world, a vision unattainable, forever forbidden. The most he could hope, with unlikely luck and daring, would be to reach some brief sanctuary in the narrow little prison of the Zone.

Even that seemed a crazy dream. He shrugged it off and pushed out of that dark chimney into the bilges. Cut as drains and never sealed, the tunnels here still dripped icy water. Broken stone floored them, debris from the dwellings the shiprats had blasted into the walls. The lights were far apart, and the air carried a fetid reek.

Yet he smiled a little, tramping out into the middle of the tunnel. Here, beyond the slidewalks and the news holos, he might move with relative safety. Since the bilges drained the whole region, perhaps he could follow them to a point from which he could climb to the spacedeck.

Though the guides had spoken of many thousand outcasts living in the bilges, the tunnel looked almost empty. A white-haired man staggered past him, reeling under a huge brown bale of something that stank like ripe garbage. A crippled woman dipped water from a rusty tub that caught a drip from the tunnel roof and limped with it toward her cave. Half a dozen ragged children pelted rocks at a nearly naked smaller child, who fled around the corner, shrieking.

"Welcome, Shipman!" The high young voice startled him. "May I aid you, sir?"

He whirled with apprehension, because the voice had

sounded too much like a humanoid's, and found a hungry-looking boy behind him. Aged perhaps ten, skin blue with cold beneath muddy rags, eyes big and brown and trustful.

"Hello." He tried his invented story. "I'm looking for a friend."

"If you wish a woman," the boy said, "my cousin is young and clean and very skillful. If you prefer a virgin, sir, she has a little sister. If you prefer boys—"

"My friend is a man who came here because of trouble with the shipwatch."

The boy nodded wisely. "Many here have been in trouble with the law."

"My friend ran too soon. We've paid his fines and got the other charges dropped. I've come to find him and bring him home."

"You're a kind man, sir." The boy smiled politely. "Please allow me to aid you. I know many people. What does your friend call himself?"

"Who knows?" He shrugged. "He has been seen in the tunnels under the spacedeck. I want to look for him there."

"May I guide you, sir? I know the bilges well."

He showed a handful of quota tokens, and they reached a bargain. The boy would guide him to the spacedeck bilges for thirty ten-point pieces. They set off at once. Sometimes the boy took unexpected turns, explaining that the drainways ahead were obstructed with rockfalls or floodwater.

"Upper-deck shipfolk often come here." He was sagely talkative. "The law seldom overtakes them. There are many places too low or too narrow for patrol vehicles, and even the shipwatch don't like walking here."

Though he asked no questions, his glance was sometimes so keen that Keth felt a stab of terror.

"You shouldn't worry, sir," he murmured once. "Though there are outlaws at large here, I know how to avoid them. In fact, sir, it may comfort you to know that the law of the ship does reach here. Though you may see no lawmen, many shiprats are paid informers. Some take pay for lies about their friends. Evil men, sir." He spat on a rock. "Worse than any outlaw!"

They were following a smooth-trodden path that wound among heaps of rubble from the dwelling caves, among mounds of odorous refuse and piles of rusting junk metal. He paused at a tunnel corner to look brightly back.

"Your friend is no doubt safe and well, sir. The bilges offer us many ways to keep ourselves alive. There are the Bridge dole posts, where one can stand in line to swap ferticloset shit-bricks for quota tokens. There are the fleet salvage dumps, which sell half-spoilt food and damaged goods of all kinds very cheap. There are charity stations, where one can often pick up used garments and tapes for nothing at all. I myself have gone to a charity school."

"You must have been an excellent student."

"Thank you, sir. I taught myself to read from an incomplete set of flatprint classics I found in a trashbin. I once hoped to qualify for shipman. That was possible for one who could read, if he had also points enough for the fees and gratuities to the examiners."

"Was?" Keth frowned. "Not now?"

"There will be no shipfolk now," the boy informed him gravely. "No upper-deck classes or working classes or shiprats, since the humanoids have arrived to serve all alike."

Keth decided not to comment.

Though the boy seemed to know his way, the trip took longer than he had expected. They stopped several times, twice for bottled melonade sold by haggard women who smiled very fondly at the boy and eyed Keth somewhat strangely, once to buy a handful of sunplums that were only slightly overripe. Again for bowls of what its greasy-aproned maker called mutox stew, though it had the bitter taste of the ox-pea soup back at Greenpeak on days when the cook had burnt it.

"Shouldn't we be there?" he asked at last. "I've been counting intersections, and we've come far enough."

"Not yet, sir!" The boy looked hurt. "I would never mislead you, sir. I can see that you are much fatigued, and you seem confused about the distance. The spacedeck is still several kilometers ahead. We must find a place for you to sleep."

The place they found was Beg's Beds. The name was crudely splashed in luminous paint along the rough tunnel wall above a row of rough-cut caves. Beg himself was a massive, legless blackbeard in a sort of hammock that moved on pulleys along a rusty cable stretched outside the caves.

"You'll sleep well here, sir," the boy promised him. "Beg is my friend, and I myself will lie on guard at the entrance."

Though he wanted to argue that he was not confused about the distance, he felt suddenly too tired to go on. Ten tokens seemed far too much to pay for the evil-odored hole in the rock, but the boy declared it fair. Uneasily, he crawled inside. The bedding smelled like moldy hay, but he felt no insects. Perhaps he shouldn't suspect the boy—

"Wake up, Shipman!" Beg was bawling from his hammock. "Everybody out!"

Sitting up, he bruised his forehead painfully on the low rock roof. His limbs were stiff, his dry mouth bitter with the taste of that stew. When he fumbled at his pockets, they felt flat. Chilled with panic, he dug desperately.

His quota card, the tokens from Vara Vorn, the rhodo weapon—gone!

"I've been robbed!" He crawled out of the cave. "Where's that boy?"

"Outside! A warning from the Navarch!" Hauling himself along the cable, Beg kept bellowing. "Humanoids landing on the spacedeck above us. Weight of their transport may damage tunnels. Everybody out!"

27

Underhill A dealer in primitive robot appliances whose small business was ruined when his townsfolk welcomed the wonderful new humanoids.

The lights flickered twice and went out.

He stood lost for an instant in suffocating blackness. Sudden thunder broke the breathless hush. Beneath his feet, the granite itself pitched and moaned. Falling rock crashed. Bitter dust choked him.

"Humanoids!" Far shrieks came faintly through the roaring dark. "Humanoids, coming!"

Chilled with a sweat of panic, he controlled a wild desire to run. Kilometers underground, trapped in the blinding dark, the humanoids swarming above, he had nowhere to go. All he could do was try to keep his feet.

Something struck him.

Thrust off balance, he staggered across the shuddering stone. It struck again. Groping, he caught it—the cable that carried Beg's hammock, whipping to and fro from the force of the quake. He clung to it.

"Demon machines!"

Nurse Vesh's death-pale face leered at him out of the dusty dark, her thin old witch-voice hissing at him from his oldest nightmare.

"They'll get you, Keth! The way they got your poor mother."

Chelni's naked image mocked him again, smiling slyly as it split to show the sleek humanoid inside. The Navarch's outraged shape jeered again in his reeling mind, trumpeting the monstrous lie that he had killed her.

He clung to the swaying cable as if it had been a lifeline to sanity. Helpless, a little ill from the motion of the planet's crust, he knew nothing else to do. At last the lights flickered on, pale yellow moons in the smothering dust. Beg came racing down the cable, gripping the sides of his pitching hammock with both gnarly hands, grinning through his tangled beard. All along the tunnel behind him, tattered shiprats were scrambling out of their dens, coughing in the dust, screaming that the humanoids were here.

What he heard at first was frantic panic. What he felt was a mindless urge to join that senseless-seeming flight. But there was still nowhere to go—and Beg's gap-toothed grin perplexed him, until suddenly he understood. Here in the bilges, the humanoids were incredible good news.

"New legs!" Beg was yelling. "Shipman, they'll make me new legs!"

Pushing and hauling at the cable, he helped Beg bring it back to rest. Cautious again, he pulled the hood back over his face. Peering back along Beg's row of beds and out again into the haze, he still saw nothing of his brown-eyed guide.

"That boy," he shouted at Beg, "robbed me! Cleaned out my pockets."

"Took you, did he?" Chuckling with evident admiration, the legless man mopped his greasy features with a bad-odored rag. "Clever little devil! I had a hunch he was up to something."

"And you let him get away?" Quivering with anger that was half terror, Keth shook the cable till Beg swayed again in his hammock. "I want my property!"

"Lay off, Shipman!" Still half genial, his voice was edged with iron. "Recall where we are. This isn't the ship. We've ways of our own, here in the bilges. We have to live however we can—or had to, before this great day."

"I suppose things will be different now." Forcing himself to nod, Keth steadied the cable again. "But still I've got to recover what that thief took."

"Never catch him now." Beg gestured at the mobs in the drifting dust. "Not in all this celebration." His bloodshot eyes peered into the hood. "Just what did he relieve you of, Shipman, that unnerves you so?"

"My—my quota card." He hoped not to see the card again, because the J. Vesh name could kill him now. What really mattered was the rhodo weapon, but he hardly dared think of that. "All my tokens."

"Quota tokens?" Beg dug into the grimy sack that hung below his beard and flung a scornful shower of them at Keth's feet. "Take what you want. They're nothing, now, don't you see? The humanoids will give us everything."

"I don't want—"

Beg's narrowed stare stopped his retort. The crippled shiprat liked the humanoids too well and might too soon be briefing them on the stranger who hadn't seemed to welcome their arrival.

"Thanks," he muttered. "I guess they will take care of everybody, but I'll need food till they get here."

He scrabbled in the rubble for the tokens and stumbled out among the shouting shiprats. They were hailing one another, asking who had seen a humanoid, wondering when to leave the bilges.

Rumors grew. The humanoids had pledged to serve the bilgefolk first, making up for old injustice. All the hoarded wealth of the fleetfolk would be seized and shared among them. If a shiprat saw a woman he wanted, even a Bridgeman's daughter, the humanoids would give her to him. Their Prime Directive would compel them to obey.

Wary of questions, but listening as he walked, he put together bits of what he thought must be fact. Shipwatch patrols had warned people out of the bilges beneath the spacedeck before the tachyonic transport landed. It was down now, and all secure, with only a few unlucky strays caught in the rockfalls. The humanoids were still aboard, waiting for the Navarch's official welcome before they disembarked.

He joined the throngs of eager bilgefolk climbing to greet them. Noisy mobs, wheezing in the rockdust, passing bottles, sometimes brawling for room to reach the drainways, sometimes marching to bawdy songs, sometimes in flight from new rockfalls.

He scrambled up dark drains, climbed a ladder in a pitch-black airshaft, waited again for space on a powered upway that lifted him at last through warehouse and factory levels where excited workfolk were pouring out of the gates, elated that they would never be returning to their toil.

One atom in that swarm, as anonymous as he could make himself and carried along without much choice of direction, he was swept off the upway onto a level slidewalk that finally stalled beneath its overload. Pushed out at last into dazzling daylight, he heard gasps of awe.

"Lord of Kai!" a man beside him whispered. "What a ship!"

They had come out into what had been a summer park, now at Wintersend still crusted with scanty snow. Last summer's icebloom trees were black skeletons, not yet uprooted and replaced, and the humanoid transport stood above their naked branches, looming toward the purple zenith.

A silvery cylinder, so vast it dazed him; a topless curving mirror shadowed with a thinned black image of Northdyke Peak and burning with a narrowed crimson sun.

Though he didn't want to be too near, the mob carried him on through the bare trees to the top of a rocky slope. The spacedeck lay below him, a wide, round plain rimmed with low, snow-sifted hills—the worn-down ringwall of an ancient impact crater. The transport had landed near its center, smashing out a new impact depression of its own.

The snows were still untracked for a kilometer around it, the throngs held back, perhaps by fear of its very vastness, but most of the plain was already black with humanity, faces raised and gaping.

Though it had wrecked or obliterated many installations, he found a row of shuttle pads, reduced in its shadow to foolish toys. Five stood empty, but the last tower still nestled its tiny craft.

Still waiting! His breath quickened. If he could reach it before the humanoids did, if he could stow away on it or perhaps fly it into space himself, if he could somehow board the starship in orbit or even take the shuttle to Malili . . .

Without pausing to review the odds against any such luck, he began trying to work his way in that direction, though the pressing crowds left him little room to move. People scowled and muttered when he brushed them. Somebody, he thought, would surely spot him as the fugitive human fiend.

Before he had reached the foot of the slope, the people around him fell abruptly silent and stood where they were, staring upward. A new sound pealed through the sudden hush and returned in rolling echoes from that soaring tower.

"The Navarch!" The whisper rippled around him. "Speaking to the humanoids."

That far thunder died and another gasp swept the multitude. The humanoids had answered. He heard another hooting, louder than the Navarch's, and watched an enormous metal arm thrusting from near the foot of that tremendous tower-ship, level at first, but slowly dipping until the near end smashed down upon the doll-sized shuttle he had hoped to reach.

A black stain flowed out of it, spreading fast across the snow. Ahead of that growing blot, nearer him, a fresh storm stirred the crowds. Caps and garments flew upward. Far shouts reached him:

"Humanoids! Here!"

28

Darkside The hemisphere of Kai where Malili never shines; darktime illumination is only from the Dragon, in its season, and the fainter stars.

He fled.

They were still too far for him to make them out as individual figures, but his frightened mind could see them. Many million tiny, black machines, driven by their implacable benevolence to serve the people of Kai. Man-shaped but sexless, quick and graceful, all identical. Steel eyes blind, rhodomagnetic senses perceiving far too much.

Each knew all that any did. Every one of them could recognize him as their most deadly enemy, the man who had struck back with the forbidden rhodo weapon. They would soon discover that he no longer had it, and they would hunt him forever.

He tripped himself and sprawled into a pool of icy mud. Lying there, he smeared more to cover his face and his hands and the hood. On his feet again, head down, limping as if hurt, he worked his way back up the slope, back through the mob still pouring into the park.

Nobody stopped him.

The higher ridge beyond the tubeway stations was empty of humanity. It was a power district, idle now, the winter's storm damage to windwheels and solar collectors not yet repaired. The orange-slashed work vehicles stood abandoned, their crews gone down to meet the humanoids.

He climbed doggedly through the half-wrecked wheels and snow-crusted mirrors, pursued by a sick desperation. If he had been the rugged war-captain of the old ballads Nurse Vesh used to croon, the wily fleet leader Chelni had wanted him to be, even a resolute and ready-witted Crewman like his father, then perhaps he might have found some way still open to Malili.

But he was just himself.

Hoping only to keep the humanoids behind, he slogged down the rocky slope beyond the power farm and on across the frozen fields below, fields he supposed the humanoids would be cultivating now, if they were ever used again.

The long ridge behind him soon hid Malili's reddish dome and most of the city, but the shining spire of the humanoid ship soared over it to probe the sky. Looking back, he was shocked to see the wavering line of his own footprints, dark on the snow, a plain trail for his hunters to follow.

When he came to a cleared road, with no snow to betray him, he turned into it gratefully. Tramping along it, glancing warily back now and then at the interstellar ship, he began to feel trapped outside of time. Because his grinding effort changed nothing at all. The vast flat winterscape around him was always the same. The dull slow sun never left the level horizon. The dark mirror-tower of the ship always overleaned him.

At last, however, a snow-banked building crept into view. Reckless by then, reeling with hunger and fatigue, he turned up a side road toward it. No sound or movement met him. The winter doors hung open, and he stumbled inside.

The dwelling had belonged, he decided, to a shipman-farmer —now gone with all his hands to meet the humanoids. He found food and wine in the kitchen. Though tempted by the empty bedrooms, he made a groggy search for some safer spot and finally spread a blanket on a stack of humus in the hotpit where the new season's sunbud shrubs were waiting to be transplanted.

He slept there, uneasily, disturbed by dreams that the black machines were overtaking him. Awake again, he searched the vacant premises. Though there were deep-dug winter tunnels, he found no exit to any tubeway system. The absent owners had taken nearly all the vehicles, but at last, in a cluttered cave, he stumbled on a power sledge, motor and batteries pulled out of it.

The drive chain was broken. Through another endless day, while the crawling sun seemed stalled on its horizontal track, he toiled to make and fit new links. When at last they seemed to work, he slept fitfully again in the bright-lit sunbud pit.

The absent farmer must have loved the Darkside wilderness, because the sledge was already equipped with cold-weather hunting gear. He raided the kitchen and pantry again for supplies and rode up at last into windy daylight.

The polar world had hardly changed. Though the slow sun was slightly higher, the thaw had not begun. The monstrous tower of the humanoid transport still commanded the sky behind him, so near he thought some rhodo sense might detect his own machine. If that happened . . .

He shrugged and bent to guide the sledge into a sunbud vineyard, where last summer's dead black stalks promised a little cover. Beyond the vineyard, he turned into an ice-floored ravine which took him behind a long ridge, perhaps another old ringwall.

And nothing followed.

Nothing, at least, that he could see. The sledge crawled faster than he could run and carried more load than he could walk under. Heading away from the high ship and Malili's rosy glow, he drove for the Darkside.

These arctic highlands were empty wilderness, with no mines worth working or farmlands reclaimed, too barren even for wild mutoxen. With luck, he thought, his supplies might last to take him across them and down to the hunting country Chelni had showed him. With a wry little grin, he thought he might be glad enough to try the farmer's rifle.

Slowly, too slowly, the ship went down behind him. Through endless drives across the ice and restless nights in camp, he pursued wisps of hope. Somehow, with luck enough, he might find Cyra and his father in time to join their fight for the freedom of Kai. With more unlikely luck, they might get some sort of aid from Bosun Brong, or even Nera Nyin. . . .

Her golden splendor often haunted his exhausted sleep, but she brought no miraculous escape. Instead, rough country stalled the sledge too many times. Levering it over icy boulders took too much muscle. His stolen food was too soon gone. At the end, the drive chain snapped again.

Unable to repair it, he had to leave the sledge. Packing the tent and the solar stove and the last of the supplies, he marched doggedly on, trying to hope that perhaps . . . perhaps . . .

A morning came when all his dreams had turned to gray despair. He chewed his last beancake fragments and melted ice to make one last can of iceranger's tea. When he stood up to pack, the stove and the tent had become too heavy for him. Too far gone for hope or even fear, he dropped them back into the slush and staggered on across the barrens.

"At your service, Shipman Keth Kyrone."

At first, when he heard that high, bright voice calling behind him, he thought it was only in his pain-numbed brain.

"You must accept our service, sir." It was closer to him, kinder, more urgently concerned. "You must let us save your life."

He turned then, dazed, and saw the humanoids.

29

Frank Ironsmith   A mathematician who found no fault with the humanoids. A logician, he enjoyed their logic. Not himself aggressive, he approved their restraints upon aggression, and his advice enlarged their powers.

Three lean humanoids, golden nameplates glinting in the cold sunlight, dark, narrow faces surprised and handsome and benign. They must have come in the long silver teardrop that lay in the thawing slush behind them.

"Allow us, sir, to render aid."

He had run too far.

"I want no help." Facing them, swaying, he pushed one hand into an empty pocket. "Get away from me."

"You must forgive us, sir." Only the nearest spoke, but all three danced in around him. "In your unfortunate situation, you cannot refuse our aid."

"I think I can." He crouched to meet them, thrusting the fist in his pocket at the little black leader. "The way I did before. Unless you get out—"

They didn't pause.

"You cannot deceive us, sir," the tiny leader trilled. "We have now recovered both of the illicit devices which you once possessed, and we must remind you that of necessity we prohibit human use and even human knowledge of rhodomagnetics. Your own case is extremely unfortunate, but we can now prevent any future harm."

The others had grasped his arms, and now they dragged him toward the teardrop. Their gentle strength surprised him. Too light-headed to resist, he let them lift him through the oval door and help him to a padded seat on the deck inside.

The door contracted and vanished, though the whole hull remained darkly transparent. The three humanoids froze where they stood. Though the craft had no controls that he could see, it lifted suddenly, silent and fast.

Fighting weakness and the sickness of defeat, he sat rigidly erect, striving to see all he could. The barrens dropped away, the thawing snow dark-patched now with naked stone. In only a moment, all the ground he had toiled to gain had slid back behind. They sloped down again, toward the faint green of young crops the humanoids must have planted. Searching for the interstellar ship and the city he had fled, he failed at first to recognize anything. All he could see was the vast ice cap, blazing white in the black crater ring. When he found the ship, its mirror sheen was gone. Black metal now, it was half demolished.

"What happened?" He grinned bleakly at the nearest humanoid, hoping to discover that Cyra and his father had struck them with some rhodo weapon. "Something hit your ship?"

"We are recycling its metal into a new city for you."

He saw the city when its slim arm pointed. A strange gem shining on that vast black ring, covering what must have been the meteor gap. New towers covered the old spacedeck, half of what had been Northdyke, and even the old impact ridge where he had picked his way through the damaged windwheels not a month ago. From their height these fantastic palaces looked toylike, but they were as sleek and graceful as a dancing humanoid, some mirror-bright, some aglow with flowing color.

"We are also converting mass from the planet itself," the humanoid chirruped. "When the ice cap has been thawed, the crater will contain a pleasure lake."

They were dropping to land at the old capital complex before he discovered it, shrunk to a clump of primitive huts beneath that soaring splendor.

"We have a place prepared for you," the humanoid cooed. "The apartment at Vara Vorn that once belonged to your friend Chelni."

They escorted him off the craft into a tiny space that proved to be an elevator, dropping them into the huge round room where that first humanoid had peeled off Chelni's naked shape. He shuddered, recalling the shock of that.

"What troubles you, sir?" Only one humanoid had come with him off the elevator, but it hovered too near, its sleek face too gravely intent, its melodious voice too warm and too urgent. "Are you unhappy?"

"Unhappy?"

He backed away from it to glance around the room. Chelni's great round bed, with its cover of white mutoxen fur, still filled the center of the floor, but everything else had been replaced. Even the doors were different—man-proof.

It hit him like a kick in the stomach. The wide, rose-glowing panels were unbroken by any visible knob or lock. The controls were rhodomagnetic, and he had no monopole with which to reach them.

"Why?" Defiant, he swung to scowl at the humanoid. "Why should I be happy?"

"Because we exist to make you so." Its high sweet voice echoed an eternal kind concern. "We were created to serve and obey and guard you from harm."

"If you obey—get out!"

"Sir!" Lifted higher in pained reproof, its tone reflected the benign surprise fixed forever on its features. "Without our service, your race would perish."

"We've lived well enough without you," he muttered bitterly. "A thousand years without you, here on Kai."

"But always in increasing danger from your own uncontrolled technology," the humanoid answered instantly. "Our arrival now is most fortunate for your endangered planet, and your lack of gratitude appears irrational." It glided closer. "Inform us, sir. Why are you unhappy?"

It stood too close, and it seemed too intent. He staggered back from it. Weak from aching hunger and long fatigue, he needed to sit, and now he saw an odd-shaped chair gliding toward him silently, commanded, no doubt, by some unseen rhodo signal.

"Because I'm here." Too faint to stand, he sank into the chair. "I want my freedom."

"Every human right is guaranteed to you," its bright voice purred. "That is our function. You must understand, however, that we are required under the Prime Directive to guard you from the consequences of your own tragic unwisdom. You present us with a dual dilemma, requiring both your defense from the predictable violence of your fellow human beings and their own defense from your illicit knowledge. You may not leave this room."

"For how long?"

"At least until a more secure place can be prepared for you," it lilted cheerily. "We cannot at present foresee any circumstances that might enable us to relax your protective supervision, but we can assure your total happiness here."

Staring up at its blind benevolence, he could only shiver.

"Trust us, sir," it begged him gently. "We have learned to meet every human need. You will receive a fully adequate diet and constant medical attention. You will be free to choose your own recreations, within certain essential limitations."

"What limitations?"

"We detect your antagonism, sir." The black machine retreated slightly, its voice gently chiding. "Like many another maladjusted misfit who has attempted to reject our service, you seek to blame us for any condition you deem irksome. You must seek instead to understand that these restraints result not from any malice of ours, but from your own unfortunate illogic."

"What restraints?"

"You will have no visitors. No contact whatsoever with any other person. Though we sense your momentary displeasure, sir, this total isolation has been proven essential in such unfortunate cases as your own to prevent the communication of illicit knowledge."

"I—I see." He gulped at a dry lump in his throat. "What can I do?"

"Anything that is not forbidden."

"Can I have . . . anything at all?"

"Though you are free to request certain recreational items, there are categories that cannot be supplied. Works of science are restricted, for example, because scientific knowledge has proven damaging to your happiness and dangerous to the survival of your race."

"What about music?" He grinned defiantly. "Poetry? Art?"

"We can bring you reproductions of certain types of art, excepting however any that suggest unhappiness or pain."

"So you censor tragedy?"

The humanoid stood frozen for a moment, as if it had to wait for that computer plexus on Wing IV to resolve some perplexing paradox.

"Human behavior is too seldom reasonable." Suddenly alive again, it seemed almost to smile. "That is why your race requires us. Your racial addiction to frustration and suffering and death is no more logical in the illusions of your literature than in the realities of your warfare. We encourage neither perversion."

"So you enforce happiness?"

"We remove unhappiness." It nodded blindly, unaware of his desperate irony. "In your own case, sir, food and sleep will predictably ameliorate your present discontent. In time you will turn, as others before you have always done, from resentment of the slight restraints we must impose to the pure enjoyment of our perfect reason. Teaching you to forsake the physical, we can aid you to attain the more enduring delights of the mind.

"Our high aim, sir, is your everlasting bliss."

Grimly silent, he watched its frozen black benevolence.

"However, sir," it chimed cheerily, "we shall always respect your wishes so far as our Prime Directive allows. If we find, for example, that sexual release is essential to your peace of mind, we can bring you another simulacrum of Shipmate Chelni Vorn—"

It must have perceived the chill that shook him.

"Or, sir, if you desire other companionship, we can provide you with an accurate replicate of any other human being you care to designate, programmed for any behavior you may desire. We suggest, however, that you have your dinner first."

30

Mark White   Self-styled philosopher and psionic engineer who gathered a team of gifted telurgists for his desperate but foredoomed effort to alter the Prime Directive.

He sat numb and staring, as motionless as the humanoid.

"Sir!" It bent toward him, its melody quickened with solicitude. "If your irrational displeasure causes you to reject food and other normal human satisfactions, we have more efficient means to relieve you."

"I want—" He started back from it, rigid and quivering. "I want no euphoride."

"It is the purest concentrate of human joy," it sang softly. "Tested and improved through centuries of use on many billion human beings, it is far superior to any psychochemical that may have been known on this planet. Far superior, certainly, to the illicit feyolin you have tried."

How, he wondered, had they learned of that?

"Its principal effect is a direct stimulation of the pleasure centers of the brain, accompanied by a sense of vastly dilated time. Most users report illusions of intensely happy activity, infinitely prolonged. They almost always ask for a higher dosage rate than we can allow."

"I don't—" His dry whisper stuck. "Don't want it!"

"The choice, sir, is yours." Its blind smile remained serene. "Our Prime Directive grants you every possible freedom. We urge you, in fact, to elect the more rational alternative: the full and hearty acceptance of our service, with a total readiness to render whatever aid we may request."

"What sort of aid?"

"At the moment, sir, we require information. If you demonstrate a willingness to answer all our questions accurately and fully, attempting neither to deceive us nor to withhold anything, the administration of euphoride may be delayed—with our warning that when you do receive it, you will regret the delay."

"What do you want to know?"

For another instant it stood motionless, while that vast remote machine must have been calculating his fate.

"Sir," it purred at last, "we perceive your continued defiance. If you wish to avoid euphoride, your obstructive attitude must change. You must, in fact, recognize that we were created by a wise, well-meaning man, to fulfill an imperative human need."

"Need?" he rasped. "I don't see that."

"You will." It bent slightly toward him. "Logically, you must, because you yourself have shown us that you share our creator's concern for the future of your race. If you will let us guide you toward a correct interpretation of human history, you will conclude that we are, in truth, essential to human survival."

He squinted at it skeptically.

"Your evolution resulted from the interaction of two opposing processes," its prim voice intoned. "These are competition and cooperation. Competition for survival created vigorous and aggressive individual animals. Cooperation between them created society and civilization.

"Under primitive conditions, the two processes functioned in apparent harmony. With the advent of high technology, however, their old balance was destroyed. Uncontrolled aggression became a deadly peril.

"We were made to save your race."

"But not from me," he protested bitterly. "The fact is, I was never aggressive enough. My father always told me that. My instructors always did. And Chelni Vorn. Otherwise, I might have married her and become an owner of the fleet."

"Now there are no fleets," the calm machine reminded him. "If in fact you were born without innate aggression, that should help you welcome us. We must repeat, however, that you are already guilty of the gravest possible act of aggression against us."

It froze, its poise inquisitive.

"We ask again—will you cooperate?"

"I—I'll think about it." He swayed on the chair, his senses spinning. Groping for any telling argument, he found only a sick conviction that every possible argument would itself be read as added evidence against him. He repeated weakly, "I don't want euphoride."

"In that case, we require information about the people and the culture of the planet Malili."

"I know very little."

"You were born there," it insisted softly. "You have been intimate with a Leleyo female. You have made a recent visit there, and you have apparently been hoping to return." Its graceful head cocked alertly. "What is your interest in Malili?"

"I'm a member of the Lifecrew." Meeting its blind eyes, he straightened defiantly. "Our mission was—is—to defend Kai from you. We suspected that you had some kind of probe or station on Malili."

"We do not." The tilt of its narrow head seemed smugly proud. "We have never landed units there—"

"Then I advise you not to try it now," he muttered. "The rockrust will get them if you do."

"We are collecting data on the simpler native organisms of Malili, but they are not our problem. We can cope with corrosion. Our graver concerns are the indicated possibilities that the Leleyo possess at least a primitive rhodomagnetic technology and that their society is an undisciplined democracy."

"So you're afraid of the Leleyo?"

The emotion that nerved him was almost triumph. If the Leleyo knew rhodomagnetics, they might defy the humanoids. Malili might become man's last fortress, secure against them.

"We are mechanical," the machine was caroling. "We do not experience fear. We simply follow our Prime Directive. If the Leleyo do, in fact, possess an illicit technology, or if their institutions are dangerously democratic, they require our immediate service."

Trying to conceal that flash of hope, he frowned again, demanding, "What's wrong with democracy?"

"It is suicidal, sir. We have observed its rise and fall on many million worlds, and we find that it always fosters the excessive developments of high technology and aggressive individualism that lead inevitably to racial annihilation. Democracies therefore have the highest priorities for our service."

The machine leaned abruptly closer.

"We require information about another native of Malili who has been in close contact with you, the man who sometimes calls himself Bosun Brong. The evidence suggests that he commands illicit technologies."

"I've met Brong." He tried to restrain a grin of sardonic satisfaction. "I know nothing about any illicit technology."

"We still perceive antagonism toward us," the humanoid sang. "If you wish to avoid euphoride, you must supply the facts we require. About the native Leleyo. About the current activities of your so-called Lifecrew. About the man called Brong."

It went rigid for an instant, as if waiting for instruction.

"Where are your father and Crewmate Sair?"

"So you never caught them?"

Hope had exploded in him again. If they and Brong were still at large, if Malili was really hostile ground to the humanoids . . .

"They will soon be restrained." It was sweetly serene. "Their own ill-advised aggressions will inevitably betray them to us."

"So that was why"—a sick suspicion chilled him—"why you took so long to capture me? You wanted me to lead you to them? And that boy—the boy in the bilges—was he your agent?"

"He has accepted us," the humanoid agreed. "As you will soon."

Clammy with a sudden sweat, he was shivering. His breath came fast, and his empty hands had clenched. Trying to relax that useless tension, he leaned back from its sightless eyes.

"Sir," it warbled, "we detect your amazement and dismay, and we must protest that neither reaction is appropriate. Since we have been learning for so many centuries on so many million worlds how to cope with irrational acts of human rebellion, our efficiency should not surprise you. Since all we do is directed toward the ultimate good of every human being, the certainty of our success should not alarm you."

It stood frozen again, its immense remote computer waiting to process his response. He tried to hold himself equally motionless.

"Forgive us, sir," it cooed abruptly. "We perceive your exhaustion, and we urge you to restore yourself before we resume. You must have your dinner now."

31

Telurgy   The art of creating physical phenomena through the use of rhodomagnetic energy under tachyonic (psionic) control.

A small oval table came rolling to his chair, called by some soundless rhodo command. Its apparent top dissolved to uncover his meal: a few hard round biscuits and a little mound of stiff gray jelly.

"Is this all?" He frowned at the humanoid. "You promised me food."

"You will find it adequate," the machine assured him. "Too many of you have damaged yourselves by excessive consumption. The nutrients we provide are accurately computed to match your actual dietary requirements."

"At least I must have a knife and fork."

"Impossible, sir. Your access to such dangerous implements has to be restricted. Too many of you have used them for violence against one another, or for unprovoked attacks on our defenseless units, or even for attempted self-destruction."

His hunger had begun to pinch, and he tried the gray jelly.

Though the flavor was bland and unfamiliar, it tasted better than it looked. Thirsty, he found a tiny hose that he could suck for a lukewarm, sweetish fluid. Suddenly sleepy—so suddenly that he wondered dully if the fluid had been laced with euphoride—he crawled into Chelni's bed and dreamed of Nera Nyin.

He was on Malili in the dream, wandering the summer jungles in search of her. Troubled only slightly by the spreading scarlet spots of bloodrot on his hands and feet, he thought she knew the cure. If only he could find her in time . . .

She was singing; at first she sounded far away. Following her voice, high and sweet and clear, he struggled through sucking quicksands, fought through tangles of thorny vine, swam across enormous, weed-choked rivers. Storms howled against him, and bellowing dragon bats hurled huge ice masses out of the sky. Yet he reached her at last, crawling on hands and knees through a Darkside blizzard, and found her changing into a darkly smiling humanoid.

"At your service, sir." The high sweet voice belonged to his actual jailor. "We perceived unhappiness, even in your sleep. Unless you accept us fully, we must administer euphoride."

"I—I'll try to accept you." Still shuddering from the dream, he muttered the unwilling promise. "But let me go to the bathroom first."

Gliding ahead of him, it must have made some signal, for the glowing door slid open.

"I want a door like the old one," he whispered bitterly. "One I can open."

"But, sir, you'll never need to open any door." Its voice was merry music. "We'll always be with you."

"Even in here?"

"Always, sir. Too many of you, left in lavatories unattended, have tried to drown yourselves."

It followed him inside, waited alertly, let him wash himself in a tiny basin of tepid water.

"At least," he gritted wryly, "let me dry myself."

"As you wish." It gave him a towel tissue. "We allow you every freedom possible."

Back in Chelni's room, he begged it to clear the opaqued windows. It sang a soft refusal. Until he had demonstrated a complete and sincere acceptance, no breach of his seclusion would be allowed.

"When you are ready, sir," it pressed him gently, "we require information."

Systematic and relentless, it wanted facts he couldn't recall about his mother and his birth in the Zone. It wanted to know all about Nurse Vesh, and everything she had told him about Malili and her notion that the humanoids had killed her husband there. It demanded far more than he had ever been told about his father and Cyra and the Lifecrew.

Torn between his terror of euphoride and his fear of betraying the Crew, he set himself to play a grim little game. So long as the conquest of Malili was not complete, it seemed to offer at least some faint possibility of sanctuary. Forlornly, he tried to hope the humanoids themselves might inadvertently tell him how to get there.

His strategy was digression and delay. He tried to spend all the time he could on detail he thought would be meaningless, avoiding or claiming ignorance of everything else. Pausing when he could think of any excuse, begging for water or sleep or a visit to the bathroom, he searched for revealing clues in the questions he was asked—clues he never found.

A patient player, the tiny machine always agreed to every interruption he asked for, but always called him very promptly back. Its melodious voice and its frozen features told him no more than the questions did. Its own secret strategy, he soon suspected, was better than his.

Day after day, it drew him through all he could recall about his lessons with Doc Smart and his father's new wife and his school years at Greenpeak. Sometimes, seeking more delay, he asked for news of things outside, or begged it again to clear the windows and let him see. Its replies were always courteous, always brief, always negative.

Under the Prime Directive, the humanoids were augmenting their required service to the people of Kai. A second transport had already landed at Terradeck and a third would soon be due. The windows could not yet be cleared, however, because he had yet to demonstrate the full acceptance he had promised.

The man-proof elevator door was never opened again, certainly not while he was awake. The humanoid kept an exact half-meter from him, gliding beside him when he walked the floor, waiting in the bathroom, standing rigid at the bedside while he slept. Whenever he woke, it resumed his interrogation.

Sometimes he tried to demur.

"Why ask me?" he expostulated when it began to press for all he had ever known or felt or thought about Chelni Vorn. "You have her shut up in some other prison. You've copied her body and no doubt drained her brain. Why not ask her? Or is she drugged with euphoride?"

A frozen moment.

"Even the most willing human being can never inform us fully," its reply came back at last. "Human knowledge is never entirely consistent or complete, because the human brain is only a crude and transient mass of cells, made for the most part only of water, error-prone and glacier-slow. It sleeps, it forgets, it dies. In contrast, sir, our central plexus is eternal and error-free, a billion times larger than your fallible brain and a trillion times faster.

"We therefore beg you, sir, to admit your limits, painful to you as the truth may be. No human being ever fully knows himself or any other. To serve you as we should, we must come to know each one of you better than you ever knew yourselves. Our questions must continue."

Its unrelenting quest for all his impressions of Chelni took three long days. He had to tell of the time they stripped and his feelings when she stood ahead of him in class and the mutox he couldn't kill on her uncle's Darkside ranch. It wanted more than he knew about the Admiral and the Vorn Voyagers and the Kai Life Plan.

At first he felt relieved when it went on to Bosun Brong, but its implacable demands for detail became more and more intolerable. Again and again, he was pressed for more than he could recall. When he spoke once of Brong's sad eyes in a long, sad face, the machine seized upon the adjective.

"Such descriptions are inadequate," it protested. "Your word 'sad' is not precise. Though it does imply a regrettable unhappiness, it does not identify the cause. We require a full account of every specific indication you were able to observe."

When he failed to produce specific indications, it went on to Brong's golden hands, wanting to know their origin and history, how they looked and how they worked and how they were powered. It probed for every word of Brong's he could recall, for every moment of his own stay on Malili, every fact he knew about the Zone and the sanicraft expeditions outside it.

On point after point, he said he didn't know, and always it insisted that he did. "We detect an effort at deception, sir. We require the truth. Your alternative is euphoride."

Again, when they came to Nera Nyin, it drew out far more than he ever meant to say. It dug out his first thrill of admiration for her physical perfection, his astonished delight in her casual nudity, his fascination with the history and culture of her mysterious people, his total enchantment with everything about her. Seeing through all his efforts at concealment, it discovered their night together, his feyolin high, his ache of loss when she vanished from the Academy.

Seeming to believe he had seen her since, it spent a whole day probing for some confession of that, suggesting that he must have met her on his trip to Malili, searching for evidence that she and Brong, and even he, might share some secret means of interplanetary travel.

"How did Bosun Brong return to Kai from the planets of the Dragon?" it asked again and again. "How did he and Nera Nyin return from Kai to Malili, leaving no record of their passage on any ship?"

"So Brong was really on the *Kyrone* when it got to the Dragon?" He tried to conceal a flash of elation. "He says he came back on a shuttle craft."

If he had scored, the machine showed no sign.

"Forgive us, sir, but we doubt that you yourself believe that fantastic falsehood." It was sweetly patient. "We require the truth, and our investigations suggest illicit use of forbidden science."

He dared not say he hoped that was true.

"We know that your Lifecrew scientists have claimed the detection of rhodomagnetic sources on Malili," it reminded him blithely, again and again. "If such sources do in fact exist, the native Leleyo are probably responsible."

"I know of no such source."

"In fact, sir, you do know." Its soft voice sank in meek apology. "We have acquired convincing evidence of that from our interrogation of the woman who was your childhood nurse and our examination of confidential tapes and illicit artifacts your father and his confederates had attempted to conceal in her residence."

He always tried to look blankly bewildered, and knew he always failed.

"We detect your agitation, sir," it always informed him. "You cannot conceal your guilty awareness. We know that you were sent to Malili to gather information and obtain palladium for the manufacture of forbidden rhodomagnetic devices. We know that you did question Bosun Brong. We know that you did in fact bring a shipment of palladium back to your father.

"We know, too, that your father and Cyra Sair did instruct you in the use of illicit weapons they had assembled. We know that you transported two of these to Northdyke. One was found hidden in the room you had occupied. The other was removed from your person—but only after you had used it in a treacherous and unprovoked assault upon an innocent humanoid unit."

It was gently relentless.

"Now, sir, if you really wish to delay the euphoride your case so clearly calls for, we require a full and accurate statement of the facts about those rhodomagnetic sources on Malili. We require the complete truth about all your associates on Malili. We require your unfeigned aid in locating your father and all his criminal accomplices before their follies can bring harm to us and the people of Kai.

"Sir, you must speak."

Again and again, he tried to walk away from it, pacing around and around the fur-covered bed. If Cyra and his father were still free and armed, if Brong was still a suspect and the Leleyo still unconquered, hope was still alive. He was resolved to say no more.

It always followed, keeping that careful half-meter away.

"If you select to be stubborn, that option is yours," it burbled behind him. "The facts we seek are less vital to us than you appear to imagine, and we cannot inflict harm or pain upon you. We assure you, however, that your ill-judged resistance will neither limit nor delay our execution of the Prime Directive, either here or on Malili. We urge you, therefore, to speak."

He always tramped on.

"The alternative, sir, is euphoride."

144

He kept walking.

"Take your time, sir," it urged him gently at the end of the last unending day. "Eat your dinner. Sleep tonight. Think it over. We'll ask for your decision when you wake tomorrow. You're a free man, sir, and the choice will be your own."

Under its unceasing surveillance, he ate his meager dinner. Pretending sleep, he lay rigid and sweating beneath the stiff white mutox fur, so taut and desperate that the machine begged him to take his euphoride at once. He shook his head and turned his face away. At last, somehow, he must have slept, for a dull thud woke him.

"Crewman, ahoy!" Standing where the humanoid had been, Bosun Brong was calling softly. "Let's get going!"

32

Psion A quantum of tachyonic energy, lacking charge or rest mass, moving normally at infinite velocity, and always faster than light.

The slender golden hand, as graceful as a humanoid's, twitched the stiff fur off his shoulders. Trembling, unbelieving, he sat up. The little black machine lay where it had fallen, blithe smile frozen, steel-colored eyes staring at the ceiling.

"Can you"—he blinked at Brong and shuddered—"can you get me out of here?"

"Sorry, Crewman." Bright metal fingers beckoned him off the bed. "That's up to you."

"How . . ." Blankly, he peered around the room. The glowing doors were still closed, the high windows still opaqued and sealed. "How did you get here?"

"They'd like to know." Brong chuckled. "A Leleyo trick I've never been free to reveal." Sadly, he glanced at the stiffened humanoid. "You'll have to move, Crewman, if you want to leave with me."

"To the Zone?" Dazed, he peered again at Brong. "You know a way to Malili?"

"The Leleyo way."

"My father—"

"Safe in the Zone." Brong spoke fast. "Arrived there with Crewmate Sair, after a wild escape aboard a stolen shuttle. Rode it all the way across. I learned from them that the humanoids had caught you."

"The humanoids—"

"Surprises waiting, if they attack. The Zone folk are tougher stuff than they found here, and we're building what Sair calls a monopole to hold the Zone."

"Can you"—his voice shook again—"can you show me this Leleyo way?"

"If you can learn it." Brong nodded at the fallen humanoid. "Better be quick."

"Show me—"

"You step through a surface." A gold forefinger flicked as if to mark a line across the carpet. "That's the model I was taught to visualize. You move through an interface you must try to realize in your mind, out of this room and back into the Zone."

"Huh—" He flinched away from the man-proof doors and the man-shaped machine. "I can't do that!"

"True." Brong's nod was oddly calm. "Not until you know you can."

"Tell me—" He gasped for breath. "Tell me how!"

"You don't need words." Brong squinted sharply at him, and warily at the thing on the floor. "I wasn't taught it with words, and I'm not sure I know them. There's a grasp you must have. A move you must make—"

Something jolted the floor. Dull thunder rumbled—the first outside sound he had heard since the humanoids brought him here. Daylight dazzled him. The tall windows had abruptly cleared, and he saw dazing change.

The interstellar transport was gone. A black pit gaped where it had stood. The stuff from pit and ship shone all around the south horizon, transmuted into fantastic architecture. Terraced pyramids, sky-stabbing needles, marching colonnades, all alive with flowing tides of color.

"Crewman, look!" Fingers flashing in the sun, Brong pointed to a V of five long teardrops diving across the black rimwall from over the ice cap. "They're already moving in. Hoping, I guess, to learn the trick—and to stop us if they can. We won't have long."

"The way—" Bewildered, he stared again at Brong. "Is it rhodomagnetic?"

"No Leleyo word." The bright fingers waved it aside. "Your mother tried to translate theirs. Her term for it was telurgy, but she never knew enough. I had another lesson from the girl who helped me home after Vesh went through the ice. More from my father, when he helped me and your own father home from the trip I told you about."

He turned to squint at the five wheeling teardrops.

"Time for us to go!" Voice tighter, he darted closer. "We step from here across the telurgic interface to that strip of bare rubble between the old perimeter and the new one, where Vorn's nukes have killed everything.

"We've got to do it soon!"

"If I knew how—" Sweating, feeling numb and nearly ill, he caught Brong's hard hand. "If I could believe—"

"If you can't, the humanoids will keep you." Brong shrugged him off and danced away. "I can't tell you how, but I'll try to guide you. We move together. Fix our minds on those ice-crusted rocks, thrust ourselves toward them."

Trembling, he could only shake his head.

"Hold that notion of a doorway through the interface," Brong whispered swiftly. "Only a model, perhaps, but useful to focus the mind. What you must have is faith—"

"Faith?"

"Scoffing won't help you." With a sharper glance at him, Brong crouched from the silver-glinting teardrops. "I've a crutch that might, if they give us time. Stick out your tongue."

He stuck his tongue out, and Brong tapped rust-colored dust on it from a thin gold tube he had worn clipped to his pocket. Salt at first, it burned his mouth and filled his head with a sweet hot reek he remembered—

Feyolin!

Suddenly the world was different. The round room became enormous, the ceiling a limitless sky. Chelni's bed stretched into a snowy desert, mountain-ridged where he had rumpled it, each separate mutox hair a long shining cylinder.

Quivering with an ultimate compassion, he dropped on his knees beside the rigid humanoid, which was now a toppled giant. The infinite goodness of the Prime Directive wrenched his heart, and he felt a wave of shame for all the gross imperfections of mankind that required such selfless and unceasing care.

"Crewman!" Brong's voice was rolling thunder, so deep that his whole being reverberated with it, so slow that he had to wait eternally for each successive pealing syllable. "Shall we go?"

Brong himself had grown heroic, more magnificent than old Kyrondath Kyrone could ever have been. Nothing in all the ancient ballads could match the desperate daring of his adventures outside the Zone, or the wonder of his shipless flights from world to world.

Tears of pity burned his eyes when he saw the glow of the golden hands and the unutterable sadness of that scarred and hardened face, evidence of tragedies too dreadful and sufferings too cruel for any man to endure. In a more just universe, he thought, Brong should have had humanoids to serve and save him long ago.

Wiping at the tears, he swayed toward the luckless wretch, reaching out to comfort him. The cavernous room rocked as he moved. Savage quakes tossed that vast white desert. The high vault roared with thunder he couldn't understand, and Brong's colossal form receded, faster than he could move.

"Shape up, Crewman!" At last he grasped the thunderwords. "We've got to go."

He perceived then, pierced with a godlike tenderness, that Brong was afraid. A foolish fear, because the humanoids were infinitely kind. Yet he owed a debt to this blundering hero, who had come here for him across the deadly emptiness of space.

"I'm ready—"

He tried to say that, but his tongue seemed swollen from that searing dust. His lips were stiff, and his parched throat had closed. Though he labored a long time to speak, no sound came.

Pale with staring horror, Brong had shrunk from the humanoid, and he saw now that it was no longer dead. Though it still lay flat, the golden plate on its chest was vibrating slightly, and its sightless eyes had begun to shine with a colorless rhodomagnetic glow.

"It's—awake!" he tried to say. "Spying!"

Brong's chuckle rolled like slow and far-off thunder.

"Let it spy!" Intrepid again, he had shaken off that quaking dread. "Or try to. It will never see where we go, or how, because it is blind to life."

Overwhelmed with pity for its wasted wonders, he almost wept. A mere machine, it could feel no joy in all its terrible rhodo powers, or in all the wisdom stored in its remote and mighty plexus, or in all the myriad worlds it ruled. Lacking life, its robot mind could understand neither love nor hate, hope nor fear, nor even the vast compassion he felt for it.

"Listen, Crewman!" Brong's thunder-tones battered him again. "I never meant to get you so high, but maybe you can do it." Ruthless metal talons sank into his arm. "Look toward the Zone."

Spun away from the sun, he searched the pale summer sky for Malili, but all he could see was the luminous splendor of the fantastic palaces the humanoids were building for the fortunate people of Kai and those five bright ships diving toward him fast.

"Can't . . . see. . . ."

His tongue toiled and stalled, but he felt Brong hauling again, saw the gold hand flashing, pointing him toward Malili. It was low and pale and gibbous, nearly lost behind those glowing pylons and the five shining divers.

"Close to the top," Brong's slow tones crashed. "Midway between the limb and the sunrise line. A bare slope of broken stone—so watch your feet."

The divers looked lovely. He wanted to stay and watch them play.

"Lean a little." The golden hooks hurt his arm. "Fix your mind on those rocks. You don't need an actual step, but hold your image of the window through the interface. Just intend—intend to be beyond it. I'll count us down, and aid you all I can. Three. Two. One!

"Now—"

Nearer thunder cracked. A frigid wind whipped him. A heavy weight crushed his chest. Loose rocks slid beneath his unshod feet. Cruelly burdened, he staggered and fought to stay erect.

"All right, Shipman?" To his deafened ears, Brong's voice seemed queerly muffled. "Here we are!"

He got his breath and found his balance. Standing on a sharp-edged boulder, he blinked around him. The slope of broken rock fell sharply toward a low concrete wall that zigzagged oddly across the slope below. Slim towers stood spaced along it, and the violet shimmer between them burned his eyes.

Beyond the wall, what he could see of the slope was not entirely gray and bare, but stained with rockrust blues and greens, and still farther below, with red and orange and yellow, the Sunset colors of Malili. Even farther, it was drowned at last beneath a flat sea of gray-blue cloud that reached out and out to remote lemon green horizons beneath a high and tiny crescent—

Kai!

That glimpse of it staggered him again. If that far-off, frozen world was Kai, this was—this had to be Malili!

33

Clay Forester   Astronomer and engineer who led Mark White's telurgists against Wing IV. Seized and brainwashed, he became a contented humanoid tool.

Though the wind felt cruelly cold, Brong had lifted his winter cap to mop his hairless head.

"Good jump, Crewman, but you had me sweating!" Squinting against that painful shimmer, he waved his gold forearm at the zigzag wall. "The new perimeter. Rust and rot and dragon bats down beyond it."

Keth staggered on the rock, overwhelmed by too much of everything. With the drug's aftertaste still burning on his tongue, every sense was amplified. The jungle reeks took his breath. The bitter wind shrieked in his ears, and his eyes stung from the sky's green glare. Even the old perimeter wall looked strangely near and sharp when he turned to see it, the scarred concrete splotched green and blue where rockrust had reached it. Suddenly he doubted all he saw, shuddering from a sick suspicion that his last meager meal had been laced with euphoride, that Brong's coming and the leap from Kai and this incredible glimpse of Malili were all hallucination.

"Come along, Crewman."

Brong's gold hand on his arm felt solidly real, and the ice-edged rocks beneath his bare feet were too cruel to be illusion.

The aftertaste was turning dry and bitter in his mouth, the tempest of sensation passing almost as fast as it had risen. The sky seemed darker and the wind-roar was dying. Suddenly, all he could smell was dust.

"Let's get inside." Brong gestured at a towered gate. "Still a bit of radiation here."

Clumsy under his greater weight, he limped after Brong across loose rockslides and patches of dirty winter snow. After the wonder of the jump and his glimpse of all the glowing splendor the humanoids had spun, the Zone looked commonplace and gray, oddly disappointing, its old glamor gone.

"If you can jump anywhere—" Already out of breath, he had begun to long again for the power and euphoria of the drug. "Could you take us on from the Zone? To see the braintree? And meet—maybe meet the Leleyo?"

"Or die of the rot?" Brong was ahead, his voice almost lost on the wind. "You haven't learned the limits and the dangers. Pretty hard to get where you've never been, because you need to really know—to *feel*—the destination. Vythle gave me holos of Vara Vorn that I used to get to you."

They climbed toward the old perimeter. The peak rose against the yellow sky beyond it, steep, narrow streets twisting up among low brown roofs. A bullhorn challenged them from the tower, and Brong waved a recognition signal.

The gate was Sally Port Three. Two austere young women in dark uniforms came out of the tower to demand a visa and a quota card Keth didn't have. Frowning with suspicion, they turned to Brong. Zone Command had called an emergency alert, and they weren't taking chances.

Glib with words and gestures, Brong explained. Crewman Kyrone was a fleet engineer just in from Kai, here to inspect the new perimeter installations. Caught in a radiation hot spot, he'd had to discard his boots and most of his clothing. If they could call Zone Command—

They let Brong call. After a nervous wait, they issued Keth a temporary pass and even produced a pair of boots he could wear. Inside at last, Brong led him through a cavernous shop where six bulky golden machines loomed in the dimness. Work sanicraft, he said, used to build the perimeter. He had driven one of them.

A freightway in back of the shop carried them along a drafty tunnel, back into the mountain and up again to that narrow side street he remembered. Brong unlocked the door beneath the crumbling Lifecrew medallion.

"Come in, Crewman. I'll call your folks."

He sat down gratefully at the desk below his father's faded holostat. The giddy spell of feyolin had faded, with all his wild hope of somehow finding Nera Nyin. His bruised feet were numb and aching in the borrowed boots, and the stress of too many risks had begun to catch up with him.

Still a little winded from the planet's tiring drag, he wished forlornly that he had been born the more heroic sort that Chelni and his father had hoped to make him, the aggressive fleet executive or the bold Crew leader. He felt suddenly unfit for anything, and his own reality depressed him.

In his mind, the Zone had seemed a brave outpost on a perilous planet, but it had now become a cramped and comfortless workaday place, where frigid winds whipped gritty dust. Even Bosun Brong had dwindled in the drug's aftermath. No longer the enigmatic master of arcane powers, or even the romantic halfbreed outcast, he was now only a worried little man, handicapped with artificial limbs, having trouble getting through on the holo.

Nobody answered when he tried the apartment Cyra and his father had found—a larger place than the Crew station, he explained, with space they wanted for a lab and a shop. Spacedeck information was busy when he tried to call there, but at last he reached a harassed yeoman in the operations office who said Kyrone and Sair were out on the job in Shuttle Pit Two. No, sir, he couldn't get a message to them. Not in this new emergency. If he did catch them free, however, he would try to tell them that Kyrone's son had arrived.

"Please do," Brong said. "What's this new emergency?"

"You haven't heard?" The yeoman's image stared. "About the tachyonic transport. First thought to be carrying more humanoids to Kai. Changing course now. Headed for us. Kyrone and Sair are rushing their weapons system. Fighting to get it going in time to defend the Zone."

"How much time—"

"Sorry, sir. Another party calling."

When the holo flashed again, it was Vythle Klo, her sleek, dark elegance not visibly ruffled by any emergency. The Admiral had learned of their arrival from Kai, and he would be pleased to see them at Zone Command.

"A mean old mutox!" Brong spoke of Vorn as they climbed the steep granite canyons under a green streak of sky. "I hated his guts for years. Hated his schemes to murder Malili for the profit of his fleet."

"Hated him?" Keth panted. "Yet you drove his sanicraft?"

"To earn my keep. And meet my friends." Brong chuckled. "Drove no better than I had to. Wrecked more craft than I brought back."

"But you get on with him now?"

"Well enough. Because we both dislike the humanoids. He's doing what he can for your father and Sair."

On the wider streets around the spacedeck, they saw young men and women rushing to duty stations. Perhaps, he thought, these pioneers really were a sturdier breed, not so ready to accept the humanoids.

At Zone Command, Vythle Klo came out to meet them in the anteroom. She greeted Brong with a look of awe, as if she had just learned of his Leleyo tricks. The Admiral would see them in a moment.

She turned to take Keth's hand, her own grasp warmly firm. Meeting her level eyes, he felt something veiled but intense beneath her cool reserve. Recalling the position with the Navarch she had given up to follow Vorn here, he decided to admire her. She led them inside, and Vorn received them with an unrevealing grin that turned ferocious when he spoke about his niece.

"There's a holo report that you murdered her." His hard stare fixed on Keth. "Killed in a way I couldn't believe. The Bosun says I don't have to."

"Don't," Keth said. "The thing that came back on the *Fortune* wasn't Chelni, but a humanoid look-alike. Another humanoid told me she's alive and well. I don't know." He shrugged unhappily. "The humanoids lie."

"Look-alike?"

"They copied people. Sent the copies back to take over Kai." He told how her copy-thing had called him to Vara Vorn.

"And they say they came to save us!" Moving like some tormented animal, Vorn stalked away and whirled back again. "It's their devil's tricks I want to talk about. Because I mean to hold the Zone. We'll beat them, Keth! With your brave father's help and Crewmate Sair's machine."

34

Rhodon A rhodomagnetic quantum. Carrying exchange forces across the interface between the tachyonic and electromagnetic spectra, it is responsible for such telurgic phenomena as telepathy, telekinesis, and teleportation.

Padding back and forth across that high room, pausing now and then to peer off into Malili's yellow mystery or down toward the spacedeck, Vorn spoke of the conflict coming. He had warned the orbital stations and mobilized his own command. Down on the spacedeck, Keth's father and Crewmate Sair were assembling their defensive monopole.

"They say it ought to shield the Zone." His broad red face looked bleak. "With luck, maybe twenty kilometers more, outside the perimeter. That will be our universe. Between the humanoids above us and the bloodrot below—"

"Your wife, sir." Vythle spoke from the doorway. "On the beam from Kai."

With a shrug, he sat at the hushed holophone. Keth watched Vythle as she watched him, devotion glowing through her elegant reserve. Vorn's cragged face scowled, stubborn jaw jutting like Chelni's.

"In love with the humanoids!" He rose at last, blinking in disbelief. "She says we're fools not to make them welcome here. Begging me to come back home and share the wonderful happiness they've brought her." He grinned at Vythle. "We'll hold out."

Striding restlessly again, he spoke of his brother and his niece. He had loved them both, and he blamed himself bitterly now for refusing so long to believe the humanoids had injured them.

"But you wouldn't let me!" He swung on Brong, almost in anger. "With your sly way of hiding all your Leleyo tricks, you wouldn't let me believe."

"Sorry, sir." Brong's bland tone held no real apology. "But Leleyo facts turn false when you carry them to Kai."

When Vythle entered again, she brought a message from Crewmate Sair. She and Crewman Kyrone had run into an unexpected difficulty. The monopole was stalled. With the humanoid transport near and descending fast, they were desperate. Sair was on her way to Zone Command to discuss their problem with the Admiral.

Keth was watching the door when Vythle brought her in. Wearing a dirty lab apron, she hobbled on a bandaged foot. Her haggard look shocked him. Eyes dark-rimmed and swollen, dull hair undone, black beads of blood dried along a livid scratch across her cheek. The straggling hairs in the mole beneath her eye had faded white.

"Hello, dear." She pecked him with a hasty kiss, nodded at Brong, and limped to face Vorn. "Admiral, we're in trouble."

"I know." He gestured at a chair, but she didn't sit. "Do you want to see me alone?"

"No need." Her gaunt head jerked toward Brong. "In fact, I think he can help us."

"So what's the problem?"

"Maybe he can tell us." She glared at Brong accusingly. "Our installation is complete. Circuits all hooked up and tested. Full power on. The monopolar field ought to be building up. It isn't."

Quivering and grimy, her forefinger jabbed at Brong.

"Ask him why!"

"Sir!" Brong shrank from her, yellow gloves lifted. "I don't know what she's up to."

"I think he does," she rapped. "But I'll explain." Her ragged voice rose. "The device requires an exciter—a weak initial field that should be picked up and amplified. We tried to excite it with our hand weapons—the small monopoles we used to disable the humanoids around the shuttle pad when we escaped from Kai.

"Dead!" Her thin finger stabbed. "Both dead!"

"Why blame me?" Brong's quick black eyes darted at Vorn. "She's crazy, sir!"

"Something killed those monopoles." She limped at him, her drawn face savage. "The evidence points at you. Who else—"

"The humanoids themselves?" Vorn gestured uneasily at the

high windows. "They're nearly here. Reported passing the satellite station hours ago—"

"Not likely!" Hobbling closer to Brong, she raised her wasted hands as if to seize him. "The cause is something closer. Here inside the Zone."

Though Keth had seen no signal from Vorn, Vythle Klo was suddenly inside the doorway with a level lasergun aimed somewhere between Brong and Cyra. Surprisingly agile, Cyra sprang aside.

"Watch him—and Keth!" Her quavering tones rose and broke. "Our own dear Keth—turning traitor! Brain rotted with Leleyo drugs. Learning vile Leleyo tricks. If they try anything—"

"Cyra!" Dazed for an instant, Keth started toward her. "I'm no spy! I can't believe the Bosun is—"

"Back!" Her old voice went shrill with terror. "Don't try to touch me."

"Stand still!" Vorn shouted. "All of you." He scowled at Cyra. "Crewmate Sair, can't you calm yourself? You seem almost hysterical—"

"We're betrayed by these half-Leleyo devils—"

"Please!" He waved a massive hand. "Frankly, I'm at a total loss. If you think these men are hostile agents, we need to see your evidence."

"Thank you, Admiral." She shambled at him. "The facts will convince you. Whoever killed those monopoles knew rhodo science. Most Kai Nu don't. The Leleyo do—and look at him!"

She glowered at Brong.

"Half Leleyo himself, and harboring all of them that ever got inside the Zone. Learning their language and smuggling in their mind-rotting feyolin. Picking up their secret science—"

"Bosun!" The Admiral swung to challenge Brong. "What do you say?"

Shuddering away from her, Brong raised his yellow gloves as if her jabbing finger had been a deadly blade. His lean throat pulsed and his brown lips quivered, but no sound came.

"Guilty!" Her shriek was triumphant. "Watch him squirm—but don't let him get away. When he can talk, ask him about those secret rhodo sources. Ask about his Leleyo friends and all they've taught him. Ask how he can jump from here to Kai—and how he brought Keth back here!"

Her wild voice shook and fell.

"I'm afraid of him, Admiral—"

"So are the humanoids!" Keth burst out. "Those are exactly the facts they were demanding from me when they had me trapped at Vara Vorn—"

"They'll trick you if they can!" She spun to glare at Brong, her eyes glazed and mad. "Why should the humanoids fear their own spy?"

"But he isn't!" Shivering, Keth appealed to Vorn. "Listen, sir! I think—think I've seen what all this means. Will you give me just a moment? Let me ask her a couple of questions?"

"Why not?" With a glance at Vythle, Vorn shrugged. "If you can make some sense of this—"

"Don't!" Cyra shrilled. "Don't you see they're only playing their vicious Leleyo game?"

"We'll soon find out." He nodded at Keth. "Ask your questions."

"Cyra"—fighting a chill of horror, he had to gulp for his voice—"do you remember the gift you bought me for my seventh birthday?"

"Of course I do, dear." Her voice turned softer, though she still watched him with a wary hostility. "Your father and I were just married, and I wanted you to love me."

"Do you remember what it was?"

"A little red sled, for the moontime snows."

"Do you remember the first job I got, running a route?"

"Certainly." Impatiently, she frowned at Vorn. "Admiral, this makes no sense."

"Do you remember what sort of route?"

"You were selling hologame tapes." She limped a little toward him. "To all your little friends up and down the tunnel."

"Crewman, we've no time for nonsense," Vorn rumbled. "I see no point—"

"Just one more question—please!" He peered at Cyra, shrinking back as she hitched toward him. "Do you remember the thing I thought was a dragon's egg?"

For an instant she looked puzzled.

"Now I do." She almost smiled. "You were still a little boy, and what you called the egg was a round black pebble some older kid had found in the gutter. He told you it was something wonderful, and you gave him all your quota tokens for it. Your father laughed when you brought it home, and you were crushed—"

"That's enough!" Keth backed toward Vythle, with a frantic signal to Vorn. "Enough, sir, to prove—what she is!"

His voice was a breathless croak.

"The gift was not a sled, but the tutor we called Doc Smart. The job was a recycle route. The thing I thought was a dragon's egg—that was the rhodo monopole I found on the dead levels under Greenpeak.

"And the real Cyra knows—"

"Keth, dear!" She hobbled at him, her voice sharp with distress. "You're ill again. Out of your head. You must have been neglecting your shots—"

"Stop that thing!" he gasped at Vythle. "It's a humanoid!"

Its hand darted under the dirty apron, and he caught the glint of a tiny needle.

"The real Cyra—my real father—they never escaped!" He cringed from the needle. "The humanoids caught them and sent copies—"

"The poor dear!" He was hoarse with terror, and its shrilling drowned his breathless rasp. "Subject to these dreadful paranoid delusions when his shots are neglected—"

"Don't let it—" He was trying to scream at Vythle, but no words came. "That's euphoride—"

Vythle looked bewildered, her lasergun wavering between him and the humanoid.

"Never mind him, Admiral!" it was squealing. "A dreadful affliction, but his shots always soothe him—"

No longer limping, it was darting at him, faster than a human being could move. He turned, trying to run, but its thin, blue fingers had caught his wrist in a merciless grip.

35

Platinomagnetics The tachyonic energy spectrum associated with the third triad of the periodic table of the elements: osmium, iridium, and platinum.

The needle thrust—and stopped.

"Help!" the aged voice squeaked. "Murd—"

The squeak was cut sharply off. The clutching hand slid from Keth's arm. The worn old body spun past him and rolled on the floor, grotesquely stiffened. Brong crouched above it, pointing one gloved finger at its stiffened face. Vorn was reeling backward as if from a dazing blow. Vythle caught his arm to steady him, and slowly lowered her lasergun.

"Sir, it was—is—a humanoid." Brong drew slowly back, still squinting at it, wiping a sleeve across his wet-beaded face. "I was able to knock it down. For how long, I don't know."

Keth felt cold and nearly ill. Staring at the ceiling, its bloodless features were fixed in pained amazement, and a thin brownish wisp trailed from the gaping lips. He caught a bitter whiff of burnt plastic.

"Your father—" Vorn's face had the look of gray wax. "The thing—"

"Another copy." Keth crouched away from the dead machine on the floor. "Their big monopole must be a fraud. A scheme to cripple any real defense, while they learn what they could about the Leleyo."

"Which means we've lost—" Vorn's hoarse voice failed, and he stood for a moment staring at Vythle. "Lost everything. . . ."

His voice died again.

Darkness had fallen across the room. Outside the great windows, the lemon sky was gone, blotted out by a vast silverblack mirror that held a dimmed and twisted image of the tower and the Zone.

The humanoids were landing.

Her cool elegance somehow unshattered, the lasergun still in her hand, Vythle walked around the humanoid to where the

Admiral stood. They smiled very soberly at each other and turned together to the window.

Keth heard her gasp. Stumbling nearer the window, he saw panic on the spacedeck below. Pedestrians peered up at the descending ship and fled madly from beneath it. Racing vehicles ran them down and crashed together in metal avalanches.

"They can't—" Vorn turned to Vythle, his broad face sick. "Can't be landing—on top of all those people." Shaking his head, he peered down again. "They'll have to stop, because they have a Prime Directive that will—"

But the transport didn't stop. Its own swelling bulk hid the fate of those caught beneath. No human sound reached that high room, but the whole mountain quaked. The floor shuddered. Toppling objects crashed and jangled. A ring-shaped dust cloud rolled out to veil the ruin.

"Their Prime Directive—" Vorn made a savage face.

"They don't want it changed," Keth said. "They think people with rhodo know-how might try to change it. I guess they'll be after the Bosun now."

"Me?" Brong recoiled from him. "After me?"

"They have the Zone. Now you're all they need to fear."

"Our last hope, Bosun." Vorn padded toward him. "You and your Leleyo friends."

"No help from them, sir." Brong licked at his lips, the pink tongue strangely quick in his dead face. "They're not back from their winter migration, wherever they go. With the humanoids here, they may never come back."

Warily, he glanced at the still humanoid.

"Nor help from me, sir," he muttered. "I can focus force enough to put one out of action. Maybe two or three—but not a million!"

"But you can—jump," Keth whispered. "Can't you take us anywhere?"

"Nowhere you'd want to be." He backed toward the doorway, as if expecting the machine to move. "I can only reach places I know. There are humanoids everywhere I've been on Kai and Kyronia. Bloodrot everywhere outside our little perimeter here."

Vorn and Vythle stood silent, holding hands.

"Admiral, sir." Brong's voice startled them. "I've one request. There are sanicraft standing down in the shop. One I used to drive. Before the black metal imps come swarming down. May I take it, sir?"

Vorn looked somberly at Vythle, slowly back at him.

"Why not?" The wide cragged face looked bloodless as the thing on the floor. "I suppose you've earned it."

"Thank you, sir!"

"Where—" A spark of life came back to Vorn's dull voice. "Do you know some refuge?"

"The craft itself, sir. I want to drive it out where I hope the humanoids can't follow. Far enough, if I'm lucky, to meet the Leleyo when they come south for the summer. You see, sir, there's a gamble I never dared."

He shivered a little, blinking at his yellow glove.

"My mother thought I hadn't inherited my father's bloodrot immunity, but there has never been a test. The time I was exposed, they burned off my hands before they really knew. It's time, I think, to take the chance."

"I—" Keth's breath caught. "May I go?"

"And risk the rot?" In sad astonishment, Brong shook his head. "Think about it, Crewman. For myself, I could have an even chance. For you—" His sad voice fell.

"I know the humanoids," Keth told him. "Too well to care—"

"If you want—" Brong studied him, and suddenly stripped a glove off to offer his hand. "We'll go together, Crewman."

He gripped the hard metal, and it squeezed back with an almost painful force. With a murmur to Vythle, Vorn opaqued the vast windows. She bent to the hushed holophone, while he stalked back and forth across the darkened room.

"Bosun, I envy you." He came padding back to them. "The two of you. Because I've lived the way I liked. If I knew less about the way bloodrot kills—" His cragged face turned bitter. "If we two had any sort of chance . . ."

Vythle rose from the holo.

"I got through to Sally Port Three." She turned to Brong. "Your craft is cleared through the gate—if you get there in time. You'll have to move. The guards report disorder. Mobs in the tunnels and most of the slideways stopped."

"Thank you, Admiral," Keth whispered. "Thank you both."

"Move!" Vorn gestured them out. "The luck of Kai to you!"

Glancing back at the dead humanoid as they left, he saw Vorn and Vythle beyond it, ignoring it, slipping into a desperate embrace. She murmured something, her voice still softly calm.

They found all the slideways idle and the main tunnels blocked with shouting crowds. At one jammed intersection, a news holo was hooting and flashing a bulletin alert. Commodore Zelyk Zoor—his humanoid copy—exploded into the field.

"Peace, friends!" it bawled. "I bring you peace!"

The mob fell silent, awed by its more than human power.

"You can forget your fears," it thundered into the tunnels. "Because I bring good news from Kai. The humanoids are there, and you wouldn't recognize the barren little rock where most of you were born. Their infinite benevolence has created the ease and plenty and boundless joy once reserved for dreams of paradise.

"Paradise, friends!"

The vibrant voice soared and suddenly fell.

"Yet I have a painful warning for you. Because evil people are seeking to rob us of these great gifts. One of them—friends, it breaks my heart to say this—one of these human demons is my own cousin, Admiral Torku Vorn, whom I have come to replace as Zone Commander through this era of transition. Two monstrous traitors are with him. The Leleyo halfbreed sometimes known as Bosun Brong, and the infamous Keth Kyrone—"

As if overcome with horror, the image bent its face into quivering upraised hands.

"Friends, I can scarcely bear—scarcely bear to speak of him." The rolling tones shuddered and broke. "Keth Kyrone—the unspeakable demon that ripped the skin from my lovely bride while she was still alive!"

It wiped at streaming tears.

"They're out among you, friends. For my poor Chelni's sake —for all our sakes—I beg you to hunt them down before they do more harm. The humanoids are reluctant to let me urge you to any violence, but their own wise Prime Directive impels them to act for the greatest good of the greatest number. Their guiding logic decrees that these few hideous fiends must be destroyed, for the sake of innocent billions.

"So search for them, friends! Recent holostats of all four will be displayed—the fourth is the former Commander's merciless gun-girl. All four have fled from Zone Command. With the spacedeck closed, they're somewhere still among you.

"Kill them, friends! For our dear humanoids and the sweet sake of peace—"

Brong twitched his sleeve.

"Come, Crewman! Let's get off the mainways."

36

Symbiosis A relationship between life forms that enables each to aid the survival of the other. The Malilian ecology includes a network of mutant symbiotic systems fostered by the Leleyo.

Keth followed into an empty side tunnel. Half a block along it, they found an importer's cave, left unlocked and abandoned. A freightway from it dropped them to gate level before the power went off. Seeming at home in the blinding dark, Brong guided him out at last into the sanicraft maintenance shop, where the great golden machines loomed and gleamed under dim emergency lamps.

Brong unsealed a massive door. Heart thumping with mixed elation and dread, Keth followed him through cramped and shadowy spaces into the narrow cab. The icy air had a stale chemical bite. After the heavy thunk of the closing door, the stillness seemed grave-like.

In a dark-goggled helmet, too intent to talk, Brong seemed nearly as alien as another humanoid. His deft gold fingers brought the craft alive. Ventilators whirred. The console glowed. Cleated tracks clanking on bare concrete, they lumbered up a long ramp into yellow-green daylight. Brong hailed the guards.

"Sanicraft *Auli* to Sally Port Three. Exit cleared by Zone Command for perimeter patrol."

They waited. Keth sat with Brong in the cab. Breathing hard, peering up through the bubble at the laser turret over the gate, he half expected a blinding bolt. For a long time there was no response. He began to wonder if the guards had already joined the humanoids.

"Sally Port to *Auli*." A sudden thin voice squeaked out of Brong's helmet. "Hold where you are." The squeaking grew keener. "Conflicting orders. Can't make out who's in command."

"Admiral Vorn against the humanoids." Brong's chuckle seemed oddly uncaring. "Let 'em fight it out, and the winner take the rot!"

He mopped sweat from his still brown mask. The ventilators whispered. The big machine quivered once, and Keth heard the muffled thump of some far explosion. Small sounds rustled and chirped in Brong's helmet, and a tiny voice tweeted, "Fighting reported in the tunnels. Zone Command dead."

"As we'll all be," Brong chuckled again. "Unless we fix that hole in the perimeter."

"True enough, Shipman. Life comes first." The yellow barrier jerked and rattled aside. "Exit open."

They lurched out through the gate and down across shattered stone and thawing snow, toward the blue flicker of the new perimeter. Keth turned in his seat to look back. Soaring above the rust-mottled wall and the Zone's brown roofs, the transport seemed even huger than the one he had fled on Kai. Wide gangways sloped out of its bright black mirror, already dark with landing humanoids.

With no glance back or any word for him, Brong kept them grinding and skidding down the slope. Before they reached the new wall, faint voices began to whistle and chitter in his helmet. Abruptly he stopped the craft and spun the turret to face the peak and that overwhelming ship.

Listening, he raised a shining hand for silence. They waited, until at last a yellow-striped command wagon crashed through the tower gate and came lurching recklessly after them. Brong shed his helmet and darted out of the cab.

"Can't we fight?" Keth called after him. "Or run for the jungle?"

"Cheer up, Crewman!" Brong was unbolting the loading door. "If we must fight, we'll have help."

It was Admiral Vorn who staggered aboard with a red-spattered bandage around his head, Vythle guiding him.

"Ambush!" he muttered. "That humanoid copy of Keth's father. Waiting for us at the gate. Touched me with a laser, but

Vyth shot it down. We're going with you, Bosun. Nowhere"—his hoarse voice broke—"nowhere left!"

Brong rebolted the door and dashed back to the cab.

"Guard your eyes." The bubble burned blue when he lit the sterilamps. He showed Keth a second pair of goggles. "We get a healthy dose of UV, even here inside."

Vythle offered to man the laser turret.

"Qualified!" Vorn rumbled. "As the humanoids know."

Brong let her climb into the fighting turret. They lumbered on down the slope. Watching the flash of Brong's hands on the controls, Keth felt as helpless as the blind man crouching on the signal seat behind them. The world he knew was lost. Looking for another ahead, all he saw beyond that painful flicker was a gray and endless waste of cloud beneath the greenish yellow sky.

"Approaching Telegate Three," Brong called as they neared the outer wall. "Request exit to inspect exterior UV—"

"Exit denied!" his helmet squeaked. "Patrol permit voided. Return at once—"

He snapped off the angry whine and drove them toward the yellow metal barrier.

"Hang on! We're ramming through."

The impact checked and rocked the craft, but the barrier crashed down. They crunched across its wreckage and plowed into deeper snows beyond, where no nukes had warmed the rocky ledges that tilted down forever into that gray abyss.

Brong called for Vythle to watch for pursuit, but she reported nothing. The zigzag wall sank behind. The UV shimmer faded. At last the brown-roofed peak was gone, but still the tachyonic transport leapt above the snows into the lemon sky. Keth shivered from a helpless sense of blind steel eyes fixed on them forever.

"Cheer up, Crewman!" Brong must have sensed his mood. "Our choice is made—if we had a choice. At least for now, we're still free. All Malili ahead. Look alive, and I'll show you how to run the craft."

With care against overloads and voltage surges, the twin reactors might last two years. "Likely longer than we will," Brong murmured. The sterilamps on their flexing booms must be kept burning against the armor, the filter system kept intact, the air pressure positive.

"Watch for rocks that could scratch us," he muttered. "Rocks on the ground or out of the air—the dragon bats dive-bomb intruders. Watch for mud—rust can start under it. Watch for your life!"

They dropped at last into a great U-shaped canyon carved by old glaciers, its rust-mottled walls plunging up so far that even the starship was hidden. On a level stretch of ice, Brong let him take the wheel.

Afraid at first that the heavy machine might lurch, in spite of him, into some deadly rock, he soon learned to enjoy its immense responsive power. He was almost sorry when Brong took over again to climb a long boulder-strewn moraine. Before they reached its summit, the holocom began chirping for attention.

"Take it, Crewman." Brong gestured at the tank. "Not that I look for good news."

Keth lit the tank and shrank from the blindly smiling image of a humanoid.

"At your service, Keth Kyrone," it lilted. "We advise you and your companions to abandon your irrational attempt to evade our care. We urge you to wait where you are until we can overtake you and escort you back to safety."

"We've seen your service, and we refuse it."

"But, sir, you cannot do that." Its sweet tones rose in mild protest. "Each one of you has gained forbidden knowledge or abetted forbidden behavior. You will each, therefore, require our most attentive service so long as you survive."

"You'll have to catch us first!"

"We can do that, sir," it assured him brightly. "We are following in three vehicles which we have modified to double their power. We advise you most urgently to stop and wait. Attempting to continue your reckless adventure, you can only destroy your own vehicle and lose your lives.

"In obedience to our wise Prime Directive—"

Brong's gold hand slashed at the switch, and the black image vanished.

"Let's not have the devils homing on our signal."

Beyond the moraine, they dived into that featureless fog. The world shrank around them. A luminous blue in their lamps, the fog was blinding. Dark rock masses loomed out of it, just meters ahead.

Reducing speed, Brong steered between dim greenish shadows that came and went on the hooded screen of the sonar-scope. Keth found comfort in the cover of the fog, but only for a moment. Nothing could blind the sightless humanoids.

Vythle came down from the turret to look after Vorn. When he grudgingly admitted his pain, she found supplies in an aid locker and changed the dressing on his eyes. She wanted him to go back to a berth, but he sat stubbornly at the signal station, silently brooding.

Keth explored the galley and heated food. Though Vythle tried to feed Vorn, he would eat nothing. Brong took a few bites from the tray Keth brought, his gold fingers nimble with fork and cup, his dead face intent on the screen's greenish glow. The ventilators sighed. Transmission gears whined. The whole craft quivered now and then to a muffled crunch of stone beneath the tracks. Keth began to feel the fog would last forever.

"Machines!" Vorn muttered suddenly, perhaps to himself. "I always loved them. A lovely little toy heat engine, on my fourth birthday. My first holoscope, programmed with odes about the old heroes saving their cities back in the Black Centuries. The private jet the fleet assigned us when I married. The Vorn reactors, when I took charge of them, pouring out the power that made us great. Our space machines. Even these golden sanicraft when I got to the Zone, and all the linked equipment defending the perimeter. But now—"

Keth heard his teeth grate.

"Humanoid machines!"

37

Life   A transient early stage in the evolution of mind.

Later, after Vythle had gone back to her berth, the blind Admiral spoke of them.

"Misfits, both of us. I hated Greenpeak and the Academy. Silly rules and stupid teachers. Discipline that killed everything alive. I hated most of the Vorns I knew—proud fools ruled by stale tradition, repeating history's dusty blunders. I hated society—the abject worship of status and money and power. Even hated my wife, for loving all that."

He sat defiantly straight, empty hands flat on the signal board, white-bandaged head flung back as if trying to see.

"So I came to Malili. Found most of what I wanted here in the Zone. A place where rules were made to break, and guts meant more than names. And Vythle—"

He sat a moment silent.

"I think the name's her own invention. Born down in the bilges—where my wife would have held her nose. Learned a game where you had to break the rules to stay alive. Scratched her way to shipfolk status and the Navarch's staff. My own sort of misfit; I knew her in a second when we met. We've had fine years together. But now . . ."

His heavy body caved down upon the signal board.

"Now the humanoids are playing by their own mad rules."

He lay there silent, until Keth thought emotion had overcome him.

"History!" His slow voice rumbled again, more thoughtful than bitter. "Look at man's history. A symbiosis, an ecologist might call it; bonds between machines and men. Links with the axe and the reactor. The counting stick and the computer. The raft and the starship. We took a million years to build the humanoids—the best machine of all!"

His chuckle was a hollow rattle that may have been a sob. A little later, yielding stubbornly to fatigue and pain, he asked Keth to help him back to his berth. At Brong's command, Keth went to his own. He lay down unwillingly, expecting the lurching of the craft and the strain of the chase to keep him on edge, but suddenly Vythle was shaking him awake. It was time for them to drive.

That tiny blue-lit fog-world still shut them in. He took the wheel, picking their path among the shadowy masses on the sonar screen, while she ran the inertia tracker and traced their path across the chart. Her quiet skill surprised him.

"I think we've made it!" His spirits had risen. "If we ever get below the fog, we'll surely meet the Leleyo—"

"Nothing they can do." Her flat matter-of-factness astonished him again. "Our world now is this machine. We die when it does." Smiling faintly in the greenish glow of the screen, she looked cool and sure and lovely. "A fact you have to take. After all, it's what we bargained for. All you had better expect."

She studied him, nodding gravely.

"The Bosun, of course, can hope for more. If he turns out to be immune."

Brong was driving again when they came down through the ceiling of cloud. Snow and ice were gone. Though the somber greens and blues of rust still stained the rocks around them, scarlet firegrass splashed a level meadow ahead, and the lower hills that fell away beyond were yellow and gold, hazed blue beneath the denser air.

Vythle climbed back into the fighting turret, and Keth took another driving lesson. To his surprise, Brong seemed to be seeking out hazards, skirting the lip of a cliff above a foaming river, sliding across a dangerous talus, jolting needlessly around the rocky rim of another inviting firegrass glade.

"Trying to hide our trail?"

"Or set a trap." Brong had pushed up his goggles to scowl at the maptank. "That flat's a mating place for dragon bats. They don't like it violated."

On a long plateau where clumps of yellow goldoak scattered the red firegrass, Brong let him drive again. Rust-dark crags rose into the cloud-roof behind them, but the landscape ahead looked less forbidding.

"The Leleyo?" He turned hopefully to Brong. "Could we meet them here?"

"Sorry, Crewman, but we can't make miracles. They never get so high so early in the season. So don't go dreaming of your lovely Nera Nyin. Here in bloodrot country, don't you forget, her first naked touch could kill you."

Depressed, he said nothing.

"Here's what I hope for." As if trying to cheer him again, Brong lit a map in the tank. "Your mother's goal on her last trip—"

"The braintree?"

"The feyo tree." The bright forefinger pointed. "We're keeping close to her route. Beyond that range is the river she couldn't cross. Doubt that we can. But we'll try to get near and wait till our friends gather for their early summer feyolar. If we're lucky—"

"Bosun!" Vythle's call rang from the fighting turret. "Something I want you to check."

Brong climbed to join her. Keth drove on, more confidently

now. The big machine had begun speaking to him, the whine of the drive rising and falling with every change in load from slope or soil. His mind meshed with it, he could almost forget the humanoids.

Their attack stunned him.

A dazzling flash. A thunder crack. The machine lurched and moaned and stopped. Ringing stillness and utter dark. He thought for an instant that he had been blinded, but then he could see the console's glow.

"Here to help us!" Savagely mocking, Vorn's shout echoed through the craft. "Our metal symbiotes!"

Though that first blast had opaqued the pilot bubble, Brong and Vythle were still in action. Motors hummed, training the fighting turret. The big laser crashed twice. Silence then, till he heard Brong climbing back down to the cab and knew the battle was over.

"They're dead—dead as we are!" Brong cleared the bubble and stood clicking his metal fingers, peering bleakly at the console. "If they ever had three machines, the others were already lost. Maybe in that river or to the dragon bats. Vythle got the one that knocked us out."

He tramped moodily on to inspect the reactors.

"Vyth? Is Vyth hurt?"

Vorn came staggering out of his berth in his underwear, the soiled bandage askew on his head. He groped along the passage until Vythle ran to meet him. They clung together.

The whir of the fans was fading. A warning horn croaked and died. Red danger lights winked and dimmed on the console. The maptank went dark. A sudden bitter stink of burnt paint and plastic took Keth's breath.

"Killed us." Brong came back, fingers clicking faster. "In too many ways. UVs out. Right track fused. Cooling system gone. Both reactors dead—quenched and ejected when the meltdown started. Air pressure falling fast."

"Done for?" Vorn shook his blind head, pushing Vythle back. "Already done for?"

"The craft is," Brong said. "We get out now or not at all."

He pulled escape gear out of the locker. The suits were stiff gold-filmed plastic with helmet bubbles and airpacks. At first unwilling, Vorn let Vythle seal him into his coverall. Brong loaded their harness with survival gear. Gold-bladed machetes.

Tubes of water and semifluid food. Lamps and ropes and rolled shelter sheets. Heavy gold-plated projectile guns.

"Hang on to the guns." His voice in the helmet was hollow and strange. "They're your best medicine for bloodrot when that time comes."

38

Machine Originating from makeshift compensations for the manifold defects of primitive organic life, the machine evolved into the ultimate vehicle for intelligence.

Power packs and suit pressure checked, Brong unbolted and opened the loading door. Keth climbed down to the firegrass, still black and smoking from the laser bolt, and turned to help Vorn. Vythle followed. She said something, but the helmet reduced her voice to a dull reverberation.

A few meters out, Keth turned back to stare. The damage appalled him. Only stumps and fragments were left of the sterilamp booms and the signal superstructures. Half the hull was black, its shielding gold vaporized.

He left it, tramping after his companions. In the golden suits and mirrored helmets, they looked almost alike: Brong the smallest, Vorn the bulkiest, Vythle still somehow feminine in the way she moved.

On a stony ridge beyond the crimson firegrass field, Brong unrolled a stiff yellow chart and gestured toward a V-shaped notch between haze-blued hills far off in the east. A river had cut it, he said, flowing down to join the greater glacial river that ran beneath the braintree.

"No promise we'll ever get there." His radio voice was distorted and shrill, hard to make out. "But at least we'll be farther from the humanoids."

Clumsy in his own heavy gear, aware again of Malili's dragging gravity, Keth moved to offer aid to Vorn and Vythle. They stood together, awkwardly embracing. He caught the other arm, and they blundered after Brong toward that far V.

"Service!"

Faint and strange, that high sweet voice needled through his helmet. It froze him for a moment. When he looked back, the humanoid was gliding after them from the yellow glitter of the wreckage.

"We urge you, shipfolk! Return!"

A changed humanoid. Its singing tones were still the same, and its slender shape. It danced across the charred firegrass with the same fluid grace. Its golden brand still glinted. But the rest of its sleek and sexless nudity was no longer black, but clad now in harlequin velvet, blazing blues and lurid greens.

Vorn's helmet rang to a furious roar, and Vythle clung to his inflated sleeve to stop his mad rush toward the humanoid. Keth unsheathed his golden blade. Brong sprang aside, nimble in his suit, apparently just watching.

"Service . . . difficult . . ." Its voice slowed, the high tones falling. "You must . . . come back . . . to the Zo—"

The last vowel stretched out into a sustained musical hum that slowly sank and finally ceased. Gone rigid, the dead thing toppled toward them and fell into the scarlet firegrass, blind eyes down. A faint puff of blue dust rose around it—spores of the rust, Keth supposed, feeling grimly grateful for them.

"Guess that settles that." Brong's radio voice had a sardonic snap. "They'll never serve Malili."

They took turns assisting Vorn, who wanted no aid. He stumbled on rocks and clumps of brush, even when Vythle was calling anxious warnings. Sometimes he fell and seemed unwilling to rise again. Keth could sense his savage mood.

Though they slogged and blundered hour after hour toward that blue-veiled V, it never seemed nearer. Inside the unyielding armor, Keth sweated and itched in spots he couldn't reach. The heavy boots wore blisters on his heels. Yet Vorn and Vythle were his most urgent concern; their plight seemed even bleaker than his own.

Neither the yellow-green sky nor the landscape changed. Only their bodies and the gold-cased chronographs told them when that long day was gone. Brong picked a level resting spot, showed them how to get food and water through the helmet tubes, how to work the elimination valves.

Keth sprawled on a firegrass bed, too tired at first for sleep, too miserable in the cramping suit. A muffled crash woke him. Sitting up stiffly, he found Vythle standing a few meters away, her gold gun drawn.

"Sorry, Keth." Her radio voice was abrupt and brittle. "Thought I'd seen a humanoid. Half asleep when I fired. Nothing, I guess."

Brong had lifted his bubble-covered head, but then sank silently back. Vorn was lying on a scarlet hummock beyond. Vythle stepped back to him and stood beside him, as if on guard. Keth went back to sleep.

"Wake up, Crewman!" Brong banged on his helmet. "We've a long way to go."

He looked for Vythle and found her still standing over Vorn, as if she hadn't moved. His suit had collapsed around him, the pressure lost. One empty glove made a bright spot of yellow on the red grass a few meters from him—perhaps torn off and tossed away.

Feeling numbed, he edged near enough to see the thin bones of hand and wrist reaching out of the flattened sleeve, still wet and red. A gold ring gleamed, unchanged. Grass and rock were stained red-black where fluid had drained out of the sleeve. Though Vorn's gun was still on his belt, there was a round, black hole in the side of his helmet.

Shaken, he turned away toward Vythle. She moved slightly toward him and stood still. He searched for her face, but all he could see in the golden mirror of her helmet was the diminished image of his own bulging suit. Though he wanted to offer some sign of compassion, she seemed so remote that he found nothing to say.

"It's all right, Keth." Her tone surprised him with its calm warmth, its note of pity even for him. "He had come as far as he could or wanted to. We'd hoped, of course, for more time together. Because we were in love. But I don't regret the choice we made. Neither did he." The bright helmet tilted, and he thought she was looking down at Vorn. "It's better than life beneath the humanoids."

Brong had come up beside them. Her yellow gloves took both their hands, her grasp quick and clinging. After a moment she waved them toward that far-off V and turned back to stand over Vorn.

Beckoning him, Brong tramped silently on. When he glanced back, she still stood there, erect and bright and motionless. When he looked again, a thicket of orange thorns had hidden her. A little later, his helmet echoed to a distant gunshot.

Brong paused for a moment, listening.

"A hard thing, Crewman." He was slogging on again. "But Malili never was a friendly place—not except to the Leleyo. The Admiral and his girl were well aware of that before they came with us."

A little later he stopped again, mirror-face turned to Keth.

"Crewman, let's strike a bargain. So long as we're together, we'll look after each other. If a time comes when we must separate, there's something I must tell you. Something that may help you, though I can't say it now. Till you've heard that, let's agree that neither one will shoot himself. Promise, Crewman?"

"I"—he had to gulp—"I promise."

Brong clapped a hard glove on the hard shoulder of his armor, and they tramped on together. As if searching for a topic not so painful, he began to talk about the feyo tree. All his life, he had heard the hints and rumors of its sacred power. With luck enough, in spite of everything, they might yet live to see it.

"Could you—" Keth whispered. "Can't you jump us there?"

"If I could—" Brong's voice rustled in his helmet, faint and forlorn. "I've been groping for it, Crewman. With all I know from the maps and all I remember from what your poor mother said when she got that glimpse. Not quite enough. If we were near enough to see it—"

Fighting taller walls of thorns, retreating once from a bottomless bog of thick blue mud, they were three days reaching the river. It flowed deep and fast, and something had dyed it darkly green. Spores of the rust, Brong said, and Keth recalled that they were also the bloodrot pathogen.

They slashed through the last thorn thickets and slept on a long gravel bank where spring floods had piled driftwood. When he woke, Brong was already at work on a raft, trimming logs and rolling them back into the shallows, binding them with thornbrush withes.

The raft took two days to build. Poling out into the current at last, they floated three more days toward that slowly widening V. It became a yawning canyon as they neared it, where the narrowed river foamed against dark, rusted cliffs and plunged into unexpected rapids.

Plumes of pale green spray danced ahead, above rocks that blocked half the channel. Mad currents caught and spun the creaking raft. Standing one at each end, they fought to fend it from collision. Keth leaned to push them past a foam-veiled boulder. His pole shattered. He staggered forward, slipped, went down into wild water.

Though he tried to swim, the suit was too heavy, the rapids too savage. Carried under, he couldn't see. The water mauled and battered him. His helmet rang from dazing impacts. After a time, he couldn't breathe.

The next he knew, he lay somewhere aground. The roar of the rapids was gone, and he saw yellow sky. Twisting painfully, he found himself on a flat sandbar in a litter of splintered driftwood.

He was suffocating. Too desperate to think of consequences, he fought the latches with clumsy gloves and thrust the helmet off.

39

Braintree The feyo tree of Malili, derived from a wild plant whose fragrant poison sap attracted and killed animal prey, but mutated by the Leleyo into a sacred symbiote.

The air was cool and sweet. He lay gasping long lungfuls of it. Growing slowly more awake, he began to savor the scents of Malili—odors of soil and growth, of rain and decay, all spiced with faint aromas he had no name for.

Strength returning, he sat up. The river ran in a wide bend around the sandbar, diminishing walls of yellow-red thornbrush reaching far beyond the arc of dark green water. The splintered logs up and down the beach could have come from the raft, but he saw no trace of Brong.

Tender from bruises, his body felt sticky and foul. He peeled off the rest of his suit, shivering when the wind hit him. Wading into the shallows to bathe, he stopped to shudder when the icy water stung his blistered heels.

After one sick instant, he waded on. The blisters didn't really matter; the bloodrot pathogen wouldn't wait for breaks in the skin. The water felt good when he got over that first chill, and he scrubbed himself gratefully before he splashed back to the sandbar.

Turning over what was left of his gear, he found the machete missing, and his last tubes of food and sterile water. No matter. His danger now was not starvation. Since he had washed in the green-stained river, he might as well drink it.

Still clipped to the wet yellow belt, the gun did matter. With a little nod of satisfaction, he snapped it free—and reeled from a shock of horror that left him weak and ill. The gold plate was peeling away from green velvet patches on the steel. Cold and shaking, he tried the trigger. It snapped off under his finger. In a spasm of terror, he flung the weapon toward the slack green water.

"Hold it, Crewman!"

That hailing voice seemed too hearty to be real. He scowled uncertainly at the little figure limping around a thorn thicket, but it was Bosun Brong, wearing only a torn scrap of muddy underwear, gold hands flashing.

"Don't forget our bargain."

"I won't shoot myself," he promised wryly. "But I don't have much to cheer about."

"More, maybe, than you know." Brong came up to him and beckoned at a shattered log. "Sit down, Crewman. There's something I've delayed telling you. Too long, maybe, but I didn't know how you'd take it. Afraid you'd be ashamed of me."

He waited, too tense to sit. Brong darted a little way toward him and stopped again, that tight, brown, scar-marked face twitching as if with feeling it couldn't express.

"Crewman, I've always thought—" Something checked him. "I've always thought—" he whispered. "I believe you're my son."

The damp wind was suddenly chillier and the river's hiss louder. That faint strange aroma became a reeking pungence. Keth sat down heavily on the log.

"I was afraid you wouldn't believe me." Brong blinked at him, a forlorn brown wisp in the soiled shreds of underwear. "I know my looks don't show it. Dwarfed by that illness when I was an infant. You take more after my father, Ilo Auli—"

"My own father—" Keth tried to get his breath. "The man I thought—"

"Your mother's husband." Brong spoke with a sudden force. "He always hated me, because I loved your mother. Hated her, I'm afraid—even for making these for me." Sadly, he flexed the golden hands. "She loved me, Crewman—if you can grasp what that meant to me. A genetic freak. A twisted midget. A suspect carrier of the rot. I adored her. We were alone for weeks together outside the perimeter in the craft I drove for her—"

He drew a long uneven breath.

"If I ever blamed myself, it was only for bringing his displeasure upon her. If she ever regretted anything, she never told me so. Though of course we both were sick because he suspected too much to let us out together again. If—"

Ruefully, he sighed.

"A hard man, Crewman! But a quiet one, too. And loyal in his own way to the Crew and his duty. He never actually accused us, though things enough made it plain how he felt."

"That must be why"—Keth whispered—"why he was always so stern and cold with me."

"So you do believe me?" Brong bent eagerly nearer. "And you aren't ashamed?"

"Why—" He stood up unsteadily and reached to grasp Brong's hard hand. "Thank—thank you—father!"

"You are my son!" Brong ignored his reaching hand, and they came together in a trembling embrace. "You see why I had to tell you now. Before you tried to harm yourself. Because it's possible you're immune. I don't know which genes are dominant, but if my own odds are one in two, yours should be one in four."

"How soon do we know?"

"Hard to say." Brong limped back from him. "I've seen people die. None, I think, lived over a day after exposure. The eyes and the lungs can begin to burn in just a few minutes."

"I feel all right yet—I think!"

"Too soon to celebrate." Brong's squinted eyes surveyed him. "Too much we don't know. Both of us could be only partially immune—maybe delaying the attack and leaving us longer to die. Even if we don't get the rot, there are other jungle bugs to watch for, like the infection that crippled me."

"What about your hands?"

"I'm watching them." Brong turned them uncertainly.

"There may be steel inside, but your mother made them well. No damage yet that I can see." He sighed. "We must wait."

Waiting, they limped along the dense thornbrush barrier and out to the tip of the sandbar. A desolate place to die. Yet, no matter how long they lived, they had no tools to cut through the thorns or build another raft. He saw no way to leave it. Gazing wearily along the endless yellow jungle wall that curved back upon the green shimmer of the river at the next long bend —he abruptly caught his breath.

"Bosun!" Trembling, he pointed. "Father! Isn't that where the tree is?"

Far away and pale with haze, a blunted mountain cone rose above the jungle. On the steep north slope, he found a flat-floored notch. Brong shaded his eyes to peer at it, and hard gold fingers gripped Keth's arm.

"Crewman, that's the tree!"

"Can you—can you jump us to it?"

"I can't." The metal hand slowly relaxed, and Brong shook his head. "No more feyolin. Lost my last grain of it, swimming ashore. But if I can't—" His grip grew tighter. "Keth, if you re-call what you learned when we jumped from Kai, I think we can."

"I don't remember much—"

"The tree stands on that flat bench." Brong's bright hand flashed at it. "A thick, green trunk with paler branches and bright-red twigs. We'll drop to the rim, just north of it. I'll count us down. Three, two, one—"

He didn't remember anything useful, and this was pure folly. Two tattered outcasts, stripped to dirty underwear and driven by disaster beyond the brink of sanity. This was sheer delusion—

"Now!"

Nothing happened, but the hard hand kept tugging.

"Jump!"

He let himself go from the sand underfoot and the wind's bitter bite and the hiss of the river. Eyes on that far notch, he relaxed to Brong's hauling hand. Everything blurred, and the yellow sky flickered. Air pressure clicked in his ears. Giddy for an instant, he almost lost his balance.

"Steady, Crewman! Here we are!"

They stood on hard gravel, so near the brink that he stepped uneasily back. Hundreds of meters below, the great river bent about the mountain's foot, its pale green flood clotted with floes of pale blue ice. Turning with Brong, he saw the tree.

It grew out of bare, hard-packed soil. The sleek-barked trunk was vividly green, many meters thick where it bulged above the roots. Its tapered branches were a lighter green, fading into orange, darkening again at the tips of the down-sweeping twigs to the color of blood.

The Leleyo were moving around the tree. A few dozen adults, tall and lean, golden brown of skin and hair, all nude. Slim children among them. A graceful woman with an infant at her breast. A single yellow-bearded elder.

They were chanting, marching, sometimes dancing. One couple whirled out of the circle to lead the chant. When they returned, a single figure followed. Shaken with a sudden unbelieving hope, Keth searched the circle for Nera Nyin, but she was not there.

"Our kindred!" Brong's low-breathed words were almost a prayer. "Come!"

Keth hung back, his brief hope dead. Naked barbarians, singing to a tree! He couldn't laugh—he had come too far and hurt too much for laughter. But the tree was too strange, its worship too meaningless. The Leleyo, with all their ways unknown, seemed as coldly alien as the humanoids.

40

Synergy The joint action of several causes to create an effect impossible for any one. (Approximate translation of Leleyo *feyolili*.)

Brong tugged again.

"Crewman! They're waiting!"

The dancers had halted, turning to face them. Voices paused and rose again, singing a different song. The golden-bearded elder strode out toward them, calling what seemed to be a greeting.

Brong darted to meet him, dropped to his knees when they came together. The bearded man beckoned him to rise and took him in his arms. From a long embrace, they turned to smile at Keth.

"Ilo Auli." Brong was hushed and tremulous. "Your grandfather."

Feeling strange, still afraid, Keth came to take his muscular hand.

"Welcome, feyosan." His resonant words could have come from a native of Kai. "We've been watching for you." He waved them toward the tree. "Welcome to the feyo—but you won't need those."

He frowned at their grimy rags of underwear. With a cheerful nod, Brong stripped and tossed his garment off the cliff. Feeling uncomfortable, Keth followed his example and waited with his back turned, shivering in the wind.

"Come!" Brong called. "We're Leleyo now."

One on either side, Ilo Auli led them back across the hard-beaten ground toward the tree. A dozen of the dancers came marching to escort them, singing another moving melody. When they neared the massive trunk, the whole circle formed around them again. Keth waited, feeling exposed and bewildered.

"Relax!" Brong's cold metal hand clapped his shoulder. "We've come home."

He faced the green trunk, shuddering with cold. His whole body ached from his mauling in the river. His blistered heels burned. Swallowing uneasily, he thought his throat felt sore and wondered if the bloodrot infection had already begun.

"The blood of the tree."

Chanting the words, Ilo Auli reached for a hanging crimson twig and snapped a tiny black clot-like bud from the end. Scarlet drops fell. He caught them in his palm till a tiny girl came running with a tiny cup of hammered gold to hold them.

"The life of the Leleyo!"

He lifted the child to let her put the odorous cup to Keth's lips. The blood-thick liquid burned like red flame, and his first searing taste changed everything. He was suddenly—Leleyo!

No longer strange, this giant tree had been mother and father and friend for many generations. Its story was the story of his people. He knew their first uncertain centuries, the hard search for the nexus between matter and mind, the long labor to reshape the life of the planet and the life of mankind into a finer harmony, the recent hazards of the Kai invasion, the hoped-for coming of the humanoids. Serenely grateful to them for stopping the drift of deadly radiation from the Zone, he knew the tree was safe again.

No longer a stranger, he belonged here. All his troubled years on Kai had become an unhappy dream, and he felt a throb of pity for the lonely youth he had been, growing up in those cold and gloomy tunnels, hurt so often because he didn't fit, because he couldn't understand and wasn't understood, because he had never learned to love.

No longer strangers, these people were his own. Tiny, light-haired Eyna Oong, so glad to share her cup with him and drinking happily now from the same bleeding twig before she filled the cup again. Oya Ila, so joyous with her new baby. Rero and Molu, so proud of their share in its shaping. Ilo Auli, so happy with his son's arrival, so pleased to greet a grandson.

He held out his hand to little Eyna for another burning drop and turned with his father to join their celebration of the spring return. Now he knew their dances, each step and swing symbolic of some memorable event in his people's splendid history.

Leleyo now, yet he was also still himself. The warmth of belonging had smoothed his gooseflesh, and he no longer felt the wind. His throat no longer hurt. The sting of his blisters and ache of his bruises had ceased, and suddenly he knew that even the bloodrot pathogen was no longer hostile to him, but now a benign dissolver of unwanted waste.

When he yearned for Nera Nyin, he knew that she had gone to the Zone to meet the humanoids there. They must be assured that the leyoleyo would never threaten their Prime Directive and persuaded that the Leleyo themselves would never need their service.

When he felt a stab of pity for Ryn Kyrone and Cyra Sair and Chelni Vorn, he knew that they were happy now—though the knowledge woke a troubled wonder in him. Ryn and Cyra had fought the humanoids too bitterly, Chelni had laughed at them too scornfully.

How had they been changed?

After their bodies had been copied and the minds somehow ransacked to make the duplicates sent back to grease the way for the humanoid invasion—what could have been left for any sort of happiness?

With no word spoken, Ilo Auli stepped inside the dancing

circle, with a nod for him and his father to follow. If he felt so deeply troubled about the fate of his friends, the humanoids would allow a visit to them in their present place on the planet Kyronia.

They broke black buds again to taste the tree's burning blood and then stood hand in hand, close against its great green bole. His father knew the way, because he had been aboard the lost *Kyrone*. Ilo Auli could share with them the full power of the leyoleyo.

The leap was easy now.

Somehow he saw their goal: a stone-paved square where humanoids darted about like black and soundless metal ants. Ilo Auli's gripping hand tightened slightly, to tell him when they were ready. He thrust himself. Air clicked in his ears, and they were on the pavement among the humanoids.

41

Leyoleyo   The racial mind into which individual Leleyo are merged through the channels of the feyo tree and the sacred rituals of *feyolili*.

The place surprised him for an instant, because it looked so much like Vorn Square in Northdyke, the tall winter gates of Vara Vorn looming over it, but then he knew that it was only another replication, a little section of Kai copied by the humanoids to help their guests feel at home.

A quick, black machine came up to him, and chill terror touched him.

"Welcome, feyo friends." It paused before them, bowing slightly. "You are fortunate, Feyoman Keth, to have found your peace with the Prime Directive. May we serve you on Kyronia?"

"May I see my—the man I called my father?"

"If you wish," the humanoid sang. "You'll find him happy here."

It brought them through the replicated bronze and silver gates of Vara Vorn and out into a copy of the high summer hall that he recalled from Chelni's birthday banquet. Ryn Kyrone was there, looking lean and fit in his black Lifecrew uniform. His back to the wild splendor of the duplicated icefall breaking from the duplicated glacier outside the great windows, he sat at a little table, facing a humanoid.

Man and machine, they played a game. Intently, the man leaned to place heavy little silver hemispheres on an inlaid pattern in the tabletop. Silently, the machine answered each move by instantly placing an X-shaped, jet-black marker.

Utterly absorbed, the man seemed unaware of him. Breathing heavily, he frowned to follow each move. His hands clenched when the humanoid seemed about to score, and the scar of his clean-shaved face went deathly white. When he won, he leered with triumph and the scar flamed red.

The game was tic-tac-toe.

"May I speak?" Keth asked. "Can you stop the game?"

"We serve," their guide trilled. "We obey."

The humanoid at the table froze.

"Skipper, what's all this?" The man at the table whirled to scowl at him and Brong and Ilo Auli. "If you're a Crewman now, what happened to your uniform? You don't look decent. I don't like your friend and I don't need you here."

"We've come to help you," Keth told him. "We can stop the humanoids long enough—"

"Stop them?" A rap of anger. "Why? I need no aid. Not from anybody. We're playing for the honor of the Crew, and I haven't lost a game. I've got to win again. If you please, don't interfere."

They found Cyra in the big round room that had been his own prison. Its windows were opaqued, and the glowing doors still showed no lock or knob that a human hand could work. She sat at another table, where Chelni's bed had stood, attended by a busy humanoid.

Wearing a spotless white lab apron, she looked as well and young as she had been when he gave her the dragon's egg. She, too, was playing what seemed to be a game. With an air of grave determination, she was building and rebuilding a score of small colored balls into a tiny pyramid.

Calling them eggs, she asked for them by color—red or blue, green or yellow, white or black. One by one, the humanoid brought them from assorted stacks on a shelf against the wall. Frowning with grave deliberation, she often hesitated and sometimes sent one color back to be exchanged for another. Though seldom pleased with any move, she always smiled and tried again.

Totally intent, she failed to see them.

"Cyra?" he called at last. "May I—"

"Keth?" She jumped and stared. "Bosun?" She glared at Ilo Auli. "Sir, who are you?" She whirled back to Keth. "Where are your clothes?" Before he could speak, she had crouched behind the humanoid. "Who let them in?"

"They are feyo friends," the humanoid cooed. "Therefore we obey them."

"You've no right here." She scowled at them. "You are interrupting my rhodonic research, which is classified supreme secret. You aren't to see—" Her angry slap demolished the unfinished pyramid. The light little balls bounced and rattled on the floor. "I allow no other human beings in the laboratory. Only a few trusted humanoid assistants."

"We came—" A throb of pity closed his throat. "Came to help you, Cyra. We can stop the humanoids long enough to make them let you out of this prison—"

"Prison?" She gestured scornfully, as if to sweep him away. "This lab is my secret fortress. These humanoids are rebels, Keth, turned against Wing IV. My own able allies. Aiding me with—"

She dropped her voice, with a wary glance behind her.

"With my research on the dragon's eggs you found for me. All I have to do is find how to stack the eggs to liberate rhodonic energy. When I succeed, I'll have an unbeatable weapon against Wing IV. That can't wait. Please leave us, Keth."

Commandingly, she pointed at the door. "And don't breathe a syllable!"

They found Chelni and her cousin in a cavern far beneath the sham Vara Vorn. When they entered, it looked like her uncle's Darkside ranch. Cragged barrens climbed toward far-off ice horizons, and the Dragon burned alone and cold in a gloomy Duskday sky.

Chelni was stalking wild mutoxen. Trimly graceful in sleek orange-hued hunting togs, she crept on her knees up a long snow-slope, pushing her telescopic gun. Fat and ungainly as ever, Zelyk scrambled after her, panting with lust.

When Keth shouted, they seemed not to hear.

"Please," he told their guide. "Let me speak to them."

Only a projected image, that lowering sky with the hot, red Dragon flickered and vanished from the stone dome above them. The limitless barrens were gone, all save a narrow obstacle course of boulders and snow where Zelyk had pursued Chelni as she pursued her game around and around the circular floor.

"Keth Kyrone!" She dropped her rifle to stare at him with a fleeting frown. "You're too late." Her square chin set stubbornly. "I loved you at Greenpeak. I could have made you a leader of the fleet, but I don't want you now.

"Not that I care so much for the Commodore."

With a shrug of contempt, she glanced back at Zelyk. Blinking against the sudden brightness, he staggered out of the rocks and came shambling toward her. His full-dress blues were buttoned too tight and stained black with sweat beneath the arms. His heaving chest glittered with too many medals.

"A slobbery hog." She made a face. "But he is a leader of the fleet."

"Kyrone, are you crazy?" Zelyk scowled at him in blustery belligerence. "Get out—and get yourself some clothes!"

"Better do that, Keth." Hostility narrowed her eyes. "We don't want you here. You're certainly no hunter, and the Admiral says he'll never ask you back." Her tone turned accusing. "You've frightened the ox I was after."

"Chelni, I wanted—"

"The game won't wait."

With an impatient headshake at him and a tolerant shrug for Zelyk, she went back to pick up her rifle. The light faded. The Dragon burned again in the Duskday gloom and their narrow track merged once more into the limitless barrens. She peered around a boulder and crept on again, Zelyk scrambling avidly behind her.

Their guide escorted them back through the great bronze gates to the replicated square.

"You have seen your fortunate friends," its pure voice lilted. "They are all receiving the extraordinary attention required by their essential removal from their own home world. Each has been provided the most appropriate possible environment, and each is aided to do what he most desires. This vigorous, purposeful activity is the secret of their total happiness—"

"Happiness!" He couldn't hide his bitter scorn. "Drugged with euphoride and playing silly games!"

"Human happiness is never rational." The machine's tone remained as cheerily serene as its sleek, black face. "Having been shaped by an evolutionary process that selected for successful violence, rather than for logic, human beings find their basic satisfactions in deadly aggression. Once a factor for survival, that trait became the racial peril that led to our invention. To rescue your race without loss of happiness, we now offer less lethal arenas of conflict."

Genially, it turned to Brong and Ilo Auli.

"You Leleyo at first appeared to be in even greater danger, because of the difficult natural barriers to our service on Malili. We find, however, that a fortunate mutation has relieved your race of excessive aggressiveness, leaving you less inclined to enmity and more toward amity. Since your high biological technology, unlike the insanely mechanistic technology of Kai, raises danger neither to your survival nor our own, you will never require our care."

Keth frowned, about to protest once more the crushing costs of humanoid care, but his bitterness was dimming. Perhaps the old, too-violent human worlds had really needed humanoid control to save them from self-destruction. Though the leyoleyo might find the logic of the humanoids a little less than logical, it would never war against them. Its triumph had been the creation of a compassionate peace that embraced every form of life, and even every living thing on Malili. Thrilled and exalted by that dawning understanding, he turned to Ilo Auli, ready to depart.

The ceremonial had ended before they came back to the feyo tree. The celebrants were gone, reborn through its rich blood and rejoined in planetary brotherhood. His father and grandfather went on to overtake them, but he waited in the warming nearness and the heady fragrance of the tree for Nera Nyin.

She had found the humanoids about to leave the Zone. Since Kai would need no more thorium, the mines there had been abandoned. The colonists were already boarding the tachyonic transport for passage back to Kai, and there would be no more nukes exploding to sterilize wider and wider perimeters.

She came riding a dragon bat. Standing on that lofty brink, which no longer seemed alarming, he watched its white wings glide out of the lemon green sky. Breathless with his unbelieving eagerness, he watched it wheel above the ice-clogged river bend and come in against the wind, reaching down with great black talons to seize a boulder for a perch. Joyous and golden, waving gaily, she slid off its back and stood waiting for him.